INTIMATE BEINGS

INTIMATE BEINGS

JESSICA INCLÁN

ZEBRA BOOKS
KENSINGTON PUBLISHING CORP.
www.kensingtonbooks.com

ZEBRA BOOKS are published by

Kensington Publishing Corp.
850 Third Avenue
New York, NY 10022

All Kensington titles, imprints, and distributed lines are available at special quantity discounts for bulk purchases for sales promotion, premiums, fund-raising, educational, or institutional use.

Special book excerpts or customized printings can also be created to fit specific needs. For details, write or phone the office of the Kensington Special Sales Manager: Attn. Special Sales Department. Kensington Publishing Corp., 850 Third Avenue, New York, NY 10022. Phone: 1-800-221-2647.

ISBN-13: 978-1-4201-0114-0
ISBN-10: 1-4201-0114-5

First Printing: October 2008
10 9 8 7 6 5 4 3 2 1

Printed in the United States of America

Chapter One

Claire Edwards had just absolutely had it, again, for about the sixth time that day. She wanted to scream and shout and stomp her feet, but since that reaction was exactly what was bothering her in others, she could not do any of that. She didn't want to roll around on the floor in tempera paint like Annie or pee in her pants like Thomas. She didn't want to fall into instant and hysterical weeping and cling to a pillow in the corner like Sam. Maybe she wanted to stand shocked still in the corner with the rest of them, but theoretically, she was in charge.

She was—Claire finally realized as she picked up the thrown barrel of blocks in order to get to Sam—the adult. She was the one paid for keeping things flowing educationally and psychologically for Annie, Thomas, Sam, and the twelve other children in her charge, all of whom were staring at her right now with wide, frightened eyes. Claire was in charge of "environment" and "attitude." Claire was in charge of "educational outcomes."

"Sam," she said, her voice like the blanket Sam was missing, the one that his mother insisted he go without "cold turkey" this very morning, "I promise you that when you get home, your mommy will give you your blankie. It's just that it needs to stay at home for now. While you are at school."

"I want my blankie!" Sam wailed. "I want it now!"

Annie rolled toward Claire, smearing primary colors everywhere. Thomas clutched his pants, whimpering.

The rest of them chimed in, crying in sympathy for this horrible scene; all of them suddenly wanted their blankies, their mommies, the toilet, an afternoon snack, their pets, anything but this classroom.

Claire knew that she shouldn't do it. Couldn't do it. Really, really, mustn't do it, but she wanted to close her eyes, think of a spot, any spot on the planet. She wanted to focus on the Kelani Resort in Maui or the Mendocino Hotel in Mendocino. She wanted to think about the Tuileries Gardens in Paris. Frankly, she would be happy at the Starbucks on the corner of Masonic and Fulton. Or the French Laundromat on Stanyan, the air thick with steam and soap. Anywhere but here.

The problem always was, of course, that she could go wherever she wanted to. Anywhere on the planet. Just like that. Just by thinking. By picturing a place, she could be there, and she had performed this trick for herself a hundred times or more since she discovered it when she was six. She could send herself anywhere, but coming back home wasn't easy. Claire wasn't sure why she just couldn't bounce herself back home, but there really wasn't a resident expert on this kind of thing. There was no *Teleportation for Dummies* at the local bookstore. There wasn't anyone she could call up and ask, "Hey, can you tell me why I can't get home the way I got here? You can't? Oh, well, could you just explain to me why I can't get even close?"

Sure, she could triangulate her way around, flinging herself from place to place until she ended up closer to home, but mostly she had to do it the old-fashioned way: bike, car, bus, cab, boat, train, plane. Of course, when she decided on a whim to disappear, she hadn't managed to pack a thing (not that she could take anything with her) and on one sad day when she failed a college exam in statistics, she'd ended up in Hawaii without a bikini or a credit card. She cringed when she thought of the phone call she'd had to make to her mother, though the two days' wait for her driver's license at the Oahu Holiday Inn had actually been fun.

But who cared about that now? In less than a second, she could be away from all of this and drinking a mai-tai on the veranda of Kelani Inn—assuming, of course, the staff took pity on her credit-cardless self. Annie, Thomas, and Sam would think they blinked too long and Claire had just stepped out of the classroom. The children would stop crying, surprised and then excited that they were left all alone, by themselves, no adult in sight. After a moment of exhilaration, they would start crying again, this time even harder. Chaos would ensue. All the children would throw paint, pee in their pants, and sob in the corners. They would be forever marked and ruined by this horrifying abandonment and become troubled, overpierced, drug-addicted teenagers who would look back on this class and all of their education as an abusive waste of time.

What was worse was that—if Claire wanted to—she could dive into their minds, see the patterns of shock and confusion and understanding. As quickly as she could travel to any place on the planet, she could get into the little stream of consciousness that flowed strong through Annie's mind. What would Claire find there? Images of school and home, friends and pets and siblings? Or something worse, something scary and horrible, images Claire would never recover from? After hearing things meant for no one but the thinker, after seeing grief and despair and sexual positions and partners no one should know about, Claire stopped. She didn't dip into anyone's mind but her own, clamping down tight and holding on to her thoughts and her thoughts only.

Childhood was too fraught a place, full of dark forests with evil stepparents, confusing events no one explained, and nightmares that made sleeping with the light on crucial. She didn't want to do that one last thing that would ruin everything for them. Claire knew how hard it was to overcome something from childhood. She had been trying to overcome her "gifts" since forever.

"Sam," Claire said, picking him up and cradling him in her arms, knowing that if she were a male kindergarten teacher, she could never do this. "It's okay. It will be all right."

Claire looked out at her class, all of them staring at her, even Annie, who glanced up at her with a blue smeared face; even Thomas, who stopped his incessant whimpering. "I promise you, it will all be okay."

They stared at her. The big white clock on the wall moved its long black hands in clicking seconds. Claire stayed in the classroom, held Sam who stopped crying, too.

"Really?" Annie asked, and Claire nodded, wishing she were agreeing to what was true.

"Yes," she said. "It will all be one hundred percent okay."

"Little demons," Yvonne said as they walked out to the parking lot. Yvonne Meyer taught the morning kindergarten class and was usually present in the afternoon class as Claire was during Yvonne's. There, but out of the way, prepping for the construction-paper projects that filled slow half hours of time or counting out beans or organizing colored paper or filling out the mountains of paperwork sent each day from the district. But just before the mini-explosion of emotion and incident, Yvonne had gone outside to call her son, who was at home ill.

"Thank God it's the weekend," Yvonne went on. "I can spend the next two days convincing myself to come back to work on Monday. Maybe I'll reward myself with chocolate or heroin."

"They aren't that bad," Claire said. "They're just—"

"Demons. They should be home-schooled or sent to baby boot camps. Rolling in paint! And then there are the parents. Why should we be the ones who have to potty train or wean their children off blankets? It's horrid."

Yvonne stopped at her car, putting her hands on her hips. She was forty-five, a little round, her wild red hair a puff around her face. She loved to wear outfits with bangles and beads, everything in either reds or oranges. When she walked, she emanated patchouli and spice.

"I'm sorry I left. I should have seen the Annie fit coming a mile away."

"Please don't worry about it," Claire said. "I should be able to control them by now. It's my second year here. I guess I just don't have it in me."

"Nonsense," Yvonne said. "You have it in spades. But teaching—well, it's not everyone's cup of tea, and I just feel that there's something else for you out there. Something bigger. Something—I'm not sure what it is. But I'll tell you this. Whatever it is, it's going to be just perfect for you."

"But the children—" Claire began.

"Listen, Claire, you are a gorgeous, smart, talented woman. You have beauty and brains," Yvonne said. "Not that teachers can't be all that. Not that I didn't have it all going on when I was your age, of course." Yvonne stopped to swivel her hips slightly. "But you are wasted here, love.

You are fit for some other setting altogether. I'm not sure where it is, but it's certainly not here."

"Yvonne—"

"Get out, darling," she said. "Get out while there's still time."

"That's what you say every afternoon," Claire said over her shoulder. "And I'm still here."

"I have no idea why," Yvonne called after her. "You could do whatever you wanted. You could be anywhere in the world."

Claire waved, knowing that Yvonne had no idea how right she was.

As she drove home in her used but functioning Toyota Matrix, heading down Fell Street and turning right on Cole, Claire wondered why she didn't just leave San Francisco and put herself in a place she would enjoy. After all, if she didn't like the new locale, she could change that one, too. She had a college degree, a teaching credential, the insurance money from her mother's death. She also had the house she'd grown up in, in West Portal, that she rented out because she couldn't bear to live there. She could sell the huge four-bedroom place, take the profit, and buy a house or condo anywhere she wanted to. No matter where she went, she'd be okay, whether it was Hawaii or Seattle or Boca Raton.

But every time she decided that she'd had it with teaching or the rent increases on her small, one-bedroom apartment or the parking derby with the law students across the street at the university and the tourists going to the Haight-Ashbury district on the other side of the Panhandle, she couldn't leave. Maybe it was because San Francisco was the only town she'd ever lived in, having gone to the University of San Francisco after completing high school.

For some reason, she was waiting for something, right here, where she'd always been.

Claire turned right on Cole Street, and in a small act of magic she didn't possess, there was a small but available parking space just across the street from her apartment building's door. Claire let out a relieved breath, pulled in, and pulled up on the parking brake. For a moment, she stared at the large cement wall of the law library, thinking. Yvonne was right. She wasn't cut out for teaching. But she didn't seem to be really cut out for anything. She'd majored in liberal studies, which was like a buffet of everything, perfect for a grammar school teacher and not much else. She couldn't use her one amazing skill for anything because no one would believe her if she tried to tell them. And she never had told a soul, not even her mother, not even in the last days when her mother was so sick she wouldn't have understood anything.

What would she have said? "Mom, I forgot to tell you that I can close my eyes and leave. Disappear. Really. Just like that. And I can go anywhere I want. It's a little odd when I arrive, but by the time people start to wonder, I can rush off. I've gone to Disneyland—that was when I was seventeen and you told me we couldn't afford a trip that summer because we were saving up for my college. And because of Dad. Leaving. You should have seen me trying to wangle thirty bucks for a bus ticket to get home before you got off your night shift. And I've gone to Yosemite, Round Table Pizza on Mission, and Alcatraz. I went to Stonestown Mall when you grounded me in ninth grade. Susie Thompson's house that night you told me I was forbidden to go there because Susie's mom smoked pot. Yes. All by myself. No, I can't take you with me. I can't take anything but my clothes. I tried taking a suitcase once, but it wouldn't go through. I even tried

a teddy bear. Wouldn't fit through either. Fit through, you ask?
I don't know. It's like there is a small space, space enough
for me, and that's it. Just enough room for my skin and a
millimeter. That means clothes usually make it. Not jackets
or coats. But at least underwear."

No, her mother would never have understood. Nor
would any teacher or friend or lover (not that there ever really
had been a true lover), so this skill was hers and hers alone.
Unused and unnecessary, even now, when she was all by
herself—no family, no boyfriend—and could do whatever
she wanted whenever she wanted.

Claire pulled the keys out of the ignition and put them in
her bag, carefully opening the door and slipping out, trying
not to ding the car next to her. She wished that others were
as careful. Her Toyota looked as though it had been
through a battle with rubber bullets.

The sky was a light shade of gray, warm, like a perfect wool
sweater. Claire walked across the street and sighed. This life
would have to do. She could work harder, join Date.com,
try harder with the children. She could go to more foreign
films, read more literature, go to a hair stylist more than once
a year. She could take her bike out to the Marin Headlands
and get some sun and air and exercise, not to mention a
good look at men in spandex. Things could get better. After
all, her life was a good life. Just about good enough.

That night after a dinner of leftover lemon pasta from
Beppe's and a half glass of Sauvignon Blanc, Claire had the
dream. She had thought she would never have the dream
again, the images fading almost from her memory. How old
had she been the last time she conjured forth the images?
Thirteen or fourteen? And then, when was the last time she
had thought about it? Actually, she had talked about it five,

six years ago, back in college, that one drunken night she had told her roommate Marissa the story.

"You came to Earth on what?" Marissa had burped into Claire's ear, leaning against Claire's shoulder, her body heavy with Heineken. "You came here on a spaceship?"

"That's right," Claire had said. "A big dark one full of children."

"So, um, you were, like, one of them?"

"Yeah." Claire nodded.

"You can't remember a spaceship from when you were one," Marissa said. "No one remembers a spaceship from then."

"I do," Claire said, feeling the warm soft air of the ship, the breath of the children sitting next to her, feeling it the same way she felt Marissa's now. "I was in a spaceship."

"Ha. Spaceship," Marissa said, lying down on the floor and passing out, her hair a dark brown fan in front of her, her last words a slurry mumble. "I want to be in a space-ship. It will take me away from my statistics exam."

"A big dark spaceship full of children. Two of them—two of them I know," Claire said to no one, burping herself and leaning against the wall. She fell asleep, and in the morning, Marissa and she had headaches too intense to talk about anything, much less the spaceship saga. And that had been the last time she thought of it until she woke up tonight, sitting straight up in bed, the pasta a lump of anxiety in her stomach.

The dream unfolded as it always did: She sees her knees and shins and shoes out in front of her. She moves them back and forth, imagining that her feet can talk. Her feet are her parents—the left one her father, the right her mother. But she can't remember her parents. She can't see them or feel them or smell them. For a second, she imagines a shoulder, warmth, heat, tears, but then she is looking at her feet again.

"Sophie," someone says, and she knows that she is Sophie.

Claire—the Sophie in the dream—doesn't say anything but she turns to smile, looking at the girl next to her. The girl is older, her legs longer, her parent feet bigger.

"Home?" she says, and then leans against the girl. But the girl isn't paying attention to her. She's listening to a boy, who is much, much bigger, his legs truly long. He's enormous, powerful, and Sophie is almost scared of him.

There is rumbling under her. The space darkens. The children sitting all around them quiet down. Some cry out, but there is nothing but the movement of the ship, the girl's constant breathing, the *whir whir* of some giant engine under her.

Home, Sophie thinks. *Home*.

But before she can even imagine what or where home is, the dream begins to fade, turns into a smattering of color, bursts of fading dots, disappearing altogether.

Claire breathed in the night of her bedroom, looked out the window to the blinking red eyes of Sutro Tower. Off, on. Off, on, all of them winking at her. She shook her head and lay back down, staring at the ceiling. Why the dream now? When she was little, she used to make up stories about the children, imagining they were her long-lost siblings. They were all going on a trip together, going somewhere safe and warm. She even named the other children, murmuring their names under her breath. What did she call them? Something with an *M*. Something full of vowels. *A* or *E* or *O*.

Now Claire couldn't remember what she called them, but

all these years later, she still felt as though she knew them, those children with the longer legs, knobby knees, dark eyes, the same blond hair as she has.

Not now.

Claire opened her eyes wide, straining, looking around the room. She waited, listening. Had she heard something? Or was it part of the dream still?

Waiting, she breathed into the darkness, hoping for more. No, hoping for less. For silence.

Not right. Go.

Her heart beat out a surprised rhythm, her body tense and waiting for more words. Maybe it was finally happening. She was hearing voices, losing her mind, finally succumbing to the weirdness of her life. What had she read recently? That more people than previously believed heard voices. It was actually kind of common, with support groups and everything. An adaptive behavior for those who heard voices and talked back to them was to carry a phone and talk into that, a decoy for madness.

Should she carry a cell phone now?

How would that go over in the kindergarten class?

Claire waited, listening in the quiet room, but there was no further message from her brain or the beyond. What did that mean? Was she schizophrenic? Was this the beginning of the end?

After a few more quiet minutes, Claire laughed. Probably it was a leftover thought from her dream. It had to be. And truth be told, she had more than voices to think about. Pushing off the blanket, Claire got out of bed and walked to the window. Just over that hill was her mother's house, the house she used to call home. But she had to admit to herself that lately, nowhere seemed like home. Not San Francisco, not any of the places she imagined traveling to. Certainly she didn't feel at home in her classroom, not with sloshing paints and urine a constant and permanent threat. But inside herself—in her mind or body—wasn't any better. Somewhere in her chest, her stomach, her core, she felt a place of slipping, sliding unease. Nowhere she stood felt comfortable. No one or no thing gave her that feeling she had in the dream. Every time in the dream, even though she was truly in a spaceship traveling to points unheard of and unseen, she was safe. She was happy.

Turning away from the window, Claire pushed her long hair behind her shoulders and glanced at the clock. The red 3:00 shone into the room and then flicked to 3:01. Four hours until she had to be at her Saturday morning Pilates class. Over fifty hours before Yvonne and the children would expect her at work. Hours before anyone would expect her anywhere at all.

"Okay, I want you to balance on the roller. Your hip centered just there, and then slide. Work that fascia. Stretch it, let your body elongate. Can you feel it lengthen, open, spread, release? That's it," said Nori, Claire's Pilates instructor. "Come on. All the way to the knee. That's it, folks. Work it."

Claire hated this feeling of thigh stretch more than any other, though her classmate Ruth told her childbirth was a bit more painful. Claire looked over at Ruth and wanted to roll her eyes. Ruth could take the Styrofoam roller and move her body from hip joint to ankle, stretching muscles Claire barely knew the names of. She knew they existed, however, because they all hurt, all at once, at this very moment.

"Ruth, you're killing me," she said. "Could you stop showing off?"

"Once you get to sixty, showing off is a way to stay alive."

Ruth rolled herself along the roller again. "Use it or lose it, I always say."

They both huffed through another up and down, the room filling with heat and the faint odor of sweat.

"I must have lost it before I got it," Claire puffed.

"It isn't easy. But I don't want to just go gently into that good night. When I married my second husband at fifty, I told him I wanted fifty years with him. The same amount of life I already had. So I have some work to do to stay healthy all those long years."

Claire took in a big breath, feeling the sweat running down her neck. She kept rolling back and forth, watching Nori's and Ruth's perfect form. Fifty years with someone? A man? A husband? A long-term boyfriend? A lover? In college, she'd had boyfriends, boys she dated for three, four, five weeks, half a year, all of them sort of falling away without any big breakup, fight, or tears from either of them. There were no screaming matches or songs from the sidewalk below her apartment window. No love letters, no smashed dishes.

It wasn't that there was anything wrong with any of the boys, men. There hadn't been a drug addict, narcissist, commitment-phobe among them. They were artists, pre-law, pre-med, teacher-tract types, who took her to movies and plays and parties and meals. Over and over again, Claire just felt disinterested, wanting to say, "Look, this coffee is just fine, but would you mind if I went to Barbados for a while? I'll be back. Keep my seat, though it might take a while for me to get home. I just can't listen to you for one more minute. I don't want to hear about the people in your office or that html or xml or C plus code you are talking about. But really, it's not that you're boring, it's that I'm bored. Bored out of my mind. *Au revoir!*"

But she never left them sitting there. She never quieted her mind and thought: Majorca, Ibiza, Aruba, Belize. She sat through bad date after bad date, pretending to be part of a couple until one or both of them just stopped calling each other. No real good-byes, no true breakup. Only apathy and confusion.

And though there had been moments of desire with a few of the men, her body rippling in a tender line of mouth, breasts, belly, thighs, she never felt the need to open herself up to any of the men she'd dated. Kisses, fine; a little skin, okay. A feel here, a feel there, nothing more than a biology experiment going nowhere.

And it wasn't that she had some kind of moral or philosophical argument for not having sex. She didn't think it was wrong or outrageous or reprehensible. It was just that she had never really felt the need, as if she were waiting for the man who would make her want to turn to him, kiss him back, say, "Yes."

"Shift to the front of the thigh. Quadriceps," Nori called out. "Work those big boys. Biggest muscle other than that thing on your backside. Come on, people!"

Claire shifted, wincing as the Styrofoam dug into her thighs. She stared at the beige and green carpet as she rolled back and forth, her hair dangling in front of her.

"Fifty years," she said to Ruth, slightly panting. "Won't you get sick of him? Won't you just want to be alone?"

Ruth looked up, her biceps firm and strong as they held her up. "Being alone is overrated. I know, I know. People say we have to do it. So important to stand on one's own feet, yadda yadda yadda. Rite of passage. Whatever you want to call it. But when I met Jim, I just knew. Every single day with him is a blessing," she said, finally allowing some huffing and puffing to enter into her words. "Every single day is a gi-ift."

*   *   *

Claire waved to Ruth as Ruth pulled out of her parking space and then drove out of the garage. It was a crowded Saturday morning, everyone trying to work off a week of carbs and fat in one kickboxing session, three people eyeing Claire's space as they pulled up from different directions. She knew she had to get out of the spot and didn't want to see the battle for the one remaining spot begin.

She started the Toyota and backed up, putting the car in first and ignoring the cars jockeying for position. But just as she began to move slowly toward the exit, she heard a voice slip through the garage and car noises, whirl around her, and slip into her ear.

"Sophia," the voice said.

Claire pressed down on the brakes so hard, a squeal peeled itself off her tires, echoing in the cavernous space. The cars waiting for her space honked, her car stalled. Claire swallowed, blinked, tried to start her car again. But the car wouldn't engage, and she was sure that she'd flooded the engine or just gone mental. She tried again, sweat trickling down her neck. She stepped on the brake, thinking it was the accelerator. Panic slipped through her body like a spider.

"Sophia," the voice said. "Imagine this. Try putting it in first gear."

"Huh?" Claire said, looking around the car. Nothing. No one. But the voice was right. She was in fourth gear, her rushed shifting keeping the car from turning over.

She shifted the car to first and started the engine, every-thing working. The three cars honked, and Claire wished she was clever enough to throw out some retort or at least flip them all off convincingly. But what she needed to do was get home and eat something. She was obviously suffer-ing from low blood sugar. That and stress. Fatigue. She needed rest. And maybe wine. Maybe some of the leftover Percocet from when she had her wisdom teeth extracted two years before.

"What you really need is to pull this car over," the voice said. "All I need is for us to have a crash, and then what would my heroic rescue be worth? All this travel, all this time to spend the afternoon with a Triple A tow truck driver and then a mechanic named Al who smokes a cigar in a recliner and barks out orders to a skinny guy with no teeth."

Claire whipped her head around, looking in the backseat, the passenger's, swerving as she did. What was she supposed to do? The car lurched, and she felt an invisible hand grab the wheel, setting the car straight.

"You are really pissing me off!" she said.

"I'm sorry about that, but you need to stop."

"Because a voice in my head is telling me to? I thought that last night's voices were just from a dream. But I am seriously insane."

"Sophia. Pull over. Please."

"God dammit, no," she said, the car slowing and starting as she did, people behind her honking. "Get out of my head or my car or both!"

Claire gunned it down onto Brotherhood Way and sped onto Nineteenth Avenue, hoping that she'd left the voice behind. She drove close to the steering wheel, looking in her rearview mirror every few seconds, expecting to see some kind of person following after her, like a terrible balloon with its string caught in her back window.

But there was no bobbing body floating behind her, and as she passed Stonestown Mall and then slowly crawled toward Irving Street, she relaxed slightly, her back almost touching the seat.

Okay, she thought. *Okay. Just a few more miles and all this will disappear.*

As she rounded the park, heading toward Stanyan, she wished for the nth time that her mother were alive. Like so many things, she wouldn't be able to tell her mother about the voice, but she could at least sit by her and maybe watch a TV show. Or work out in the garden, digging up weeds or planting the latest in heirloom vegetables. Anything to take her mind away from the craziness.

But, of course, her mother wasn't here anymore, and there wasn't a person she could confide in. Claire was pretty sure that Yvonne would listen politely and then call 911. Ruth would likely do the same. Maybe it was time to go to a therapist and just spill it all and wait to see what a trained professional would suggest. Maybe she would do it. Maybe she would just finally take care of this problem.

"You don't have a problem, you nut," the voice said.

"Stop it!" Claire shrieked, braking hard at the corner of Stanyan and Hayes, a Muni bus squealing to avoid hitting her.

"Shit, shit, shit," she said, turning right onto Hayes and stalling right behind a FedEx van.

"You need to stop this car right now," the voice said.

Breathing in small, shallow breaths, Claire pulled over, parking in a rare open spot, ignoring the stares from passersby and the FedEx driver. The voice might be a product of her own imagination, but it was right. She was a danger to herself and others.

"Who are you?" she whispered, convinced now that she was talking to nothing but her own sad thoughts. "Where are you?"

"Due to the powers of others, I have managed to render

myself invisible this once," the voice said. "But I don't hear that well."

"Who are you?" she asked again, her voice louder, clearer, even though she felt her heart pounding in her throat.

She looked down at her hands in her lap, shaking her head, almost wanting to laugh out loud. Was she this lonely and sad that she was conjuring up a voice? A male voice. A man. A man who was focused on her. She had finally cracked. All these years she really had been crazy. Those times she thought she'd gone to another country or town or place had been psychotic breaks. A psychotic break. She had been delusional, was so right now. When she thought she could hear other people's thoughts, she was merely deep in some horrid fantasy of her own creation.

She was paranoid, schizophrenic, maybe bipolar with an affective disorder. Top it off with panic and anxiety, and she was a psychiatrist's dream. A master's thesis. A doctoral dissertation.

So it was clear. She had no choice. No more debate here. Nothing else to argue about. Claire knew she needed to drive herself right now to Langley Porter Psychiatric Institute at UCSF and check in. Forever. Get some kind of commitment. What did they call that? A 5150. At least she'd never have to deal with Annie and Sam again.

"Oh, what a drama queen!" the voice said, and as she heard the words, a body began to take shape and form in a waver of pixilated air.

"You are a jerk," faded from her tongue, and she blinked, tried to focus on what she could hardly believe was happening next to her in the passenger's seat.

For the moments it took for him to appear, Claire knew that even though she had felt odd her entire life—even though she'd made herself appear with a *poof!* all over the place—she'd never really believed that magic existed. She never really thought about the concept of super powers or abilities. Everything truly odd was contained in her and her alone—she was the holder of the world's weirdness. Actually, she thought she was some kind of genetic anomaly, a creation of some weird fluke in a DNA strand. No one else was like her. No one on the planet.

"I would have to say that no one is like you. But you aren't alone in this power business," said the man now sitting next to her. "Believe it or not, soon you are not going to be all alone anymore, ever again."

Claire couldn't focus on what he was saying. Instead, she slowly moved her gaze from his thigh (a very nice thigh in what seemed to be cotton pants) to his body (strong), shoulders (stronger), neck, and then face. His face. Claire wanted to stop breathing because if she did, she would die, and she wouldn't have to sit there completely embarrassed, her body roiling in heat, her mind just about everywhere.

"You are just some kind of delusion," she said, relieved in a strange way that at least she knew what she was dealing with. "Some kind of sad last gasp of hope in me."

"Really?" the man said. "Strange how I feel so *here*. You know, like in my body."

"Sorry. You're not," Claire said. "It's all about me. Finally, the cliché comes true. Hold on to your hat. We're going to Langley Porter. It's close by, so that's good. Put on your seat belt."

"I don't think that's where I want to go. From the sound of it, there are madwomen screaming in the attic there," he said, and for a brief second, she allowed herself to look at him. He was so—so perfect. His eyes were dark, looking at her with an intense, humor. Like he liked her and wanted to laugh not at but with her. His dark brown hair hung in soft curls to his shoulders, gleaming in the sunlight coming through the car window. He smiled, his teeth white, his lips full. As if hearing her, he licked his lips, his eyes sparkling, his hand almost reaching out to touch her.

"Whoa, buddy." Claire started giggling, laughing, resting her forehead on the steering wheel and then sitting up and looking back at him. "Keep your fake hands to yourself. If I'm going to be crazy, I'm not going to add to it by letting the figment of my imagination touch me. Haven't you ever seen that movie *Fight Club?*"

When the man didn't answer, she answered for him. "Of course you did, because I did and you're me, so you did. I've split my psyche. If there were a movie of this car scene, I'd be talking to air. It's Brad Pitt and Ed Norton all over again. The next thing you know, I'll be hitting myself thinking I'm beating you up."

"This is not going the way I wanted it to," he said slowly. "It would be easier if you would just be quiet for a minute."

"So you have practice in this?" Claire wondered how many other unfortunate women were out there, all certain a handsome man had just appeared one day, especially for them.

The man sighed, shook his head, and put his hands on his knees. Turning to face the street, he sighed.

"Look, I know this is weird. And I tend to be a pain in the ass. So can we start over here?"

Claire stared at him, breathing in quick breaths, nervous and scared and amazed. And then she smelled it. Him. He smelled like soap and something citrus, the tang of whatever he used to shave filling the car.

Do hallucinations have smells? she thought. *Is this a multisensory projection of all my sorrows? Can I hear, smell, see him? God knows if I could taste him, and I didn't let him touch me. But smell?*

"You know," he said slowly, "I haven't had much practice with this. You are the first person I've rescued. And, of course, I have a vested interest. But I really would like to start over. If I get out of the car, would you promise not to drive away?"

As he spoke, the man seemed to become more real. His movements had weight. He filled the car space with what Claire could only call maleness: smells, words, muscles actually rippling under his clothes. Rippling. She'd thought it was only a cliché, the men she'd dated skinny or maybe filling out their Dockers a little too fully around the middle, their expensive leather belts pulled tight.

He smiled again, his eyes so bright, dark but seeming to be full of pinpoints of light. "Do you promise?"

Claire nodded, took her hands away from the wheel and folded them in her lap. What would it hurt to listen to him? Maybe once he left the car, he would simply disappear. Hallucination over. A wonderful hallucination all gone.

"I promise," she said.

"Okay," he said, not moving.

"You don't trust me? My own hallucination doesn't trust me? Does that mean I don't trust myself?" She wanted to laugh. "Listen, take the keys with you. If you disappear, I'll just find them outside on the sidewalk."

Claire pulled the keys out of the ignition and dangled them close to him. He took them, but she jerked back before he could touch her skin.

"So you have them," she said. "Go on. Get out and we can start over."

She brought a hand to her mouth, pressing back her

laughter, the nervous sound that was growing in her chest and pushing upward. If Yvonne could see her now! Ruth, too! Her older friends would finally get how bad things had gotten.

The man shrugged, opened the door, and got out, the car suddenly empty of energy and heat as he closed the door.

I'm counting to twenty, she thought.

She looked out to see him standing on the sidewalk. Well, not all of him. She couldn't see below his thighs or above his chest, so she allowed herself to watch the grace of his body (his core, as Nori would say), the way he seemed to stand so naturally. Like an animal used to speed and comfort. A lion, a jaguar, a creature that could go from zero to sixty in six seconds.

Trust me, I take a lot longer than six seconds.

Claire listened to his thought, focusing on every single syllable, wondering how it got into her mind, and then she realized—*my God*! He could do what she did. He could hear . . . he'd heard everything she'd been thinking since the moment he appeared in her car. Before that, even. Maybe it was he who had spoken—thought—the night before in her bedroom.

You—you read thoughts? You read thoughts!

You are one quick cookie, he thought. *Now stop thinking. Be quiet and let me start all of this over again.*

Claire blinked, stared out in front of her. The person she created in her hallucination would have her abilities and would be able to read her thoughts. But as she sat there watching people navigate the crosswalk, heading toward the medical buildings on either side of the street, she wondered if this might really be happening. Was this happening? Was she really here? She shot a glance at the man's torso. This was happening. Something was actually happening to her. Could it be that her life was about to start after all?

Sophia, he thought. *For God's sake. Stop it. Quiet down.*

Okay, she thought. She closed her eyes and then opened them. *Sophia?* That name was so familiar.

Stop thinking, he thought.

Claire sighed and closed her eyes again. She swallowed hard and tried to keep her mind empty.

But it was impossible. Nothing she'd learned in Pilates or even the occasional yoga class was helping her clear her crazy monkey-mind thoughts. What could she do? How could she focus? She could probably focus on a muscle. Her calf. She'd stretch it out, imagining the sinews and tendons elongating. Claire pushed her heel down, feeling the pull, but then she knew that he was listening in on her, hearing her try to quiet herself.

She would empty herself. She'd try to be the way she was sometimes on a spring afternoon when the kids were drawing with the thick crayons on thick construction paper. In a rare moment, they were concentrating on one thing. The sun would beat down into the classroom, their little voices would merge into a lull, and Claire's head would empty, her body soften, relax, adjust into her small-sized seat.

There, she thought, feeling that warm afternoon feeling, the way it always was just before the bell rang and she could go home.

He knocked on the window, the door creaking open. Claire almost jumped straight up, blinking her eyes.

"Hi," he said. "How are you?"

"Um," she started. "Great."

"Hey, I've come a long way with a couple of messages, so do you think we might go somewhere where we can talk?"

Then the first normal thing since she got in the car happened. Her stomach growled. And somehow that feeling began to overwhelm everything else she'd been feeling.

"Do you like pho soup?" she asked.

"Foe? Like an enemy?" he asked, opening the door and sitting down. "If it's made of my foes, I'd have to say no. They aren't very appetizing. Scrawny things, really. Not a lot of meat."

Claire started the car. "No, not foes. P-h-o. Broth, noodles, vegetables, and meat. It's Vietnamese."

"Sweetheart, if it has meat in it," he said, "I'm in."

Claire felt almost perfectly normal when the server brought her the steaming bowl, the soup fragrant with chili and ginger.

She picked up the large spoon and looked at her lunch companion, his lips, his eyes, the way one dark curl twirled below his ear. He, however, was mesmerized by his food, ogling his Chinese five-spice chicken, going for the plate of meat instead of soup.

"This is exactly what I've been needing. On the safe—at home we have food, but nothing like this. Nothing that I can exactly identify."

Claire sipped her soup, trying to stop staring at him. Where had he come from where food wasn't identifiable? Had he escaped from—from what? A ghostly gulag? A special prison where people learned how to materialize? A baby food factory?

"We're starting over again," he said, forking chunks of succulent chicken. "Let's not get weird."

"My thoughts." Claire put down her spoon. "I can turn my ability off. Can you?"

His mouth full, the man nodded.

"So let's do that, then," she said. "Let's really start over. Do what normal people do."

The man was almost humming with food pleasure, probably really unaware of what she was saying. But she felt him unlink, close off, and she knew her thoughts were her own. He nodded again, and Claire watched him plow through the food. How his mother must have loved to feed him, she thought. How fun to put a plate of food down in front of someone and have him really chow down.

Claire went back to her soup, looking up occasionally as she ate. The man was smiling and eating, looking at her, the dining room, mumbling thanks as the server filled his water glass.

"Oh, I wonder what beer they have," he said finally, putting down his fork. "God, that would taste good. A cold beer."

"Order one," she said. "Why not? If you can't get identifiable food at home, I would think beer would be even harder to find."

"Yeah, it is. Sort of like a dry state. But no, I probably need to keep my wits about me, such as they are."

"For what?" she asked. Now that her stomach was full, her completely flabbergasted feeling came back, wrapping over her like a shawl. She put her palm down hard on the table. "Moving around into other people's cars? I mean, what was that? And I don't even know your name. Who are you? Where did you come from?"

"So you've moved from thinking I don't exist except in your mind? I've graduated to actual flesh-and-blood status? Am I real now? Like that rabbit in the story, gone from stuffed to hopping around?"

Claire pushed her half-empty bowl of soup away and sat back in her chair, glad there weren't diners at the next table.

"I think you're real. You eat real, at least. And fast, too."

"Always the first done. I had three siblings, so we learned to dig in fast in order to grab whatever was left over."

Claire blinked. A man who materialized in her car had siblings. Three! Having always been an only child, Claire couldn't imagine what it must have been like to fight for food.

But could his family do what he could? Could they read minds? Were there actually other people out there who were like her? Real people? People she might pass on the street?

"Are your siblings like you?"

The man sat back, a hand on his flat belly. "Not that I can tell. We never had a sit-down where I came out of the weirdo closet. Once I figured out what I could do, I sort of watched them for clues. Something kind of held me back, though, and I never said anything to them."

Claire breathed in, confused. So confused. How had she gotten from Pilates and Ruth's conversation about marriage and rolling around in pain on the floor to here, eating Vietnamese food with a man who materialized in her car?

He looked at her, shook his head, and smiled. "Come on. Let's go. Of course, I hope you have cash."

She almost snorted. "What a date. Scare me to death and then make me pay."

"Sorry, I have a true lack of dollars lately. I promise, I'll make it up to you." He winked, his face so open and handsome, she thought she might fall into it. How long had it been since she'd been drawn toward a man? She'd almost given up looking for the feeling, imagining herself the spinster kindergarten teacher Miss Edwards.

This wasn't right. Not now. Claire stood up abruptly. Her excitement was not a feeling she anticipated, and she stormed up to the cash register, wanting to somehow make it all stop. Right now. Going insane was better than falling for a man who might not even really be real and who didn't carry cash.

*   *   *

Outside on Geary Street, Claire felt her head clear. "So are you going to answer any of my questions? I think I've been very patient."

"Of course," he said. "If you're going to be with me forever, I have to start somewhere."

"Forever? Excuse me? What did you say?"

He walked toward her, and she stepped away, her back against the stucco wall. "I said I'm going to be with you forever."

"Give me a break! You can't just say something like that. It's too soon! It's too weird. It's not normal."

"Nothing about us is normal, but I've been waiting my whole life for you, Sophia."

As he spoke, she wondered if this was the same kind of magic that allowed him to be invisible. He had the rare ability to make women not want to laugh when he said ridiculous things, the things that men maybe thought but never, ever said, except in soap operas and in horrible desperation. Or maybe they were the things women wished men could say without seeming like weaklings. But these words from this man's mouth sounded real and true and, if Claire thought about it, more magic than appearing in her car.

Claire crossed her arms, but a slim, flickering part of her wanted to believe him.

"Now I know that it's you who is crazy," she said, dropping her arms to her sides. "Not me."

He didn't say a word, and she looked into his dark eyes, feeling each breath under her ribs. She didn't know what was happening, and yes, of course she did. There it was, like a fan waving a sign at the Oscars. A kiss. She wanted to kiss him. That's what she wanted to do. How sick was that? There was more wrong with her than she previously imagined. But she really had no choice but to kiss him, and then she was flooded with more heat and shame. She was thinking too loud. He'd probably turned on his mind and heard every single thought she'd had. And that's when he did laugh, for a second, and that's when he leaned over and kissed her.

Claire couldn't have pulled away, even if he'd been a toad without the prince part. His mouth was so, well, there. Warm and soft and insistent, he was telling her everything with his lips and then, gently, with his tongue. But he was also telling her things with his mind. She hadn't opened up her thoughts for years because there hadn't been anyone to hear her, but here now, as they stood on the sidewalk, was a feeling of warmth, something yellow, golden, sun kissed. Here was hope, a feeling of connection that looked like rope, thick and tightly wrapped. Here was travel, darkness and light and speed. Here was an image of bodies moving together, pleasure in the sound of an *Oh!*

His mind opened up to her, and she realized that he was right. She wasn't alone. For once, she was with someone—someone like her. She was in his mind.

You are the only one I ever hear this way, she thought, letting him put his arms around her.

Shh, he thought, stroking her arms, her shoulders, his hands running gently up her neck, his thumbs lightly skimming her jaw.

What is your name? she thought to ask, but then she almost missed his answer, her body so caught up in his touch.

Darl, he thought. *Now, shh.*

So Claire, for once, didn't think. She let herself fall back into this kiss, as if it were a soft down mattress that would catch her. As if this kiss were the last thing she would ever do on this planet.

Maybe it will be the last thing you do, he thought, pulling her close. *I've got to take you away from this place.*

His hair brushed against her face, her neck, long and soft and silken. She let her arms wrap around him, feeling parts of her body start up, heat welling in her stomach, her throat, her thighs.

Where are we going to go?

Shh, he thought again, and then the world faded to only him. Only his lips, only his breath. She stopped hearing the honking cars outside, barely saw or felt the sunlight or the breeze blowing up from the Pacific. There was nothing but him. Nothing at all.

Chapter Two

All his life, Darl James simply had to think of home, and he was there. It didn't matter where he was: working as a cashier at Total Foods in downtown Olympia, Washington, playing video games with his friends on a well-worn garage couch, skateboarding on the long, beautiful slab of concrete in front of the school library. He'd be at school at football practice, think of eating a chicken salad sandwich at the kitchen counter, and he was suddenly there standing by the Formica or the stove or sitting at the long farmhouse table.

"Shit, honey, where did you come from?" his mother Joanne would say, grabbing the kitchen counter with one hand, the other at her throat. "Whoops! Sorry. I mean, holy cow!"

Darl would blink, unable to tell her the truth, unable to say, "I was thinking about that great chicken from dinner last night and I got hungry. So I just popped in for a quick sandwich."

No, he'd make up some lame excuse about feeling sick and then realizing he wasn't sick but hungry. Starving! He'd talk about the stealth and speed and strength he'd gained from being tight end, able to block anybody, able to catch anything And his mom would end up making him the chicken salad sandwich and then insist that he stay home in case he was, in fact, sick. They'd watch a movie, sitting together on the couch, until his younger siblings Dave, Suzy, and Julie came home, complaining that Darl always got to stay home, always got the best leftovers, always got Mom's attention.

"No fair," they'd say.

And he knew they were thinking, somewhere in the very back corners of their mind, *Why is he the favorite? Why is the adopted one the one Mom loves best? I mean, she named him* Darling, *after all.*

And because the four of them shared her like a prize between them—their father Pete long since gone to his new family in Seattle, leaving them behind in the little blue house on Caton Way—Darl understood. He knew how precious their mother was to them because she didn't leave them behind, moving on to a whole new life. Because she always stayed, cared, loved them all, even him, the adopted one. Because she pushed them, challenged them to learn more, study harder, think about the future. If Darl were his siblings, he would have felt the same way.

Later, when he was in college, he'd managed to keep control of his hunger and his thoughts of Joanne's great cooking because he had been accepted at the University of Southern California on a football scholarship, and suddenly appearing in Olympia, Washington, out of nowhere for a chicken sandwich would be way too hard to explain to his poor mother.

And because his mother had not moved from the house he'd grown up in, Darl wasn't sure if it was the house or his mother or both that drew him back, just like that, all those times while he was growing up. Now that he was living in

Southern California in Encino, he found himself pulled back to his own suburban tract house each time he let his guard down. Bored at a faculty meeting? The room stuffy and airless and full of the same teacher complaints he'd heard since he started teaching? In a flash, he'd be on his couch, in his living room, blinking into the afternoon light.

Now that he was with the others on the safe house and they talked of making a home for them all somewhere, away from destructive anger of the Neballats, would that be home? Or was this, this feeling of Sophia in his arms home? Was she where he would keep his heart?

But everything was too hard to explain. He'd never even tried. How could he say, "I close my eyes, and then I'm here. I don't have to fly. I don't even feel it. I don't think one tiny millisecond goes by. I'm in one place, and then another. Just like that."

Who would have believed him? He wasn't stupid enough to think he could go around talking about crazy stuff like that and not end up on Dr. Thorton's table with a tongue depressor in his mouth and the man's concern evident in the creases on his forehead.

No, some smart part of him had kept his ability a secret, as if appearing at home were as normal as being able to make a ninety-yard punt return every single game, week after week after week. Everything had always been a secret, confusing, a mystery. And even now, as Darl kissed Sophia as they stood on the sidewalk on Geary Street in San Francisco, traffic zooming by, he didn't know what to tell her. She didn't know anything about him. And she sure didn't know anything about who they were.

She sighed, her breath sweet, light, her mouth warm. Darl kissed her harder, touching her firm sides with his hands, feeling her muscles flex slightly. This was a story that was hard to believe, no matter how it was told. He remembered what it was like when Michael and Kate showed up in Los Angeles with their energy bubble and tried to convince him that one, he wasn't hallucinating, and two, he was from a planet in space, Cygiria. As he stood there on the football field, watching the junior varsity team run back toward the locker room, he received the news that he, Darl James, was a space alien, like one of those creepy creatures from late-night Saturday television. Not only was he not Earth born, a human, a human being, but he needed to leave the planet right now and jump into this strange energy bubble and fly through the atmosphere into space to a safe house located on an asteroid. On the asteroid were dozens of fellow Cygirians, all plotting on how to reunite their lost tribe. There was a big fight going on with some invisible, murderous aliens from yet another planet, and Darl needed to help.

"What are you smoking?" he had asked them both, these two beautiful people standing in front of him. "I mean, you look relatively normal, and I hate to be rude. But you're insane and I think you should leave right now."

"Like being a homing pigeon in terms of traveling back to your point of origin isn't kinda wacky?" Michael asked. "Like reading minds isn't either? Come on, dude. Think about it. You know inside that this is all going to make sense. You've probably never felt normal until right now as you're listening to this."

And the story did make sense, even though he was petrified the entire ride to the safe house in the bubble, stars and meteors and planets under his feet like sparkling carpet. But Kate and Michael were right. Everything had made sense once he got to the safe house. He'd met people who knew him, even though they had never met him before. They knew how it felt to be different. Even with the warm love of his mother, his football team, his friends, his schooling, his job as a high school football coach, Darl had never felt there, arrived, in place. For the first time, he felt truly comfortable in his own skin. Not special or weird or secretive. He felt entirely normal. He'd come home.

So how would Sophia react to the story of their people, her life as it would unfold from this point on? How could he possibly tell her? The truth was, he didn't want to explain it to her now. The tale was too big, too unwieldy. And he didn't want to interrupt this kiss, so long and lovely and anticipated. She was so soft, so here right now, so in his arms, making the smallest of sighs and sounds. He wanted her, her lips on his, her body pressed as close as it could get on a busy San Francisco street.

Sophia moved closer to him, and he could feel the wonderful fullness of her breasts against him, her light sweat like citrus, like rain. God, he wanted her, even though it was ridiculous. Even though she couldn't yet know they were twins, doubles, paired in energy and ability. She wasn't ready for him yet.

Slowly, he pulled away from her, feeling the current of movement sliding away as he did. "Let's go to your place," he said. "Or somewhere else. Maybe we could get coffee. Man, I could go for some caffeine."

Sophia looked at him, blinking, confused. "But . . . I still don't know anything about you but your name."

"It's a very long story," he said. "And I'm pretty sure that just about an hour ago, you were ready to commit yourself to the most illustrious mental health facility in the country. That is insane in and of itself, but I think that what I have to say might not sit well right now. And we aren't in enough of a rush that I can't spend more time."

As she listened to him, he could see the parts of her personality flash in front of him. At first she seemed to agree. Then she became irritated, pressing her lips together and crossing her arms. And then she seemed to remember their kiss. Her face softened, and watching her remember what he was still feeling made Darl want to kiss her again. And again.

"We could go to my apartment, I guess," she began, but the word "apartment" made Darl think without wanting to of her bed, soft and welcoming. From her very orderly appearance even in a workout getup, she must keep a clean house. The bed would be made up with nice linens, the blankets soft, the pillows fluffy, her body . . . Darl shook his head.

"I don't know," he said. "Let's just walk."

Sophia looked up the street. "This really isn't what you might call a touristy street. It's more like Le Mans. People trying to get from downtown to the beach as fast as possible."

"Where else?"

She thought, biting her lip. "We could go up a couple of blocks to Clement. Look at the Chinese markets. Go into the kitchen supply store. Or a store. Stare at Peking ducks hanging in the window. But I don't really want to do that. I want to ask you questions. I want—"

Sophia breathed out, looked down. "I don't understand what is happening."

He lifted her jaw with his hand, feeling her smooth skin on his fingertips. She was so beautiful, her hair like something out of a story his mother read to him as a child. Was it Rapunzel's or the princess's from *The Princess and the Pea,* girly stories that his sisters had wanted to hear night after night? He didn't know, but even as a child, he'd stared at the long trains of hair more than paid attention to his mother's soothing voice. He must have remembered Sophia, even then.

He looked at her, his heart opening. He'd never imagined that this deep welling of feeling could be real. Sure, he'd known what everyone at the safe house had told him about the intensity of seeing your twin, the one you truly could not live without. Yeah, he'd seen them all matched up, united in power and in some kind of connection he associated with stupid television movies or books that women read on the beach. Of course he knew that it was crucial that all Cygirians found their twin, their mate in order to bring their people back together.

Whatever.

But here it was—she was—right in front of him. For him. She didn't know it yet, had no idea what he was about to tell her, but this feeling was real. It was true.

"Let's go look at pots and pans. You can tell me more about San Francisco. I've only been here twice, and once was for a bachelor party. I think the places I went to are not on any tourist map. Or shouldn't be."

Sophia looked up, cocked her head, and stared at him. Then she nodded and sighed. "Okay. Pots and pans it is. Maybe even a little teapot."

The morning weather had handed off the day to the afternoon, the air shifting into the brief warm lull before the fog rolled back in. Together, Darl and Sophia walked the blocks from Geary and Clement Street in silence, a couple of feet apart, each looking at the other periodically and then turning away.

No matter how weird this felt, Darl was glad to be back on Earth, on this soil, in his country. He'd never imagined that his twin was just up the state from him all this time, but San Francisco? When Darl thought of this city, he thought of the saying that Mark Twain apparently didn't even say: *The coldest winter I ever spent was a summer in San Francisco.*

"No one knows who said it," Sophia said.

"You told me to turn it off! And all along, you sneaky thing, you've been listening." Darl moved closer to her, wanting to take her hand but holding off for now.

"You got sloppy and let me right in," she said, smiling.

I can't believe I met someone else who could do this, she thought, looking at him, her eyes so full of relief, Darl wanted to read more than her thoughts. He wanted to touch her body as if it were a manuscript written in Braille.

He was reining back his thoughts now, but he saw Sophia could sense his feelings. She blushed and her walk slowed, then sped up.

"It's so weird to be able to talk about this. The way we are. My mother would have never, ever understood," she said. "She loved me. But she was very conservative. She wasn't thrilled when I got my ears pierced."

Darl laughed, moved to let a skateboarder rumble by. "Sweetheart, this is not something anyone understands. Except maybe people in Berkeley or Taos. Or *Star Trek* fans. People who like Harry Potter and *The Lord of the Rings.*"

She stopped walking, turned to him. "*Star Trek*? Harry Potter? Fantasy? Why those stories?"

"Oh," he said. "You know. Telepathy and all that. Like something Spock could do. Or that one chick in the newer *Star Trek*. Magic in general. Listen."

"You watch that stuff?" she asked.

"I had to. It was the only way I could figure things out. Nothing could completely explain who I was, but it sure helped," he said.

"This is crazy," she said. "I'm crazy. This just can't be real."

Darl took her arm, guiding her forward. "What I'm saying is that most people don't consider the things we can do as normal. Not by a long shot."

"Things?" She was interested, slowing, her leg brushing his as they walked. "What other things? What else do you have?"

Darl wondered if this was the time to tell her, here on this busy block, the bustle of Clement Street just yards ahead. Cars rushed by, shoppers carried pink plastic bags hurrying home with lunch, two cops stood at the corner talking with a bicyclist. When he breathed in, he could smell the savory heat of Peking duck, the meat succulent and spicy.

"Darl?" she asked. "What is it?"

He'd never had to flat-out tell anyone about his power. Kate and Michael had assumed he could do something—after all, he was a Cygirian and they were rescuing him. But he'd never stood face-to-face with a person and told him or her what he could do.

"Tell me," she asked. "What else can you do besides read minds and become invisible with some help?"

He swallowed, looked into the warmth of her dark eyes. "I can send myself home."

Sophia listened, blinked. "I don't understand."

"I can go home. Right now." He snapped his fingers. "Like that."

Sophia stared at him. "You want to go home. Where is that?"

"Not—"

"Where are you from, anyway? Around here?"

"No, my little dense one. Think about it. I can go home by thinking about it. By intent," he said. "All I do is let go, focus, and there I am. Home."

"Dense one!" she said, but even as she tried to get angry, his words began to bear fruit in her mind.

"I think it, and then, there I am," he repeated.

And then her face opened into what he could only call peace. She closed her eyes slightly and smiled. "No."

"Yes."

"Yes."

In this second of her acceptance of him, she nodded, once, twice. "I," she began.

"I know," he said. "That's the way it works."

"What do you mean works?"

Darl walked to her, took Sophia in his arms, the energy looping through them, their powers finding their connections just as their bodies did. She was warm and lovely and light, and her body seemed to understand, listening to the crackle of magic between them. She pulled him closer.

"Hold me tighter," she said, and he tightened his arms around her shoulders, letting one hand drop to press the small of her back.

In that instant, her body against his, everything fell away. Gone were the pedestrians, the shoppers, the traffic, the noise. It was only about Sophia and her regular, quick breaths, her warmth, her smooth lines. He needed to take her away, he needed . . . And then he felt something, a shift of air and atmosphere.

Don't open your eyes, Sophia thought.

Why?

I don't know. Just don't. I think we are going somewhere.

Darl held on to her, feeling the world whoosh by, and then he knew they were not on Clement Street anymore, not on any San Francisco street, somewhere else entirely, the air, the heat, the feel of the world, not city, not urban.

Okay, he thought. *I think we've arrived. I'm opening my eyes.*

As he slowly opened his lids—the bright white light making him almost pull back—the first thing Darl saw was ocean. Or water. A large light blue body of it, lapping up on the white sandy shore. On the horizon, birds flapped their way north, hazy clouds hung on to the sky, vague and nonthreatening. For as far as Darl could see, there was nothing but beach, water, sky, and trees, a tropical oasis. A different, hotter sun touched his neck, and so did Sophia, pulling him close.

"I've never been able to do that with anyone before," she said, looking around, her hair sparkling gold, her skin rosy in the heat. But then she looked at him, her eyes wide. "But now we're stuck. Unless your home trick works after I've done something like this. It doesn't look like there's a bus around here."

Darl smiled. "That's what I'm champ at. If I had a pair of ruby slippers, you could call me Dorothy."

She shook her head. "This is so—I don't have words. I guess amazing will have to do."

Darl pulled away from her gently, taking her hand and leading her to a small shaded patch on the beach, a date palm curving over them in a leafy umbrella. They both sat down, holding hands as they gazed out onto the smooth blue water.

He cleared his throat, trying to find the words to start this conversation, knowing, of course, that all the words would be weird. "It was always this way with me. I'd be missing my mother's cooking, and I'd suddenly be in the dining room, looking for a plate of spaghetti and meatballs. I've gotten a lot better about it in recent years about just appearing at random and unsettling moments, but for a while, I thought I was going to have to watch her for heart failure."

Sophia looked at him, her eyes slightly slit. She took a deep breath. "This is so much all at once. I have so many questions."

"Why don't you just ask them all," he said. "I remember how it felt."

"Who are you? Who are we? Why can we do this? And why did you show up now? Today? This is all too weird." She pulled her hand away from his, shaking her head. "I can't stop thinking that I'm insane. That this isn't happening at all. I've waited for so long for any answer, and I've made it up out of sheer desperation. I haven't really just met the man—" She paused, taking in a breath before continuing. "I've finally just cracked. I'm really in my car somewhere gibbering. I keep wanting to be relieved, to be happy, but then what am I supposed to do with the fact that you materialized in my car? That you read my mind? That we're on the beach right now? Thank God my mother isn't around to see this."

For a second, Darl tried to get into her thoughts, and she held up a slender but firm hand. "Don't. Stop it. No mind reading right now. I'm barely able to handle your words. So forget our thoughts for a little while, okay?"

Darl felt her close down, her mind clamping shut. He did the same, not wanting to scare her more than he already had. So leaning over, he took her hand again, feeling the fineness of her strong fingers against his. "When I first heard this story, I assumed the tellers were insane. Or that I was. I think that if you didn't think this was weird, you wouldn't be normal. So I thought, how can this possibly be real? But then all I had to do is think about my life up to that point. Sliding from one place to another. So think. Think about this. You know this is real, Sophia."

She shook her head again. "But why do you keep calling me Sophia? For some reason it feels familiar, but that's not my name. My name is Claire. Claire Edwards."

Darl looked at her, going back to the first time he'd heard the name Sophia. It had been Edan who had told him to find her. "My sister Sophia. I saw her in the Source. She's your twin," Edan had said. "Find her. Bring her home to us."

But she wasn't Sophia. That wasn't how she thought of herself. She was Claire. Clear. Bright. Claire.

"All I was told was that your name was Sophia."

"Who told you that?" she asked. "Who would tell you that? Who could possibly know me and say that?"

"Your brother," Darl said slowly. "And your sister."

Sophia/Claire turned to him, blinking, her face otherwise immobile. "Excuse me?" she said finally. "My brother? My sister?"

"Edan and Mila," he said.

Claire blinked, mouthed the names, shook her head. "Edan and Mila. My siblings. I don't have siblings. I'm an only child."

"Here on Earth you are."

"Here? Here! On Earth? On Earth!"

"Here," he said. "But where you were born, you had a brother and a sister. From where we come from, you are the youngest child, the littlest one."

"All right," she said, standing up quickly. "That's it. Enough of this bizarre beach interlude. I want off the ride. I want to go home to my boring little life. Now. Right now. Take me back. This was all more real when I thought you were a figment of my deluded mind."

Darl smiled, loving the way anger played rose on her face. "So I get to show you my trick? I sure hope it works."

But Claire wasn't laughing or happy or enjoying the banter that had always worked on women. No, she was about to bop him, her hands on her hips, her mouth a firm, stern line in her beautiful face. Clearly this wasn't going the way Darl had hoped. Slowly, he stood up, brushing sand off his hands.

"Look," he said. "I know this sounds ridiculous. Insane. How could it not? But S—Claire. Claire. You can't think that with the powers you have you are a normal Earth person. Did you ever feel normal? Did you ever feel that you were in the right place?"

She continued to stare at him, blinking once, twice, and then her face opened, fell, tears in her eyes. "No."

Moving closer to her, Darl put a hand on her shoulder. "And I know what I'm saying seems crazy, but doesn't it in some way make complete sense? You were left here in order to save your life. Your Earth parents took you in, some magic making them not question where you came from. You never suspected anything and neither did they. But all along, you had a dream—"

"Yes. The dream," Claire said. "My dream."

"Our dream," Darl said. "It's the dream we all have. Of coming here. Of being together that last time."

"In the spaceship," she said evenly, just as he had remembered saying it when Kate and Michael mentioned the dream to him the first time. Darl knew that if he wasn't the first person she'd told about the dream, he was the first person who had understood and believed her.

"Yes," he said, his voice low. "That's right."

Overhead, a seagull flapped by, its wings heavy in the hot

beach quiet. Again, she stared at him. "The boy and the girl? The ones that are always next to me?"

He shrugged. "The dream is always different for everyone. Some people have only images. So I'm not sure about the children, but I would assume they were Edan and Mila."

"Why didn't they come to find me? Why aren't they here to tell me this story?"

Darl took her back into his arms. "Because I am your twin."

"What?" she said, her voice muffled against his chest, her arms beginning to struggle. "My what? My twin? You're related to me? That would be very disturbing."

"No, no! Not that way. No, not at all. It's just an expression, though I can see how it could upset people. Give them the wrong idea entirely."

She shook her head against his shirt. "I think it should be changed."

"The planet that Edan was raised on called us doubles. They knew about us. They were worse than Earth people, though, putting everyone in the Source . . ."

Claire's breath hitched, and Darl knew he'd given her a little too much information. He could tell her about Edan's home world Upsilia later. And then somehow, he'd be able to explain the Source.

"Twins in power, not in relation. I'm your opposite. Your mirror. You and I fit together that way. You can go wherever you want. I can go home. Together, we can go anywhere. Together, we are complete. I knew what you could do with travel even before knowing you."

At those last words, Darl felt Claire begin to laugh, the sound lightly rumbling against his shirt. And then, as her laughter grew louder, he felt her tears, her relief, her body sagging against his. He could almost feel her let go of the years of struggle and worry and fear, all the unease and feelings of con-fusion slip away as she finally took in what he was saying.

Darl didn't say a word. He didn't need to right now. There was time to explain everything about their world and people after she'd been given a chance to recover from this first boatload of information. For right now, Darl wanted to sit on this tropical beach that her dreams and desires had brought them to, the water lapping at their feet, and hold Claire—his twin, his double—tight. After his long years of waiting, he wanted to float in the relief of finding her. He wanted to breathe in her skin, her taste, her smells. He wanted to touch her hair, her arms, rub his fingers over her soft lips, kiss back the rest of her questions. And he wanted more, needing all of her, even though they had met only hours be-fore, even though he'd just learned her real name.

Darl knew that his need for all her skin and touch and feel was wrong. Not wrong really, but somehow inappro-priate for the world they had both grown up on. There was supposed to be conversation, dating, decision making, and then and only then, this, this contact. But they were differ-ent. They were meant to be.

He couldn't push away his feelings, couldn't rid himself of how much he wanted her. And he wanted her. Right here on this beach. Right now.

At that last thought, Claire turned up her face, her eyes still closed, tears a sheen on her cheeks.

Yes, she thought. *Oh, yes.*

You're listening to me? he thought back. *I thought we had a deal.*

I don't have to listen to you, she thought. *I don't have to hear your thoughts. I just have to feel your body and I know what you are thinking.*

Darl smiled, knowing that his body certainly was ahead of him on this one.

Are you sure you want this? You know we're missing all the socially acceptable markers. Coffee, dinner, a movie. You're supposed to talk to all of your female friends about this for weeks. And I don't want to blow this up right when we have just started. Right when we have so much to do.

Claire, nodded, her eyes wide and clear as she looked at him. Without really meaning to, she sent him images that were only feelings: loneliness, confusion, flickering desire that burned out, slight, boring kisses on uncomfortable sofas. She had said no to more, no to it all, not because of fear but because her body had held back, kept her from feeling.

"I've never done this before," she whispered. "I mean, the whole thing."

"I know," he said. "I hear you, and I mean that literally. But why? Why would you have held back all the passion inside you?"

"I've been waiting."

"For what?" Darl asked, hoping she knew the answer.

"It's stupid," she closed her eyes and laughed. Opening them quickly, she smiled. "But it's true. I guess I was waiting for you."

"You knew I'd materialize in your car one morning and scare you into almost committing yourself?"

"I knew that I had a dream. Of what it would be like. Of how I would feel. It wasn't anything tangible, but I knew that all of me, everything, would know when it was right."

He slowly moved Claire onto her back, kissing her face, her lips, her neck. "I hope your dream is coming true," he said, letting his mouth slide down her neck, his tongue gently tracing her collarbone.

"I hope so," Claire said, sighing. "But I hope we don't have to wake up from it."

"Let's have the dream first before we decide that." Darl gently slid his hands under her T-shirt, feeling the smooth softness of her stomach, ribs, his hands finding her breasts and pushing away her bra. He wanted to awaken each nerve, each angle of bone, each soft plain of sweet skin. Darl wanted Claire to remember this—he wanted to remember this, this first of always.

Moving under him, her body opening to his attentions, Claire began to touch him, let her hands slide under his shirt, playing his ribs like an instrument. He heard her breath catch in her throat with each subtle stroke, her mouth on his taking in the kiss, wanting and needing more. They seemed to mirror each other, both needing to touch, to feel, to begin to memorize these bodies that would come together often, forever. In a way, it was as if they were already making love, their bodies in a current they couldn't control.

The world around them seemed to fade into black, nothing but their two bodies slowly rocking, pulsing, beating.

Let me take off your clothes, he thought.

Let me take off yours, she thought back.

They both smiled, opened their eyes, shuffling off their clothes, helping each other with buttons and snaps and hooks. As he took off his shirt and pants, Darl knew he'd never felt more natural or relaxed with a woman. He looked at her, his eyes so hungry for every new thing he saw. And what he saw, he could barely believe. *My God*. There she was below him, naked, her breasts and body smooth and lovely, and she was smiling up at him, her eyes alive with feeling. Not nervous, even though she'd never been with a man in this way.

Don't fool yourself, she thought. *My knees are weak. Thank God I'm not standing up.*

We can try standing up later, Darl thought, lying back down next to her, stroking a clean line from between her breasts to the soft hair with his fingertips. He let his fingers play on her skin, loving the way she reacted, pulling him closer, urging him to move on top of her.

"Oh," she said, clearly feeling how hard he was against her belly.

"Oh, yes," he said, wanting nothing more than to be inside her, but he knew—he wanted her to be completely ready for him, too.

I am ready. I've been ready for you since before I knew it, she thought, bringing her hand around his neck and pulling his mouth to hers, kissing him with all her feeling, all her thoughts—thoughts of him and her and the need between them.

There was so much he had to tell her. There was so much she didn't know about what was going to happen in her life. But as they moved together, Darl slowly readying himself to enter her, he realized that love—their love—wasn't something he had to teach her. It was as if she knew his body already, understood how to tilt her hips to meet him, how to relax to let him into her wetness.

Their kiss stopped, mouths open, her cry of "Oh" a small, lovely sound.

Are you all right? he thought, almost unable to hold still while she accepted him into her body. She was so silky, smooth, warm, no tremors of pain or fear holding her body taut. Claire was just warmth inside, warmth outside, her thighs holding him on top of her, her arms on his shoulders.

Her thought was a moan, a sound, a feeling, a *yes* in motion and urgency. Darl had made love with women—girls, really—who were virgins, but it was as if with him, Claire wasn't a virgin. She wasn't inexperienced. She wasn't naïve.

She was simply a woman who had waited for the man she wanted most.

Yes, she finally managed to think. *Yes*.

With that acceptance, Darl closed his eyes, opened his mind, let his joy at her touch, her body, seep through him and into her. They rocked together, kissing and touching, knowing that this was what they wanted most. Claire was like heat and fire under him. With his eyes closed, he could almost see her as gold, rich, warm liquid pooling around him. Oh, and how lovely she was, how exactly right. They slid, they rocked, they touched, and when she made a little gasp, a surprised sound, an amazed and startled and happy sound, Darl couldn't help but let go, his body filling hers, emptying into hers.

And then, there on the beach, taking in deep breaths, still holding each other, they slept.

It was the sun on his feet that woke him up, the heat sending hot fingers up his toes and to his ankles. Then he felt Claire next to him, her body almost as warm as the sun. As he stirred, so did she, holding him tight.

"You're awake," he said, stroking her back.

"I have been for a while. I've been listening to you breathe," she said.

Darl smiled, pulled her closer. "You should have poked me in the ribs. I don't want to waste time sleeping when there are other, better things to do."

"It was—it was," she began.

"I know," he said.

"I don't want to say anything stupid," she said. "But I'd always hoped—I'd always wanted—"

"Me, too," Darl said, knowing that he hadn't the words to tell her of his longing and hope all these years.

For a moment, they lay together in silence on the pile of their clothing and sand, the palm tree above them whisking stripes of shade across their bodies. Behind them, the tide had risen, wafts of cooler air reaching their feet with each incoming wave. Darl lifted his head and looked around, scanning the beach for people, and seeing none, rested his head back on the sand, pulling Claire closer.

"You are so beautiful. So, well, perfect."

She laughed, the sound reverberating against his chest. "You are, too. I know I should feel slightly wrong for not getting a first date out of you first, though. A movie, at least. Something that you actually could pay for!"

"Wait a minute there. Maybe it's me who should feel wrong about that. I mean, I feel so cheap. So used."

They both laughed, but Darl worked hard at containing the bursting feeling inside him, something like happiness, something like joy. He knew she was feeling the same way, her thoughts full of him. But they were both dancing around the newness, the slight bit of time since they'd met.

"So, how did you know I was your twin?" Claire asked.

"You know how to pick your tropical isles," he said. "No one in sight."

"Are you changing the subject?" she asked.

"Probably," he said. "Yes. Once we get into this, there really isn't a way to stop it. And I have to tell you everything, and you might not like it."

"Why? You've told me I have a brother and a sister. Sure, there's the whole alien trip with spaceships, but with a lot of therapy—"

Darl rubbed her back. "You won't be here for therapy, love. No time for the weekly appointment thing. We have to go."

"Go? Go where? To my siblings?"

Closing his eyes against the back and forth of fronds and

sky, Darl sighed. He remembered how he'd been when realizing that his life—such as it had been—would stop. "Yes, we're going to go to Edan and Mila. And we're going to stay there. At least for a while. And then—"

Claire pushed herself up, looking at him with her dark brown eyes, her sunlight hair hanging on his chest. "Stay there? For a while? How long is a while?"

Darl gently pushed her hair back from her face, loving the play of the silky strands between his fingers. Without him wanting it, parts of him began to stir, and he breathed deeply, knowing that no matter what interrupted this story, he'd eventually have to tell it anyway.

"This story is about us. Our home planet, Cygiria."

She breathed out, paused, blinked, and then nodded, wanting him to go on.

"Our parents—our parents saved us from the Neballats, who wanted to enslave us because of our powers and because they'd let their planet die. They needed us to do the work they'd forgotten how to. They were dying, and they were angry."

Claire bit her lip and then sighed. "I don't understand. They couldn't enslave us, so they killed us instead?"

"I know. Cutting off your nose to spite your face kind of thing. I'm not real clear on the reasoning, but reason didn't seem to be a big consideration," he said.

Above them, a flock of birds dipped and then spun off over the tree line. The water lapped at the shore; the air whisked his skin like warm cotton. Darl thought he might fall into the best sleep he'd ever had, here on this faraway beach, Claire in his arms. But he had to tell her all of this. He had to bring her right up with him, so that they both knew all there was to know.

"Go on," she said. "Tell me the rest."

"Okay," he said. "Before they had to escape, our elders managed to set up a safe house. And then they sent us on ships and put us on planets where we would survive. They left some mechanisms in place to help us. The dream, for one, the image of the spaceship, the children. And there, they left us information on how to find each other. Information about our past. Not much. But enough to give us an idea. And there was one set of twins—Jai and Risa—who got to the safe house first. They started this process of recovering us all from Earth and Upsilia."

She shook her head, her hair falling around her face again. "I have so many questions, they can't all come out. I don't know which one to ask first."

"Just try. One at a time." Darl sat up and let her lean against him as they both faced the ocean, the sun starting to glimmer and arc toward sunset. Her body felt warm and smooth against his, and all Darl wanted was to push her down and love her, taste her, feel her. He wanted to forget about the reason for this mission, about the Neballats, about the orders Edan, Mila, Michael, and Kate gave him. But he couldn't.

"Just ask."

"Okay. Back to the twins. How did you know to find me?"

He sighed. "This is confusing even to me. But when Mila found Edan on Upsilia, he was in a place called 'the Source.'"

"The Source," Claire repeated.

"Yeah, it's a sort of, well, a place where everything and everyone—um, well, a place where all souls mingle."

She looked at him, her eyes clear and focused, and then she started to laugh. "So not only are you here from another planet and not only are you telling me I'm from another planet, but now you're giving me information about the Source? Like heaven? Like creation? And how could Edan have been there and come back alive?"

Darl snorted at the amazed look on Claire's face: her mouth was open, her eyes wide. "You don't need to convince me that this sounds weird. I don't really get it myself. But let me finish. When he was in the Source, Edan saw you. He found you, part of your soul. He knew that you wanted to be found. And when he found you in the Source, he found me."

"Part of your soul was there, too," Claire said. "And we all still have managed to remain, well, in our bodies and alive and somewhere else entirely. And even weirder, we don't even know that part of ourselves is somewhere else."

"Yes," he said. "Exactly. We leave a little bit in the Source when we—"

"Please," Claire said, holding up a hand. "You just have to give me a huge break here. I've never been very religious, so the idea of a soul is hard in the first place. A soul with a detachable part is even harder. How do we decide which part to leave behind? Is there, like, a snap or a zipper and we just peel it off and incarnate? And then when we go back to the Source, do we meet ourselves there? That little piece of us that is floating around loose?"

"Look, I know. It's, well, hard to explain. But I'm not kidding," he said. "I really wouldn't make up this kind of stuff. I wouldn't know how. There is not one bit of the story-teller in me. Nothing creative except making up amazing run plays for my team. I'm into football and nachos, okay? At least, I was."

Claire shook her head, leaning her forehead into her hands. "So," she said after a long pause. "My brother went to the Source, talked to me, found you, and then what?"

"After they found me on Earth—"

"Who are they?" she asked.

"It was Kate and Michael who found me, but we're trying to gather everyone together for our fight." Darl leaned back against the palm's trunk, the bark scratchy against his skin. *Maybe*, he realized as he searched for words that would work, *we need to put together a pamphlet to hand out*. No amount of shared thoughts or feelings of connection made this part any easier.

"So two aliens named Kate and Michael found you, and then you found me because—I would assume—my brother told you to."

Darl leaned forward, pulling her tight against him. "That would be about right except for the part about me needing, having to find you, no matter who told me to do it. About the connection we have. Have always had. Will continue to have. About my life never feeling complete until now. Right here. This second."

At first, he imagined she was going to pull away, stand up, and stomp down the beach, find some willing local to get her out of this mess. When he looked in, her thoughts were quick, confused, and upset, so he pulled away from them, letting her sort it out herself. But then something happened, a shift he could feel all the way into his bones. Despite the bizarre nature of their story, she found the rope she could hold on to. Them. The two of them. The way she felt in her body. The calm, centered feeling in her mind.

"This is completely crazy," she said finally, turning to look at him. "I mean, here I am in Tahiti, finally, after wanting to be here forever. I had pictures of this—" She spread her arms out, trying to encompass the blue water, white sand, endless sky. "In my mind all my life. And now I am here with you. With a man—with someone I connect with. On levels I didn't even know existed. And you are telling me things that are so wacky that I really have no choice but to believe them. Look at who I am, for goodness' sake. Look at what I've always been able to do."

Darl put his hands on her face. "I see you, Claire. I see who you are."

She closed her eyes, put a hand to her face, breathed in. "I know."

Gently, he pulled her hand away, leaning forward and kissing her cheeks, salt on his lips. "I will hold this craziness with you. I will always share it with you. I will defend you against anything, anyone, anytime, anywhere. But come with me. Come back to our people. Let me show you what I have found."

The air began to move again in a slow, soft breeze. The day was slipping farther into afternoon, the shadows longer, the sky a cerulean blue, the sun a puddle of rich melon color, a floating tasty orb.

Claire sat up straight, smiled. "Okay, Darl—Darl what? Can you believe I don't even know your last name? Or your middle name."

"Darl Alan James."

"And Darl really stands for?"

"My mom was really happy when I showed up, apparently. So—"

"Darling?" she asked, smiling. "She named you Darling?"

"Darl will suffice, smarty pants." He ran a hand down her shoulder.

"All right, Darling Alan James. I will go with you. Other than I just don't think I can be without you, there is the big perk that we will be able to go and come as we please. Here, there, home, back again. At least, I'm hoping you'll get us back."

"That's what I'm best at," Darl said. "No matter what, I can always, always get us home."

Chapter Three

As if it were nothing—as if Claire hadn't spent a good portion of her life finding rides home from places she'd flung herself to almost by accident—she and Darl reappeared on Clement Street. Just like that. *Poof!* There was absolutely no travel time, no streaming through matter, no waiting for the continent to come into sight before landing. There was no motor over, under, next to them pushing them through air or water. Their movement together wasn't like flying or traveling or moving. It was a thought, a connected thought, the two of them holding hands. What they could do together was flick a switch and appear and disappear, moving anywhere. The two of them, their clothing, and nothing else.

"Except I find I am still full of sand," Darl said, now sitting at her kitchen table, wearing nothing but his Levi's and a pretty big grin. "In some strange places. I need to take a shower before we go."

Claire closed her eyes at the word "shower" because shower involved disrobing, and she knew that if Darl took off his clothes one more time, she wouldn't want to leave this apartment today, tonight, ever again. Already when they'd first arrived, they made it as far as her bedroom before his arms went around her and she melted in that way she'd just this very day learned how to melt. God, how he changed the consistency of her insides to something hot, molten, ready to flow. Then just when she was about to get up from her bed and begin the work of shutting down her life here (making calls to her landlord, her tenants at her mother's house, Yvonne and the school, and the bank), he pulled her back onto the sheets and made love to her again.

So now Claire closed off her mind and dug through her desk drawers for her bank records, trying to keep the image of Darl's amazing body out of her head. But how was she ever going to do that? After all these years, she had finally found the man she wanted to be with. Fully be with. Those evenings on couches with her failed dates now made sense. No one had ever made her feel the way Darl Alan James did. She hadn't been able to fake it then, even though she wished she could. Being a virgin had seemed ridiculous in this day and age. None of her friends had ever understood her reluctance.

"It's your body," Marissa had said back in college. "Sex is nothing to feel guilty about. You can make the decisions. You can be with who you want to be with."

But Claire hadn't felt guilty. In fact, if she'd had that kind of magic, she would have wished herself into her own sexuality, knowing that sooner or later, she had to move into it and take it. However, she hadn't been able to do more than push aside the apathy inside her, so she decided to do nothing, despairing even as she said no every time, that she would never find a man to say yes to.

Darl walked up to her as she stood at the desk, letting his hand slide from her shoulder down her arm. "What else do you have to do? It's not like we can take anything with us. And we can come back. You don't have to finish everything up right now."

Claire shook her head, holding back sudden and slightly ridiculous tears. "I want to—I can't just leave everyone in the lurch. I have a job, you know. I have people who count on me. We are talking about children, you know."

He turned her toward him slowly, so gently, holding her face in his hands. "That's all true. And you have so many people counting on you, you can't even imagine. A whole world of people. A whole generation of people like us needing you, needing each other. You have a brother and a sister. Here—here you have a job, but do you really have a life? A life that you want?"

For a moment, Claire wanted to push his hands away and storm out of the room. How could he say that? Did she have a life? How dare he! How could he even ask that? Who did he think he was? Showing up unannounced from the safe house and telling her who she had to live for and when and where and why? Of course she had a life. Or she'd had one, especially when her mother was alive. There had been holiday parties and visits with neighborhood friends. She had a life when she was in school and had more friends and roommates and dates. But now? What did she have? A few acquaintances and a stubborn handful of students who didn't listen to her, who screamed and peed in their pants and rolled around the room splashing paint. She had an exercise class. A nice apartment with a view.

Looking into his warm, dark eyes, Claire let the tears come. She'd been so lonely. So alone for too long, holding herself back because somehow she'd always known that life would find her. And it had, today, in her car after Pilates, on the beach in Tahiti, right now in her kitchen. And Claire knew she didn't want to live the way she had been anymore.

As she cried, he held her, rubbed her back, pressed his hand against the small of her back.

"It's all right," he whispered, and without knowing how, she believed him.

"You're right," she said. "I don't have what I want here. But I have things I need to tie up. People who would miss me. Responsibilities."

"I didn't mean to hurt your feelings, sweetheart. But we will come back, Claire. You've seen what we can do together. If you want, we can come back today."

She hugged him, breathing in his warm sun smell, a smell that she felt she'd been breathing in forever. Claire wasn't sure how she could leave this world, this place, her home, but she wasn't sure how she could not.

"I'll make a few calls, and then we can go."

"I had to come back a few times, and it wasn't easy because I had no you yet. I couldn't move as I can with our combined efforts. I had to have Kate and Michael transport me in their psychotic bubble a few times. And trust me when I say that neither of them likes Los Angeles very much. And they didn't even have to drive in traffic!"

Pulling back, she looked up at him. "What are you talking about? What bubble?"

"Oh, love," he said, hugging her tight. "There is so much that will just flip you out. Let's wait until we get there before I go into the bizarre things that everyone can do."

Love, she thought. *He called me love.*

Yes, Darl thought back, holding her, his arms tight against her back. *Love.*

She relaxed, closed her eyes, wondered for a tiny second when she would wake up from this dream. Would she startle awake, go to her nighttime window and stare out at the red eyes of Sutro Tower, waiting, as she had every night and day, for her life to start? Was all this happiness the product of her lonely mind?

But no. She could feel him, breathe in his skin, touch his wonderful flesh. She had taken him into her body, parts of her still startled, sore, and happy.

So Darl was right. They needed to be together, and in his arms, their two bodies humming together, bones and blood and flesh attuned, Claire wondered why she would have even clung to the idea of this old life.

Because it's what you know, Darl thought. *Because it's hard to let go of the known for the unknown. Even if the known isn't so hot. Because all of this—us—is frightening.*

Yes, but it's wonderful, Claire thought, letting her hands smooth his hair. *Frightening and ridiculous and wonderful.*

So let's go, he thought. *Make your calls, and let's blow this pop stand, sweetheart.*

Claire nodded, smiled, knowing that was all she wanted now. Darl and movement. Her life as it was supposed to be. Finally.

"So where are we going to go, exactly?" Claire smoothed her sleeves, looking up at Darl. She was ready to go, leave her apartment, travel away from Earth and everything. But the problem was she had to be able to visualize this safe house or they would end up who knew where. Some asteroid from her childhood imagination? Some planet from a terrible sci fi movie? It was a *Star Trek* episode, after all. "I have to have a clear picture of this place or I can't get us there."

"You know, I think I forgot my map," Darl joked, winking at her. "I think we'll have to do this by feel. Stop for directions. You know, take the back roads."

If Claire were carrying a purse or a bag—filled with things she just couldn't live without and was somehow able to take along for the ride—she would have hit him with it.

But she shook her head instead, her hands on her hips. "Darl, I have to have a picture of our destination."

He walked to her, putting his hands on her shoulders. "So let me give it to you. Close your eyes and let yourself flow into my thoughts."

"I know what you've been thinking about the past hour, and it hasn't been anything to do with the safe house."

"Can you blame me? With you in front of me, what do you expect?"

He leaned down, kissed her, and Claire wanted to just let go, pull him close, stay in her apartment for the rest of their lives.

We have to go, he thought. *They are waiting for us now.*

I know, she thought, but she didn't really know that. All of this was just a story she hadn't read yet, couldn't really grasp.

So go with me here. Follow what I can show you, what I remember, Darl thought, and then his words disappeared and his mind opened into a dark, blank panorama of space. What did she see? What could she see? Nothing at first, space empty and still and full of a vast nothingness that was so lonely, so awesome. Being by herself on a Saturday night in her apartment was a joke compared to the maw of this darkness. Space was a gnawing greedy hole that went on forever, and Claire felt herself cling to Darl, holding his arms tight as they stood together in her apartment. She didn't want to get abandoned in space—even if it was only in Darl's thoughts—floating alone forever, her oxygen ever so slowly running out.

I'm here with you, he thought, and then space began to change, moving by, lights in the distance—tiny flecks of white—growing brighter, clearer, illuminating her face. And then the scene was passing by them like an amusement park ride, the blankness of space opening into curves and spirals of bright dust and light, stars now, not dots of light, but streams.

How far away are we going? she thought, realizing as she looked back that Earth was nowhere or it was simply nothing, a pinprick lost behind all the greater brightness and light-years of time.

When we travel, it will feel like nothing. But we are in another solar system. You have to forgive me, though, Darl thought, his laughter a sound in her mind. *I haven't passed the astronomy test yet. In fact, I'd probably flunk.*

And then they seemed to slow down, the lights around them not flickering but steady.

Here, Darl thought. *Here is the safe house.*

Claire looked down at what seemed to be a chunk of rock floating solo, in no seeming orbit of any larger body. This was where the Cygirians were? How could they possibly breathe? Were they all wearing space suits or was there some kind of magic protecting them? How could anyone possibly survive on that desolate hunk of rock?

Our elders were smart. The elders hid the safe house where the Neballats couldn't find us. This is a façade.

When Darl said the name of their enemy, Claire recoiled, the memory of them in her bones and blood even though it was only mimimally in her mind. She felt the spindly, evil heat of the Neballats, could almost taste the metal of their need for the Cygirian power, see something ripping red like a wound, hear the screams of those they'd tossed aside as they searched for the most magic Cygirians of all.

We are safe here. It's a pretty darn good name. The Nebs won't find us, Darl thought. *Look. Look at how well protected we are. At least here.*

And his thoughts brought her closer to the asteroid, its

pocked face coming closer and closer. Claire wanted to turn away, avoid the crash, but then they seemed to enter something like an atmosphere. The sky lightened, opened up, a diffused sun somewhere beating down heat Claire could almost feel on her arms.

Darl's memory took them to ground, which seemed solid, safe, sound. She looked around to see ordinary buildings, flat squat things that reminded her of . . . of . . .

Government housing? Darl thought, and Claire laughed.

Exactly. I thought my first view of alien construction would be more, well, architectural, she thought. *Space age. Cool, even.*

Not a lot of time for them to construct, he thought. *They were planning on the fly, almost literally. Trying to make sure we had a place to go when we started to find each other and realize our powers.*

We, Claire thought, looking around for them, all of them, her people.

And then Darl showed them to her. There they were, Cygirians, sitting together in the fake sunlight talking, walking between the buildings, some kind of everyday life just going on even as the Neballats sought them out.

Can you show me my sister? My brother? she thought, and she felt Darl hesitate, stop, the world frozen in that moment.

I think you should meet them in person, he thought. *I think your first time of seeing your family should be when you can talk to them yourself. Hold them. Really meet them. This view would be like a terrible photo. It wouldn't be them at all.*

For a second, Claire stiffened, wanting what she wanted. A family. Immediately, this instant, in front of her. But she knew what Darl said made sense. She wanted to see her family with her own eyes, her own thoughts, hold their images in her own memory.

Okay, she thought. *You're right.*

And Edan, well, I think my memory won't do him justice. He is one kind of amazing dude.

What do you mean? Claire thought. *The Source thing you told me about? Where he went in and found out about you and me?*

She felt Darl shrug as she held him tight, both of them connected in his memory. *It sort of goes beyond that. He's like—he's different from any person I've ever met. Man or woman.*

In what way?

I—well. Claire, let's just leave it for now. You'll meet him soon enough and you'll see.

Okay, she thought softly, the mystery of her brother growing inside her. *All right.*

For a few more moments, Darl swung his thoughts around the open space of the safe house, letting her see more scenes of Cygirians talking and laughing and living. But then with the slow turn and slowing of his thoughts, the world started to break apart, the colors of the safe house blurring, fading, the world cracked into a sudden pixilated gray and then all was darkness.

Claire breathed, clung to Darl, her mind still full of this place she was going to take them both. After a second, she felt Darl's arms around her, his breath against her cheek, his strong body holding hers tight.

"Did you get it?" he asked, pulling away a bit so that he could look at her. "Can you take us there?"

"Yes," she said. "And now I want to go. I'm not scared anymore."

"You don't have to be scared," Darl said. "You have me

and you have everyone else. And, Claire, you know what they say. There's safety in numbers. After we manage to collect us all at the safe house, we will be able to fight back against the Neballats. And that's what we are doing. That's one of the reasons I'm here. Not only do I need you, we need you."

Claire nodded, wanting to both laugh and cry. God, if she could only call Yvonne and tell her that she had been right all along. Claire didn't belong in the kindergarten class. She belonged in space with an alien. At last, Claire had something to do on a Saturday night. That's right. She was going to go off into space with her date. A space date. A space battle date.

She shook her head. This was *so* not like her. She was off to battle horrible aliens who had tried very hard to kill off her entire race. From kindergarten to *Star Trek* in one step.

"Let's go," she said. "Hold on to to your hat."

And in a second, a blink of the eye, they were gone, headed to the safe house, headed home.

At first, Claire thought she had made a terrible mistake. After all, she had only just seen everything there was to see about the safe house, but when she opened her eyes, she thought that whatever Darl had shown her earlier had been an error. It was as if he'd put in the wrong tape, forgotten to eject it, and shown her the movie anyway.

There was noise, a gaping wind, a sucking sound. And cold, so cold, a fierce, bitter, icy slap of air that slung itself around her body, yanking her back and forth in its giant bony claw. She felt that at any moment she was going to be whisked away into the dead space. Somehow she managed to stay put, though she did not know why, her legs seeming to flail above her. What was she holding on to? What was holding her down? What was keeping her from flipping up and into the vast darkness all around her?

Darl? she thought.

"Darl?" she said, whispering, then yelling. "Darl, where are you?"

Hang on, came the thought, and Claire knew that barely hanging on was all she could do. Her arms were, she realized, clenched tight to something that was hard as well as malleable. But she didn't care what was saving her. She wanted to get out of there. She wanted Darl. She wanted Darl back in her apartment only seconds before, kissing her and reassuring her. This was not part of her date plan. Not this aloneness. Not this aching dark, angry, miserable cold.

Here we go, the voice thought, and there was a tugging, a slow, urgent pull away from the dark. Strangely, as she moved away from the cold, the air, the sucking sound of the empty spot, Claire began to see images of what Darl had shown her. There were the stars, the lights of the universe, the vast open panorama of space. Any moment, she felt a *Millennium Falcon* episode would occur and she would go into hyperspace. Or the Starship *Enterprise* would go into warp 10, winging through the stars at six thousand times the speed of light. But nothing continued to happen. This ride wasn't going anywhere fast. In fact, this ride seemed to barely be moving.

Are we okay? Claire thought back. *I know it's probably not a realistic question, but can I do anything?*

It's my twin, came the voice. *Michael. He's been knocked out. He is still helping me do this somehow even though he's unconscious, but this is about all I can do on my own.*

Twin. Twin! Claire thought. *I must be with Cygirians. And this Cygirian must know about Darl.*

Do you know Darl? Have you seen Darl? Claire felt her

breath and heart speed up. She wanted to run and search for him, but there was nowhere to go or run, for that matter. Looking below her through what seemed to be some kind of energy bubble, she saw the dark shape of a planet. The safe house?

There was silence from the other voice, space lurching by in slow tugs.

I know Darl.

Where is he? Claire thought. And then after she thought the words, she tried to find him in her mind, her thoughts, reaching out of herself for his words, his feelings. In the tiny amount of time they'd had together, she'd become used to his zippy, fast, yet thoughtful replies, the way he held her image in his mind even when he was doing something silly like flipping through a magazine as he sat on her couch. Since the moment he'd appeared in her car, Claire had felt as though she had connected with the part of her that had been missing for years. His mind was almost like hers; his thoughts her own.

But now he was gone. Truly gone. Nothing of him left but memory.

As Claire thought, the voice was silent. Claire felt her body still, tears well behind her eyelids.

I'm not sure where Darl is, the voice thought. *I was dealing with Michael, and then you were there, and it's lucky because we had already created the bubble when it happened.*

Bubble, Claire thought. What had Darl said about a bubble?

It almost hurt to think about the short time they'd had together, now that it seemingly was over. But she thought she knew who was tugging her through space.

Kate. You must be Kate.

Yes, thought Kate. *And you are Sophia, but I can tell that's not what you are really called.*

It's Claire. I'm Claire. I know you were all told I'm Sophia, but that's not my name. And I came here with Darl, and then he was gone and there was nothing but empty space and cold. What are we going to do? We can't just leave him there. I have to find him. We have to go back. We have to.

Closing her eyes against the darkness, Claire began to cry.

Darl, she thought. *Darl, are you there? Darl?*

She waited for a moment, clinging to the hope that he would somehow answer, but there was nothing but the whoosh of movement, the brush of space against the bubble.

Look, Kate thought, the bubble seeming to lug itself across the blackness. *I know this is probably totally blowing your mind, but I've got to get somewhere where I can look at Michael. Everything happened so fast. He's alive. He's okay, but he needs help. And then we can try to figure it all out.*

What happened? Claire thought. *What—where? I don't know what happened.*

Again, Kate was silent, space slowly starting to speed up, the lights flickering as they moved through. The bubble was rocking, rocking, slowly at first, and then more quickly, Claire holding on to the elasticky, slightly slippery electric sides of the bubble as they moved.

What happened? she thought again. *Everything seemed so safe in Darl's memory.*

But Kate didn't answer, focusing, Claire imagined, on moving them away from whatever terrible thing had happened.

Claire felt so sleepy. No, she wasn't sleepy. She was exhausted. Bone tired, every part of her wanting nothing more than sleep. And sleep was nice. None of this would be there—not Darl's absence, not this trouble in space (*space!*), not this floating around the universe in a bubble she probably was about to pop right out of. Maybe she would wake up in San Francisco, unhappy in her life, but alive. No promise of love and joy, but at least not floating around with two people, one of whom was unconscious. Not separated from the most amazing man she'd ever met because if she woke up from the dream, he wouldn't be true or real or part of her. It would have all been a product of her hopes and dreams and desires, nothing more.

As she was just about lulled into a fast, deep sleep, she heard one last thing, Kate's thought, small and thin.

The safe house is gone. The Neballats destroyed it.

Claire startled, opened her eyes and looked up into the bubble, out to where she could see Kate's and Michael's still outlines.

How? she thought.

The same way they destroyed our home planet, the way they destroyed our parents. The way they destroy everything. Kate's thoughts were as sad as a sob. *If it wasn't for our informant, we'd all be dead.*

So more than you escaped? Claire thought, hope surging through her. *There were more ways out?*

Yes, we got our ships out. Other people have powers that enabled them to escape.

Claire took in a quick breath. With their powers, she and Darl would have been able to escape on their own. If she hadn't lost him. If she hadn't let him go.

It's not your fault, Kate thought. *Something happened when you appeared, during the last blast of their attack. But I didn't see him. He wasn't where you were. I would have taken you both, though we'd be going even slower than this. So someone has him. I know it.*

Claire wanted to think so many things, to hold on to hope, to think about being with Darl again, despite all this tragedy, the ruin of the safe house, the end of the dream that Darl had given her.

But she wasn't sure she could bear it, this sadness, the bizarre landscape of bubble and space. If she had a knife, she imagined she'd cut herself out of it and float away into the nothingness.

Don't be a drama queen, Kate thought. *Worse things have happened, and worse will likely happen again. I need you to be strong. I want to go home to take care of Michael and then I think we need to go to Upsilia. That's where Darl might be. It's not the most hospitable world, but there are people there who will help us.*

Claire wiped her face, breathed in, shook herself clear of her sad thoughts. For now, she would hold strong. If there was a possibility that Darl was alive, she had to be strong, long enough to see him. Long enough to hold him tight and not let go again.

Claire had been rocked into a light, weird sleep, images floating past her as they moved. At one point, it seemed that Kate had picked up a lot of speed, and the rocking stopped, the bubble humming with speed and flight. Now and again, Claire looked up to see the stars and Kate's image, but then she would fall asleep again, just to dream of Darl.

Their entire relationship—all one day of it—was too amazing. To think that he'd materialized out of nowhere, she'd taken them to Tahiti where they'd made love on the hot, soft sand, and then they'd gone into space only to be attacked by Neballats, the aliens who wanted to kill them.

But the most amazing part was Darl himself. His smile, the way his hand skimmed the skin of her arms and legs and face. His smile, his laugh, the smooth skin of his back, the way he felt as he entered her. And though the first time had hurt a little, it had been nothing compared to the pleasure he'd given her, the deep, pure pleasure of being loved and treasured and held. She felt joy. She felt warm and safe and loved. She felt known. For the first time in her life, she'd given over her complete self to another person, and that person—Darl—had said, "Yes." He'd said yes and he'd said, "More, please. More, please, now."

And now, in her dreams, there was more. Darl next to her, whispering in her ear, saying, "We're here. Wake up. Claire. Wake up."

If I wake up, will you be there? Claire thought, and then she realized she was waking up and it wasn't Darl talking to her but Kate.

Claire opened her eyes and then shut them against the brightness. "Where are we?" she asked.

"Port Saint Joe, Florida," Kate said. "My aunt has a vacation home here, and I figured the odds were good that she wouldn't be here. I was right, thank God. My aunt Laura is a pain in the ass. And I'm pretty sure I wouldn't have been able to explain three suddenly appeared people."

Claire sat up, realizing that she was in a sun porch, lying down on a chaise lounge. Potted plants filled the space, vines creeping up the screen walls that enclosed the space. A gecko skittered up one stucco wall and hid behind a frond of something exotic. From outside, a warm wave of air pushed into the porch area, and a trickle of sweat dripped down Claire's forehead.

Next to her on another chaise was a man. A very nice-looking unconscious man, long limbed, blond, sort of built like the swimmers and water polo players Claire had only wished she could know in high school.

"Tell me about it," Kate said. "When we're on Earth, I'm forever beating teenagers away with a stick. They surround him like he's a rock star."

"Is he okay?" Claire asked. "Should we take him to a hospital?"

"He's actually asleep now," Kate said. "He has a knot on his head, but it doesn't seem to be that bad. Not a concussion. I figured we could let him rest and keep an eye on him for a while before we go off again. Maybe take a shower and have something to eat, too, though knowing my aunt, we'll have to go to the Piggly Wiggly."

Claire stared at Kate. "The piggly what?"

"Wiggly. The store. Down here they actually have supermarkets called Piggly Wiggly."

"That's maybe the weirdest thing I've heard all day," Claire said, looking at Kate seriously. For a second, Kate blinked, and then they both started to laugh. Together, they laughed hard, so hard that they both leaned over, holding their sides. Here she was on a chaise on the Gulf Coast with two people who'd pulled her across the universe in a bubble, and the Piggly Wiggly sounded strange? It was not to be believed, understood, appreciated. She could never tell anyone. Not ever.

And as she laughed and laughed, it was then that Claire felt the tears come. She was crying, Kate was crying. The safe house was destroyed, along with the hope the Cygirians had of regrouping. Michael had been knocked unconscious, now asleep with a knot on his head. And Darl—Darl who showed up and changed everything? He was somewhere in the dark universe, lost maybe, captured maybe, hurt maybe—maybe something else.

Kate reached out a hand, rubbing Claire's forearm. *It will be okay.*

I hope so, Claire thought. *Oh, I hope so.*

*   *   *

The kitchen was filled with the tang of citrus. Kate stood at the counter peeling and then slicing up oranges and grapefruit for a fruit salad. Claire sat at the counter slicing vegetables, something nagging her the entire time. It was a feeling, a shrug of irritation she had to keep off her shoulders.

I should be doing something else, she thought, holding her ideas to herself now so that she wouldn't disturb Kate. *I need to be searching for Darl. I need to get out of here.*

She knew they had to wait until Michael was recovered. He'd come to earlier, enough to talk briefly with Kate, and he was asleep in a back bedroom, the door closed against their cooking noises.

Even though Claire understood they wouldn't be in Florida long, she wanted to find out more about the planet they were going to go to, this Upsilia. Maybe she could find Darl herself. She knew that with a few clues, she could get herself there the same way Darl had helped her navigate to the safe house, or what was left of it. She could slip into Kate's thoughts right now, twist around in there to find out the details of this other planet—the spin through space, the location in its solar system, the terrain and atmosphere, the people, the buildings, the rooms—and just leave Florida. Just like that. She would forget that she had no idea about galaxies other than the one she was in right now. And she barely knew that one, having to memorize the sentence "My very educated mother just served us nine pizzas" in fourth grade in order to remember the lineup to the sun.

But that didn't matter. She'd have Kate's images. And once there on the planet, she would find Darl. She would find him alive and well and happy, and he would bring them back to San Francisco. They didn't have to save their people now. It was too late, wasn't it? The safe house was destroyed, their people scattered once again. They could live together, work, and take amazing trips whenever they wanted. Tahiti was just the first of so many. Maybe Claire would quit teaching, go back to school and get her administrative credential, become a principal and get away from the kids. That was enough. That had to be enough. That would be fine.

Claire put down the knife and stared at the rounds of zucchini and tomato in front of her. She knew she could do just what she was thinking, so why did she feel so bad about it? Why this heaviness in her body, as if she'd grabbed onto a fifty-pound dumbbell?

She scooped up the vegetables with her hands and dropped them into a glass bowl, watching Kate focus her knife on a blood orange. Claire began chopping the basil, the smell dark and green in her nose.

She couldn't leave without Kate and Michael and a plan. She loved Darl. She knew that even if they'd only just met, and though she longed to find him now, now, now, she couldn't leave. And it was because of the dream. It was because of her sister and her brother, the children always next to her as they hurtled into Claire's imagination. Maybe Claire did want to find Darl and be done with Cygiria, but she would be lying to herself. She could never go home to her apartment with Darl and forget about the dream that had been with her since she could remember. And now she knew they were real, had names—Mila and Edan—and were looking for her. If there was anything she could do to help them, too, Claire knew she would. She had no choice.

"Why do the Neballats want us dead?" she asked, putting down the knife. "Why are they after us?"

Kate turned to her, a waft of orange floating toward Claire. "Because of what we can do."

"That seems ridiculous," Claire said. "Why wouldn't they want us alive? We could have been more useful alive than dead."

"You've never seen us in a group. All together, doing what we can do? It's pretty overwhelming. Pretty damn amazing. I think when Cygiria said no to all the Neballats' requests and then threats, they decided to get rid of us all. Later, I think, they figured out there were a few of us who could really help them fix the damn mess they made of their own planet. Like Mila and Garrick. And Edan."

Kate tossed the salad and pushed the bowl aside, pulling plates from the cupboard with ceramic clicks and clanks. Claire watched her, trying to figure out how to ask the next questions.

Shrugging and now hearing what Claire was thinking, Kate turned and smiled. "Time. It's all about time. Time in the body and time in the world. Together, Mila and Garrick can go back and forth through time, all time. When they were alone it wasn't much of a gift. As with all of us, we are better in pairs."

"What can Edan do?" Claire asked. "What can his twin do?"

"It's kind of sad," Kate said, putting a folded napkin in front of Claire. "He can age himself. He thinks he's lost about ten years."

"How does he know?"

"He doesn't really, but he felt it inside. He feels a lot of things, that one."

"And his twin? I mean, together, they must be able to age and unage each other. That seems to be the system."

Kate listened for a second, seeming to search with her mind for any stirring in the bedroom, and then turned back to the counter. "He hasn't found his twin."

"Really? But Darl—Darl," Claire said, her voice suddenly soft and pale. His name was like joy in her mouth, and she couldn't believe she didn't have free rein to say it over and over again. Until she found him, she'd have to use it when she could, savoring every syllable.

She breathed in, found her words. "Darl said that Edan found out about Darl and me in that place, the Source. If he could find us . . ."

"You'd think," Kate said. "But he didn't. And then when Mila brought him to the safe house, there was so much to do, and I never heard him talk about his twin again. He is— he has, well, he's been busy. But I don't know how he could have forgotten, let it go. If I didn't know—"

Kate stopped what she was saying and shook her head. "I'm sorry. I just wanted to tell you about why the Neballats are after us. I just don't know if we are going to all make it through this time. We thought we made it. That was our mistake. We all got too happy."

Claire picked up a red pepper and turned it in her hand, liking the slightly waxy-smooth feel against her palm. "Were you unhappy growing up?"

"Yeah, but I decided to play with the herd. Act like a pack animal. Be a Hun in a group of Huns. You know, do sports, cheerleading, pretend to really care which boy liked me or not. But I always knew something was off. Wrong. I was waiting. Always waiting, and when Michael showed up at the restaurant in Boston that day, I finally got it. Everything, for once, finally made sense."

Claire wanted to tell Kate that she knew exactly what she meant. That all of Claire's life she'd known she was somehow wrong. And just today, with Darl, Claire had finally felt the understanding Kate talked about, knew who she was the moment Darl showed up in her life. But Kate knew all that already, and then there was a muffled groan from the bedroom, and Kate turned and left Claire sitting there, holding the pepper, staring out into the bright Florida light pouring in the windows. Somewhere not too far from here was sand and water and wide open sky. Claire wished she could go to the beach, lie down on the cool, wet sand, and close her eyes, opening them only to be in Tahiti and with Darl. That's where things finally made sense for her.

But there was dinner, and then Michael's recovery, and then another strange flight to another planet first. Claire would have to hold her beach in her mind, a sand globe of pleasure and joy she could shake now and again, just to remember, just to feel.

"Man," Michael said, his body slightly slumped over the table. He held a fork in one hand, a piece of roasted zucchini dangling on a single tine. "I feel like shit. Like I have a really bad hangover."

"You would know how that feels," Kate said, laughing. "From what I know, you have plenty of experience with tequila and Dos Equis!"

"You've never seen me with a hangover," Michael said. "I've been good ever since we met."

"Yes, you have," Kate said. "But there was enough of a history there for me to hear all about it. In fact, the first night we met, you had a beer in one hand and a hangover on the way, if I'm not mistaken."

"You saved me from myself."

Michael smiled, and if Claire knew him better she would be sure it was a half-smile, a wan smile. He was as tall, tan, and blond as Kate, but he looked as if someone had opened his release valve and let out half of his air. Clearly, he still needed some patching and filling.

"So about this planet," Claire asked. "This other galaxy. I guess I don't understand how we never knew about all this life out there. I mean, how did it happen?"

"Quantum theory," Michael said.

"What?" asked Claire.

"Oh, no," Kate said. "Oh, please. You had to get him started. Here we go."

"No, really," Michael said. "It's like this. Particles—particles of matter. They can pop into existence just like that. So we know that our universe popped into existence, so why not another? And another?"

"Yes," Claire said, pushing a tomato around on her plate. "I think I've heard about this. But isn't that theoretical? Isn't the possibility of another planet being able to sustain life pretty rare? And that life would be nowhere near the same kind of life. And you are telling me there are, what? Three or four? Or were three or four?"

"There are probably more, if you believe in extra dimensions. Scientists here on Earth are really trying to figure that one out, but we don't need to know. We can see it. We can go there. And there is life, so what more proof do we need? We are the proof."

Claire shook her head. "If there are universes popping up all over the place, why do the Neballats need us? Why can't they wait for a new planet to just show up somewhere?"

Both Kate and Michael were silent. Finally, Michael cleared his throat. "I don't know. It's like people want what they don't have, thinking it's what they need. Who knows what will happen if the Neballats get what they want."

"I know how I feel now that I have what I want. Or had," Claire said.

They both nodded, looking at each other and then Claire.

"So," Claire said. "Is there, like, a list of what Cygirians can do? It doesn't sound like the powers are consistent or were formed with some great plan in mind."

"There is sort of an informal one," Kate said. "It's been hard to organize."

"What are some of the things we can do?" Claire asked. "I mean, I always thought being able to go anywhere I wanted was kind of the end of the line of super powers, if you can call it that."

Michael sat back, crossed his arms behind his head. "Let's see. There's so many things. Moving through travel, flying, becoming invisible. Fire. Water. Air. All the elements. There's bringing things to life and, well, not."

"That's Whitney and Kenneth," Kate said.

"Turning on and turning off electricity," Michael said.

"Stephanie and Porter," Kate said.

"Aging oneself," Michael said.

"Edan," Kate said. "And I would make the bold statement that his twin can undo age. A veritable fountain of youth. But he hasn't met her yet."

"Darl told me about Edan," Claire said, looking down at the table.

Kate leaned over and touched Claire's arm. Claire cleared her throat, tried to smile. "So. We are going tonight? Going to Upsilia?"

"I think we have to," Michael said, his face relaxing into this conversation that didn't involve loss. "I don't think I'll be at full speed in even a day, so we shouldn't wait. If we've collected there, we need to get with everyone and figure out what to do."

"But the Neballats were there before," Kate said. For the first time, Claire could see that Kate wasn't too sure of the plan she'd described. "Why wouldn't they be there waiting for us again?"

"Those people. You know, the weird ones with the droids?"

"Droids?" Claire said. "Like robots? Like from the movies?"

"They called them Anthros," said Michael. "But they were droids, and not the little tin-can type. They were almost like people but with, obviously, artificial intelligence. The Upsilians are light-years ahead of us."

"In some ways," Kate said. "But in others it was like pre–Civil War times."

Michael gave her a glance, shrugged slightly. "Anyway, they sort of helped us when we were there. They helped us get the abandoned ones off the planet."

Claire shook her head, sat back, her plate almost totally full. Her stomach was whirling, and one more weird idea would likely make her ill. Droids? Upsilians? The abandoned ones?

"I don't understand any of this."

"I don't really either," Kate said. "But here on Earth, we don't have a group of people who've protected us, understood us. We never had enough critical mass to be recognized. Not one of us ever went off, caused a stir, sold his or her story to the *National Enquirer*."

Claire laughed, realizing that she would have made great headlines had she really gone ahead and traveled places: WOMAN FINDS HERSELF NAKED IN TIBET OR BAY AREA LOCAL FOUND WANDERING BANGLADESH STREETS.

"Right," said Michael. "No news."

"And no one to put us in cold storage," Kate said. "They really watched over us. Helped us out. Made sure they all stayed in the Source."

"I think," Claire blurted, "that the Source doesn't sound too bad."

Both Kate and Michael stared at her for a moment, their dark eyes blinking.

"Um," said Michael. "You think that having your body in a pod and your soul elsewhere is a good idea?"

Claire felt her heart beat a strange rhythm against her chest. "Not really. But it sounds like there is peace there. Like you can find the answers there. Look what Edan found out. Sort of like heaven."

"But what can you do with all that information?" Kate said. "You can't live. You can't be in your body. There's no life there."

"Sounds like there's love," Claire said quietly.

"There might be," Kate said, putting a hand on Michael's forearm. "But I want my body and love. I want the whole package. The whole deal."

Claire's heart pounded, her breath a skip in her chest. The whole deal. That's what she wanted, too, but it always seemed so hard before. The Source seemed like a place where there would be no struggle. They wouldn't be going through what they were going through right now at this very moment. No one trying to kill her. No one abducting Darl. No one wanting anything but to float by.

"I don't want to find out," Michael said, catching Claire's thoughts. "I want to get our people back together and figure out what to do."

He stood up slowly, picked up his plate, and walked into the kitchen. Kate watched him as he left, taking in a quick deep breath. She turned back to Claire.

"He's right," she said. "We need to go."

"I'm scared," Claire said, startling herself with her words.

"Who isn't?" Kate asked. "I think I've been scared since Michael appeared at Carmen's, sidling up to me at the bar, telling me my life would never be the same. But I've also been totally joyful. And amazed. And happy. But scared, too. This is what we have and this is what we can lose. What else can we do but live this life that we have, Claire? We were born like this, put here on Earth, and now we know who we are and what we should be doing."

Until this very day, Claire had been a kindergarten teacher. She'd been a woman who'd lost her mother, who had few friends, who liked to do Pilates. She had been a lonely twenty-five–year-old woman living by herself in San Francisco, eating pasta at night in front of the television or in front of an open book. Now she was a Cygirian fighting for her planet. Fighting for her love. Kate was right. What choice did they have?

"All right," Claire said. "I'm ready."

This time, the bubble was fast. Actually, Claire had no idea how fast she was going this time or the time before, but she interpreted speed by the stars. Unlike the time before, the stars were bright, quick lines in the sky, the world nothing but light and dark, no shapes, no stillness.

Kate and Michael were above her, moving them toward this world, Upsilia. Her stomach was a pinpricked mass of nerves. Half of the things—no, really all of the things—Kate and Michael had talked about seemed too amazing to be real. Anthros? And then there was the Source. The place where all souls converged. And then there was the hope that she would find Darl. In her mind, Claire played it out. They would arrive on the planet, quickly find the Upsilians, who would lead them to the large group of very safe, very alive Cygirians who were waiting for them patiently. Darl would be standing in front of the crowd, his arms open. He would move toward her, hold her tight, press himself against her.

And this was where her hope merged into two plots. If she was holding Darl, Claire could immediately take them anywhere in this ever-growing universe. Anyplace but Upsilia.

The other variation of this scene was that she would simply hold him just as tightly, and then they would turn to listen to the plan, the idea, the way for all Cygirians to be safe. After that, she would meet her sister and brother, who were likewise safe, and they would all go on to make things right.

Then she would take Darl back to Tahiti.

She wanted the sand. The heat. His skin.

Claire spun in the soft energy of the bubble, relaxing against the sides. She'd never thought she was a selfish coward, but her first fantasy sure showed that. She wanted Darl all to herself. She wanted her life and his to be separate from all this insanity and be safe and normal. But she also wanted the connection she felt even to Kate and Michael. This desire for connection, community would only intensify if she were around more of her people, and she craved that, too. She craved the safety for all of them.

Hold on to your hat, Michael thought. *We're going in.*

Claire clung on, thought, *Darl? Darl? Are you there?*

From the spinning night came no answer.

Darl? she thought one more time, imagining that she heard him call out to her, to everyone. What was she seeing? An image of a house?

But then everything grew blazing, a world in front of them spinning in its orbit, a swirl of white and blue and gray. Earth but not Earth, home to people who would help but not help. The only place they could go right now, the only place that Darl might be alive, ready, waiting for her.

Here we go! Kate thought and everything was light and heat and hope.

Chapter Four

When Claire held him tight and pushed them into the space of the safe house, Darl immediately tried to hold on to her, but she was gone, as if her body were made of flickering heat and steam. Like that, without even a second of feeling her, he was clutching air, swirling in the wild winds of the safe house. But it wasn't the safe house anymore. The environment had been destroyed, the atmosphere slowly evaporating into the emptiness of space as he looked around. Since he had never endured space flight before and because he was able to flick himself back home so quickly, he'd never felt the lightness that the sudden slow dissolving of gravity supplied.

He didn't have a lot of time. If the atmosphere and the gravity were going, Darl knew he had about a second to figure out what to do, how to find Claire. He looked around, thinking that he might have seen the flash of departing spaceships, but he couldn't be sure if the travelers were friend or foe.

Claire! he thought, all his mind forced into her name. *Claire!*

There was nothing. No thought. Nothing and no one calling back to him.

The air began to thin into a pearly gray, Darl's feet light on the smashed terrain of the destroyed safe house. Broken and burned pieces of buildings and structures began to shift, move, float off their moorings, pulling skyward, wanting to float into nothingness. Darl had only seconds of air left, only slivers of time before his insides burst from the shift in pressure. And he thought he could almost feel that pressure, his lungs, heart, spleen pulsing wide into the expanding air.

Home, Darl thought. *Home.*

And in an instant, he was in Encino, California, sitting on his couch in his living room, the television's dead black eye in front of him. Nothing had moved since he last left, nothing had changed, not even the air, stagnant from lack of air-conditioning. How long had it been? Three weeks? Four? He couldn't remember anything, the destruction of the safe house the only image in his mind. The people, the buildings, the lovely green carpets of lawn, the fake blue sky. All gone.

And no Claire.

Darl took in a huge swallow of air, grabbed the blanket from the top of the couch, and wrapped it around himself, shivering in the hot air of his house.

Blinking, he tried to find his thoughts, an idea, a plan. What was he supposed to do? Who could he contact? Where could he go? Who would have the time to come find him now that everyone was on the run again?

As always, he was useless with his stupid power. Well, at least this time he'd managed to save himself, but what had he done for Claire? He'd left her there on the safe house. Hopefully, someone had found her, whisked her away in one of the ships, taken her to Upsilia, where they might be safe. Someone had to have found her. If he wasn't such a damned idiot, he could use his power to actually go to Upsilia instead of retreating home like a coward. What could he possibly do in Encino?

Throwing the blanket off himself, Darl walked around

his living room, staring at what he once thought was so important. Trophies from football championships he'd been in; trophies from teams he'd coached. He was supposedly the one who could get things done on the field. He was the quick thinker, the one with the sharp moves. As a coach, he could see into the other team's motivations and ideas. Darl was quick, fast, sharp, strong, and stealthy. But now? He was hobbled. Useless.

He sighed, looking at photos of Dave, Suzy, and Julie, and of his mother, Joanne. For a second, he wanted to call her, tell her how he'd met the woman of his dreams and then lost her. He wanted to hear her soft, reassuring voice.

"Darling," she'd say. "You'll find her soon enough. How could you not? You can do anything you set your mind to. Just think of it, and it's yours. Like everything you did since you were a baby."

"But I think she's on another planet, Mom. I hope she's on another planet. If she's not on the planet, she's . . . she's . . ." And then Darl knew he'd have surprised her so much, she wouldn't be able to help him with Claire. She'd call a doctor instead. She'd call 911. She'd assume that he was drooling mad. His siblings would be ecstatic.

Darl wandered into the kitchen, flicked on the lights, opened the refrigerator and stared in. Before Kate and Michael had whisked him to the safe house, he'd managed to toss what would go bad, except for a bunch of carrots that looked like long, withered fingers in their bag on the shelf. He grabbed a bottle of water and cracked it open, slamming the door shut on the horrible vegetables.

"Just think of it," his mother had always said to him. "Just think of it, and it's yours."

Claire? he thought again, pressing her name into the world. *Claire! Anyone? Anyone out there at all?*

Darl waited, opening his thoughts to the world, the universe, beyond where he'd ever gone with Kate. He called out to any Cygirian, anyone who would find his or her way to Encino and help him find Claire.

He didn't breathe, didn't move, feeling nothing, hearing nothing. Darl held himself in the anticipation of a reply, his body taut and waiting.

Help, he thought. *I need your help*.

He sent out images of where he was located, throwing out an image of his house, his street, a topographical map of the greater Los Angeles basin, locating it on the continent, the planet, the galaxy.

Come get me, he thought. *We can work together*.

And then nothing. More nothing. His body slumped. Still nothing. His mother was wrong. He couldn't just think of it or anything.

Darl took a big sip of water, walked over to the kitchen window, and cranked it open, letting in a waft of warm, thick air. In front of him, life went on as it always had. And before, that was fine. People left for work in the morning, children wearing backpacks headed to school. Sprinklers went on and went off. Carpenters and plumbers and gardeners and pool service people rolled in and rolled out. The sun arced over the smog-filled sky.

But now none of that seemed normal at all. What he wanted was what he'd found. Claire. What was he going to do without her? How was he ever going to manage to find her again, much less any Cygiran to take him out of here to where the action was, where the battle was?

Darl shook his head and then finished his water. The events of the past day—finding Claire, traveling to Tahiti and then the safe house, and rushing home—had exhausted him. He needed sleep. He needed unconsciousness. If he'd had beer in the fridge, he would have drunk one, two, three to try to help him forget.

Darl walked back to the couch, sat down, and then lay down. He'd just take a little rest. He'd think hard. He'd dream an answer. He'd dream the perfect solution. And then he'd wake up and find Claire. Somehow. Some way.

A loud knocking and a persistent ringing woke Darl out of a heavy sleep. He sat up, his heart pounding against the stairs of his ribs. He wasn't sure what the sounds were, the ringing like something that could have been left over from his dream.

It was dark in the house, and he blinked into the murk of his living room. The knocking started again, and he stood up, walking toward the front door. He looked through the peephole, but he hadn't turned on the front porch light.

If possible, would you mind opening the door, a man's thought. *For all the Southern California hype, it's cold out here.*

Who are you? Darl asked, but then he realized that the only person who could be talking to him through thoughts and a wooden front door was another Cygirian.

Brownie points for you, the man thought.

Will you try to be polite, a woman thought. *For God's sake. We just got here and already he's going to want to throttle you.*

Darl smiled, opened the door, and flicked on the porch light. Standing in front of him were two people, a man and a woman, both looking a little worse for wear, their hair standing up in the back in the unmistakable airplane-seat do. The woman was pretty and tall, with dark hair and eyes, her expression full simultaneously of patience and irritation. The man was also tall, but he slouched against the doorway, almost pouting.

"Hi," Darl said. "I'm Darl James. I don't think I've met you before."

"Clearly we're strangers. We must have missed your auspicious safe house arrival. But you've likely figured out that we're Cygirians," the man said, sighing. "Well, I'm Porter. This is my twin, Stephanie."

"You must have gotten my message," Darl said, thinking that the last time he heard the name Porter it was in association with a mental health facility.

"Loud and clear, though it took a bus, a BART ride, and an ungodly trip on an airplane to get here. Then the rental car and the damn freeways around here. What is with the 10? It boggles my mind that Earth is functioning at all."

Stephanie smiled. "Let's just say that we haven't had to travel this way in a long time."

Darl nodded and opened the door wide to let them in. "Tell me about it. Come on in."

Stephanie and Porter walked inside, and as Darl closed the door, he realized that maybe there was hope. His mother hadn't been wrong after all. He'd thought it, asked for help, and it had shown up.

Porter flung himself down on a chair, crossing his legs. "Don't get too excited. I don't know who else is around here. We just happened to be lurking around San Francisco, hunting down an earthling who'd had a bad experience with a simulator."

Darl nodded, remembering what he'd heard about simulators, horrible mind-controlling devices the Neballats used. Creepy, crawly, disgusting things that slid under the scalp and worked the Neballats' bidding.

Running a hand through his dark hair, Porter continued. "We weren't having any luck finding the unfortunate fellow, and then when we called to get a ride home, nothing. Everyone with any sense had gone back to the safe house, I guess. We couldn't get anyone's attention, but then we heard your message."

Stephanie nodded. "It was weird. Just like that, nothing from anyone. We couldn't do anything. And our power with electricity is relatively limited."

"It does wonders to light up a city, but it's hard to travel home with it," Porter said.

Darl almost shuddered, thinking of the place these two called home. He remembered the terrible floaty feeling as gravity trembled into nothing just before he fled for Earth.

"You don't know what happened?" Darl asked, realizing that he must have left those images out of his message.

"What did happen?" Stephanie said, her face slowly shifting from smile to worry as Darl's feelings and thoughts broke through into hers.

"The Neballats." Darl took in a deep breath. "They destroyed it. I don't know what happened. My twin—"

He couldn't say her name without a pain in his sternum, so he stopped, taking another breath. "We showed up just afterward. But she—I don't know where she is. And I can't travel without her. I mean, I can only travel home. So here I am. Useless."

"It's gone?" Porter asked.

"Yes," Darl said. "Completely."

"Did the rest of us get away?" Stephanie asked. "Where did they go?"

"I don't know. I would assume Upsilia or here. But I didn't see anyone before I left. There wasn't anything when I got out of there."

Porter and Stephanie looked at each other, some kind of conversation going on between them. Just looking at the two of them communicate, watching their comfortable body language made Darl want to push things around, rip up his living room, scream from frustration. This was all wrong. Look at them. They blinked, listening to each other. Porter put his hand on her arm, she moved closer to him, letting her hip lean against his side. Their thoughts, their bodies, their ideas all flowed together in a river that was the two of them.

Darl's heart beat hard. He needed to get out of here. He needed to find Claire.

"I can't—" he started and then stopped when the doorbell rang again.

"Don't tell me you ordered a pizza," Porter said, and Darl thought that if he wasn't so upset about Claire, he'd want to punch the guy in the nose.

Darl walked to the door and then opened it, the light shining down on four people, all of them looking at him expectantly.

"You called us, right?" one of the men asked.

And then before Darl could answer, one of the women said, "It didn't happen, did it? I thought I saw it. I thought I heard someone sending me a message, but it flickered away before I could really grab it."

"Come in," Darl said. He looked at the four of them, and at the same time, listened to Stephanie's and Porter's quiet conversation behind him. He knew from football that the team was everything. That there was safety in numbers. That together, focused, they could make a play. This was the way to the goal, and the goal was Claire.

He opened the door wide. "Come in, and I will tell you everything."

The doorbell had rung four more times during the course of the night; each time Darl answered it, there was a Cygirian waiting on the front step, except, of course, for the time the pizza delivery man did show up.

All of the Cygirians except for one named Odhran were from Earth. Odhran's twin—Elizabeth—was from Seattle, and they'd been on Earth during the safe-house destruction so she could introduce Odhran to her adoptive family, passing him off as a foreign exchange student from Dublin, Ireland. The rest of them—Porter and Stephanie, Damon and Laura, Mark and Diane—had been on Earth looking for other Cygirians when the safe house had been destroyed. Darl had met Mark and Diane at the safe house, but the others were all new to him. Even so, their presence felt familiar, known, comforting.

So now because of his call out to the universe, there were nine people including himself sitting in his living room, the remnants of three pizzas on the dining room table.

"Fine cuisine," Porter said, his mouth a snarky curl.

"Didn't stop you from eating everything in sight," Stephanie said, rolling her eyes.

Darl laughed, but then stopped himself, feeling somehow that his laughter, his happiness, was a betrayal of Claire. He couldn't be happy until he found her. He couldn't enjoy anything until he knew she was safe.

"So," said Mark. "The good news is that between us we can create weather, electricity, fire, and change appearances. One of us can head home at will. But the bad news is that we can't do anything useful like travel through time or space. We can't make the bubble that Kate and Michael can. We can't move time back or move it forward. We, none of us, have access to a spaceship, unless we feel like going postal and breaking into NASA. But we know what they think of astronauts gone mad. We haven't managed to contact anyone off Earth, and probably Jai and Risa and Edan think we've been killed."

Darl hoped that Jai and Risa—the first twins, the first pair to remember the dream and find the safe house—and Edan had made it off the safe house. They all seemed important to the rebuilding of the life that had been stolen from them so long ago.

"Yes, indeed. Quite well put," Porter said. "Is there any more pepperoni?"

"God," Stephanie said. She crossed her arms, looked down into her lap.

"What are we going to do, then?" Darl asked. "Is there a way for all of us to send a message like I did? Something louder? Something that people off Earth could hear?"

The doorbell rang again, and Laura jumped up, now used to the ever-evolving party.

"I don't know," said Mark. "We should try. The more people show up, the stronger we'll be."

Porter stretched and rubbed his stomach, looking around the room as if he'd definitely swallowed something they all wanted for themselves.

"What do you have, Porter?" Darl asked.

"I guess none of you heard about what I saw on Upsilia. With Garrick. Quite the Cygirian show."

But before he could continue on with his story, Laura walked into the room with three people, all of whom looked a little worse for wear. The couple—and Darl wasn't exactly sure how he knew this, but their body language, their bearing, bespoke twins—was sodden, bedraggled, just about an hour past total soaking. The lone man was completely dirty, and he shifted back and forth on his feet, clearly embarrassed that with every move, dust puffed up from his clothes.

"They don't have anything that can get us there," Laura said, shrugging. "But at least they made it."

"If you feel like traveling through water, then we are your people," the wet man said, holding out his hand to Darl. "Not to mention blasting through earth at about five hundred miles per hour." He nodded toward the dusty man. "I'm Carl. This is Rebecca. And Steve."

Darl shook Carl's hand, the man's flesh cool and slightly puckered, and then shook Steve's, dry and gritty. He nodded at Rebecca. "Sorry that you can't get us out of here. But I'm glad you are here."

"A lot of good it will do us," Laura said, her body jingling with irritation or nerves or fear, it was hard to tell. "What are we going to do to get off this planet?"

"No one seems to want to hear my story," Porter said. "And it's a doozy."

Darl turned to Porter again, wishing he could bench the guy, get him off the field, or suspend him indefinitely. Maybe he could transfer him to another team altogether.

"What do you have, then?" Darl asked. "Don't just sit there if you think you can help figure this out. It's—"

"Rude?" Stephanie said. "Cruel? Stupid?"

"Well," Porter said, smiling. "If you are going to lambaste me."

Darl wanted to hurl himself at Porter in a full tackle, but it was Stephanie's clear, harsh gaze that got Porter to start talking.

"All right. Keep your skivvies on. Here's what happened."

As Porter made himself more comfortable, Darl sat on the end of the sofa and the rest of the room quieted, everyone listening. Porter seemed to feel the attention, his body language relishing the focus.

"So Garrick and I," Porter turned to Darl. "Garrick is Mila's twin. Mila is Claire's sister—"

Darl started at her name, wanting and not wanting to hear it uttered. "I know," Darl said. "I've met them all."

"And?" Stephanie asked. "Go on, Porter."

"So," Porter said after a pause. "So Garrick and I were in the cave on Upsilia with the group who thought they were Cygirian advocates. You know the ones. Put us in little pods and sent us to La-La Land. And yes, I'll move forward, my love."

He looked at Stephanie, a smile just on his lips. "We managed to make an escape from them, but then we were stuck in a hall with the Neballats coming at us. But then those of us who had been in the Source managed to do something I never imagined."

"And?" Darl asked, hearing the pause for impact in Porter's last word and not wanting it at all.

Porter gave him a quick, dark look and continued. "They pushed us together, everyone in a circle, a tight circle, and the next thing I knew, we were moving out of there, out of danger. Moving together."

The group in the living room sat still, quiet; only tiny "ahhs" and "whats" filled the air.

Mark cleared his throat. "So this group effort thing got you to where?"

"We managed to get out of the cave and away from the Neballats," Porter said, crossing his arms, satisfied with his story. "And then we were home."

"Yeah, a spaceship was involved at that point," Stephanie said. "That's a pretty crucial bit of information. The group traveled through atmosphere. Not space. And we've got a lot of space to travel through."

Darl shook his head. "I have experience going backward

my whole life, home and nowhere else. Only with . . . Claire could I move back and forth. You all know how this works. So how did they manage to do something like this together?"

Odhran, who had been completely quiet the entire time, stood up, nodding. "It's called for lack of a better name Convergence. We learned to do it in the Source. It's this idea that we are all the same energy, the same power. This arbitrary splitting of skills is just that, but if we put our minds and souls together, we can do whatever we want. We aren't limited by our abilities or our powers or what we can do with our twins or doubles. It's about intention and belief."

Darl laughed. "Belief? So you've done this? It all works on faith?"

"No, I haven't been a participant in Convergence," Odhran said. "Never. Never had the chance. In the Source, we are all just our energy, our souls. Whatever you want to call it, so we don't need to merge. We already are. I was in so long, I didn't think about it."

Odhran looked at Darl steadily. "And it is about believing in your intent. What you want and why you are doing it. That we all have the power to do anything. That's what I learned in the Source."

"How long were you there?" Darl asked.

"I was there for almost seven years. I was brought back during the escape from Upsilia."

There was a gasp. Seven years? Darl stared at the man, wondering how he knew how to use his body anymore. How did one come from a place of no body, all soul, all energy back to arms and legs and brain? How did one tolerate being forced into such a place for so long?

Odhran held up his hands. "It's all right. It was a lot better than being on Upsilia and not being able to live. We were really pushed away from daily life. They were scared of what we could do with our doubles, all the powers we had. So they sent us where daily life couldn't affect us. And where we couldn't affect it. But it's lovely there, in its way. It's kind of like heaven."

Porter shook his head. "Give me gravity and a good cup of coffee, and I'm in heaven."

Stephanie rolled her eyes again, and Darl wondered about these two. Porter didn't say anything about Stephanie in his list, nothing about touching her, and Darl felt confused about their relationship. But no matter the implications of Porter's sentence, Darl thought that for the first time, he agreed with Porter. Everything about a soul and collective energy and oneness was fine and dandy, but he liked living in his flesh. He liked touching—he liked touching Claire, feeling her smooth skin under his fingertips, seeing her eyes, sensing her heat, tasting her wetness, her tears, her lips.

For a quick second, he was almost there—her eyes gazing up at him as he looked down on her, moved in her, flashed in front of him, and he had to swallow, breathe, try to forget so he could go about the business of finding her.

"Do you think," he asked Odhran, "that this technique, this way of moving—Convergence— could get us from here to Upsilia?"

"And if it can, are we even sure that the group is on Upsilia?" Mark asked.

"Clearly, they are either here or there, and those who are here are showing up two by two like Noah's ark," Porter said. "I think we could wait a little while longer and we might have quite the crowd. Your message packed quite a punch."

"Seems so," Darl said, his heart filling again with hope. Maybe Claire would show up. Maybe she would come to his door right now, now, now! After all, she could be on Earth, too, being rescued by a group or a duo that had the ability to travel through space.

"So we should wait," Mark said. "But not for long. Not much longer than tomorrow morning."

"You're right," Darl said. "We can't wait for much longer at all. But let's give it a little more time."

The group nodded, and even as they all agreed, the doorbell rang. Darl breathed in as Laura went to the door again. Maybe Claire would be here now. Maybe she would show up later. And if she didn't, the more people they had, the better. The more people who could join with them in the process of Convergence, the better the chance he would be holding Claire by tomorrow.

A group of about thirty Cygirians stood out on the lawn of Darl's backyard. He hoped that if his neighbors looked over the fence, they'd imagine Darl was having a party. Albeit it was an early morning party, and they were all standing in an awkward circle. If they were looking out their windows, maybe they imagined it was some kind of AA meeting or new-age energy circle, something that involved Darl's group to walk in a labyrinth or chant or sing Celtic songs to lute music. Darl was sure that Max and Nancy Samuelson to the right of him and Ina Brown to the left would be a bit dumfounded. Darl Alan James involved in something spiritual? And it wasn't a scrimmage or formation practice? Or a poker party? And shouldn't there be a cooler full of Heinekens involved somehow? Maybe even a keg.

But no one seemed to be looking, and Darl stopped caring about what anyone thought of him. He wasn't the man everyone had always thought him to be. He'd had to tamp down his ability to read minds and fling himself homeward on a thought. He'd had to pretend to be normal, picking a very "normal" life and job.

"Hey, Coach," the high school kids would say. "How's it hanging?"

"Hey, Coach," they would say. "You are *way* cool."

Darl had been that cool coach, laughing at their jokes, reprimanding them for bad language and lewd talk and one too many beers over the weekend, but not too often or too much. And he was strong, as fit as they, ready to run a 440 at the drop of a hat. Able to throw any pass, to bench press 240 no problem, to do 600 crunches in less than six minutes.

"Hey, Coach," they would say. "I wish you'd date my mom."

And now Coach was heading off into space with a group of aliens. Coach *was* an alien. That was the headline in the school paper, THE INQUIRER: COACH JAMES DISCOVERED TO BE AN ALIEN.

Darl shook his head, looking down at the slightly wilted grass under his feet. If they could only see him now.

"So I want to let you into my mind," Odhran was saying. "I want you to feel the feeling I learned about in the Source. The connection between us all. That's the starting place. That's where we have to begin, the place that we will converge."

Darl nodded, understanding this connection even if he'd never felt it before. But he almost had when he met all the Cygirians at the safe house. And when he'd first looked at Claire as she sat in her car, terrified, amazed, and so beautiful.

Odhran continued. "Close your eyes and if you aren't

touching someone else, do so. This doesn't have to be holding hands. Just leaning into someone a little."

I thought this was all about the soul, not bodies, Darl
heard Porter think from his location in the circle. *But I
don't want to quibble.*

No one else paid attention, and Darl let go of the smile
that flickered in him at Porter's words. He let himself drift
into the shoulder of the woman next to him, feeling her
heat, smelling the scent of soap on her skin.

Breathe in, thought Odhran. *Relax.*

The woman wasn't Claire, but she made him think of
Claire. He imagined Claire's smells, something like flowers,
the sharp sweetness of lavender, the smell somehow light
purple and delicious. He thought about running his hands
from her shoulders to her hips, letting his palms take in her
curves. He thought of the way she watched him, seeing him,
knowing what he could do. Who he was. The only person
who had really seen him—through and through—his entire
life. The only person he'd allowed to.

*Let go of everything but thoughts of everyone around
you. Feel the connection. Think only about that. The energy
between us, within us, surrounding us.*

With sadness, Darl let go of Claire. She had not been one
of the Cygirians who had shown up last night, the doorbell
going off until three in the morning. She had not tried to
contact him, no message from anywhere. He couldn't feel
her or see her or sense her. So he needed to do what Odhran
said.

He let her go.

He let her go.

He let her go, and then there was nothing but a hum, a
vibration, an energy swirling from the woman's shoulder

into him, from him, into the shoulder of the man pressed next to Darl. There was almost a heat of thought, and it was from Odhran. But it wasn't just Odhran, it was all of them thinking together, as one unit, as one thing.

Behind his closed lids, Darl saw what looked like a mass of energy. Something huge and wide and flat, a pie of flickering particles. In the pie, there were some forms, some energy that seemed to vibrate at a different level, but really, it was all one mass, one wave of energy that included him and was him. Nothing was separate, nothing was not him.

This is what we are, Odhran thought. *And we can move. We can go. We can be wherever we want to be.*

Darl knew that this should frighten him. Move this pie? This enormous blob of energy? This mass of nothingness, with no legs, no sails, no wheels, no jets, no engines? Nothing that would seemingly get them anywhere?

But he wasn't afraid, and the next thing he knew, there was the feeling of air and speed around his body and in his body—moving through his body. In his mind's eye—in the collective eye of all the Cygirians with him—he saw Upsilia. He saw it swirling in its own galaxy, spinning around its own star so much like the earth, a tiny spot in the constellation Libra. There it was, a ball of green and white and gray.

They were going to go there, this mass of energy that needed no vehicle but this oldest vehicle, this realization of the shared quality of everything. They were going to get there to find the rest of their people. And Darl would finally be able to touch Claire again. Finally, after two days of not having her. Finally, after not having her his entire life.

Chapter Five

That, as they say, was rough.

Claire tried to open her eyes, but she couldn't seem to, her world inside her head dark and confused.

I told you to slow down, came the other thought. *Even with a concussion, you never listen to me. So damn stubborn.*

"Don't! Ouch! Damnit, Kate," Michael said, and Claire tried to open her eyes again, knowing that her friends were in trouble. But if they were, so might she be, and it was so nice and calm and safe where she was. Here in this drifting, she didn't have to think about anything except sleep. She thought to roll over and fall back into her thoughts.

"Would you stop it," Kate said. "Such a damn baby. You pretend to be such a tough guy."

"Will you just pull it out? And then we can wake her up and get out of here. Who knows what might find us."

There was silence, and some slight wind whisked across Claire's skin. Slowly, her skin seemed to awaken, and she felt sand under her fingertips, in her mouth, pitting her cheek. The sun was hot, burning into her neck, and something sharp was digging into her toe.

"Where in the hell did you drop us?" she mumbled, spitting sand out of her mouth as she did. "I thought you guys were good at this."

Claire blinked and opened her eyes into a sheet of yellow heat and light. Something alive with more than four legs—she knew that—scuttled across her ankle, and she yelped, sitting up, her hair in front of her eyes. She wasn't sure what she saw, everything was so different from where she imagined they'd be. Since Kate and Michael told her the story of Upsilia, she imagined dark caves, rows of pods, and a lineup of articulate droids wanting to probe her flesh.

"Our aim isn't exact," Kate said. "So we are here on a desert. On a cactus, actually."

"And it's in my damn ass," Michael said. "I don't remember all these cactuses last time. Now I'm injured top and bottom."

"We weren't here on a tour of local flora and fauna," Kate said. "We were only here for about a second anyway."

Claire could tell that she was irritated, upset, angry, but then even as Claire watched her, Kate calmed down. She breathed, touched Michael's forehead, kissed him on the shoulder.

And then, before Michael or Claire could see what she was doing, Kate pulled out a long thorn, Michael yelping as she did.

"There, now," Kate said. "We're good to go."

She held up a rather thick, pointed, triangular shaped thorn. Claire winced, her eyes wide. Sitting up, she looked down at her toe, glad to see that she'd only been banged up by a rock, not a thorn.

"You don't think I'm a very good nurse?" Kate laughed. "I don't blame you."

Claire smiled, shrugged, smoothed out her clothes, and stood up. They were, indeed, in the middle of a desert. For miles and miles all the way out to the horizon, there was nothing but sand, scrub, and cactus. Big thorny cactuses. And though the sun hung hot and full in the sky, it was not burning directly above them. Was it spring here? Winter? And why did they stop in the desert in the first place?

"It's a good break point," Michael said. "Before we move in. To get our bearings."

Claire started, realizing that she was not in the practice of turning off her thoughts. She hadn't had to, ever; no one seemed to slip inside her mind except for once, when a homeless woman looked at her and shook her head, saying, "You shouldn't cut class, missy. Get back to school before your mother finds out."

Claire had rushed back to school and forged a note from her mother, deciding that if a homeless woman knew she was out of class, her principal was soon to follow.

But now she was around people who could read her— quite literally—like a book. With Darl, the experience had been wonderful, a melding of inner and outer, their bodies and thoughts merging into something fluid and known. But she knew she might want to turn it off a bit with Kate and Michael.

"So the place with the people and the scary pods is close by?" she asked, her mind now sealed off and her own.

"One more little bubble ride, and we're there," Michael said.

"With the pod people," Claire said. "The ones who want to throw us away." She wished that Darl were here, right now. She knew it hadn't been long enough for her to need him so much, but she did. She wanted him to help her decide how to feel about all of this. After all, it was he who had brought her into this mess. If he hadn't shown up, she'd have gone home from Pilates and eaten a cinnamon roll, drunk a couple of cups of coffee, and then maybe taken a walk into the Haight. That night she would have watched some rerun on television, curled up on her couch. But now? She was on another planet worrying about pod people and cactus thorns.

"Look, they aren't why we are here. You know that, Claire. This is the only other place people might be. And they weren't so bad," Michael said.

"Please don't get me started on them not being 'so bad,' " Kate said. "All I can tell you is that I want to get this over. Go back to Earth. Rent out a giant warehouse and move us all into it. Buy up a couple of motels. A farm. A ranch. A small impoverished town. I don't care. Just get things back into place before the Neballats show up again."

"Who is to say they haven't already invaded Earth? I mean, why are we running?" Claire asked. "They seem to find us wherever they are. They might be here right now."

Kate and Michael stared at her, and she didn't care. Suddenly, this running around seemed pointless. She wanted nothing more than to curl up and hope that the struggle would go away. She could sleep and dream, and maybe this would all be over when she woke up.

Kate almost snorted. "Ridiculous. We have got to learn to protect ourselves. We've got to give Edan a chance to do . . ."

"To do what?" Claire asked. "Edan has to do what?"

Kate stopped, looked at Claire, and shrugged. "I don't know. Nothing. Listen, I know it sounds impossible, but it's going to be okay."

Claire breathed in, wondering what it was about this brother she had never met. What could he do that an entire planet couldn't do? What was it about him that had so many people invested, relying on him to do something, something big?

"Let's get going." Michael looked confused as to what

body part to hold as he stood up: his head or his ass. Finally, he just brushed the sand off his clothing. "Let's go and find our people."

Kate and he talked for a moment, and Claire turned back to gaze out into the desert. The light shone gold on the smooth shimmer of hot sand, light blazing off long-dead black bark of the trees. Waves of heat pulsed up from the ground in widening, flickering arcs. Somewhere past the edge of this view was a whole civilization of people who did not like Cygirians. And beyond them were the Neballats, who destroyed everything Cygirians managed to create.

She sighed, closing her eyes. All of this terrible truth was there, but there was something else inside her, something as warm as the sand, something that even her fear couldn't dampen. Now that Darl had shown up and released her ability to love, Claire couldn't keep it down. She wanted to fight in order to live to the hour she would see him again. It was so corny, but it was true. She was suddenly a walking billboard for hope, even though all the facts were out there, facts that could stop them all.

Claire swallowed down the grit in her throat and knew that despite her negative thoughts, the strange people on this planet, not to mention the enemy that wanted them all dead, and Kate and Michael's navigational errors, she would do whatever she had to, whatever it took, to find Darl.

Take it easy, Michael thought. *We're going to land soon.*

Okay, Claire thought back. She quieted her thoughts, wishing she wasn't bouncing around in a bubble. She focused, staring out the bubble at the landscape below.

But isn't someone going to notice us soon? I can see the city right over there. Aren't we going to hit radar? Don't these people have things like weather cameras like we do? They are some kind of advanced civilization with androids and the Source.

That's right, and they probably already know we are here, Kate thought. *They did last time. They let their whole little plan unfurl.*

But as the bubble slowly lowered to the ground, nothing charged out at them, spotted them, attacked them. There were no groups of people running at them with pitchforks or laser guns or bombs. Instead, Kate and Michael made a quick, soft, easy landing, and the bubble shimmered away to reveal a cool forest of trees and bushes, the sun making dappled shadow patterns on the soft turf.

"Now that was a landing!" Claire said.

"It's easier when we aren't coming out of space," Kate said, her shoulder raising a little defensively as she spoke.

"I didn't mean—" Claire started.

"Oh, it's always my fault when we crash," Michael said. "I don't have any finesse."

Kate learned over and kissed him on the cheek, touching him so gently that Claire wanted to weep. She'd missed the desire to kiss someone like that her entire life, watching others in surprise, amazement, and envy. Looking at everyone else falling in love, it seemed so easy, the leaning over into someone else, the giving of one's love to another. A quick kiss, a smile, a whiff of the other's skin. How easy.

But how impossible until Darl.

"So where is this cave?" Claire asked, pushing Darl, his dark curls, his smile out of her mind. "Where are the pod people?"

The three of them began walking east, toward the city. All around them were broken branches, shorn right off the trees. And in open spaces were black rings of singed needles and leaves.

"What happened here?" Claire asked. "It looks like some kind of weird fire."

"The Neballats were here," Michael said. "These marks are from their spaceships."

"Do you think they are still around?" Claire looked up toward the canopy, imagining the shadow of some great craft hovering just beyond them. But there was nothing but sky and trees, and she shivered, everything inside her jangling.

"They have the time it takes to destroy something before they have to get back in a protected environment to rejuvenate," Kate said. She stopped walking, pulling on Claire's arm gently. "They aren't like us. They aren't healthy. I mean, maybe they once were. But they are pretty creepy looking. Sort of invisible, except you can see their organs beating inside them. I like to be in denial about my organs. I know they are there, but I don't want to have to watch them work."

Claire blinked, trying to imagine these creatures. "What happened to them?"

"They destroyed their environment so much that they destroyed themselves. That's why they needed us in the first place. Now they just flicker across the universe, desperate to find something to make them whole."

"Well," Michael said. "It ain't going to be me to fix them."

"Let's hope not," Kate said.

They walked on in silence, the eyes of the forest staring at them. Claire kept fighting the urge to look over her shoulder, sure that someone was following them, hiding behind trunks and rocks, tracing their every step. Overhead, birds called, strange whickering songs she had never heard before. What kind of bird was that? she wondered, realizing that she wouldn't know. She was on a strange planet, an alien planet, breathing alien air and looking at alien trees.

She was on another planet! And it wasn't a cliché, something she might think when she was at a party or wandering on Telegraph Avenue in Berkeley or at a parent/teacher meeting at school when things got weird. She was on another planet in another galaxy.

Blinking, she looked up again at the trees, realizing that while everything looked normal, it wasn't what she was used to. The tree might be some kind of fir, but it was a little off, fuzzy needles when they should be sharp. The black birds flying overhead should have red dots on their wings, but instead they were dotted green. Lizards with purple streaks instead of blue flitted across the tops of logs. The rocks should be granite, but what did the people here call that kind of geologic formation? And how was the planet formed? How was it shaped? And were people's insides the same here? Hearts and lungs and spleens and livers? If the Neballats had organs visible from the outside, did that make them the same, too? Or were there fundamental differences as with the trees and birds and lizards?

All of this seemed just too weird. After a whole life of thinking that humans were the only evolved creatures in the universe—any universe—now Claire was faced with the fact that there was so much more of everything. It was as if someone flung the same ingredients into the air and Upsilia and Earth and Cygiria and the former planet the Neballats lived on formed separately, different but enough the same to breed three groups of creatures that could live on any of the planets.

And if she was Claire on Earth, was she Sophia here? Or

something else? What were people called? How did people live? Were the rhythms of life and living the same on Upsilia as they were at home? Probably not.

She rubbed her forehead, her brain unable to hold all these thoughts together. None of the things she'd learned in school, read, been taught were true. None.

"I hate to say it," Michael said. "It's such a cliché."

"Then don't say it," Kate said. "Let it go. Please. It will make us all so much happier."

"What?" Claire asked.

Michael smiled. "You aren't in Kansas anymore."

"Do you have a pair of ruby slippers to get me out of here?" Claire asked, thinking of what Darl had said to her back home. "An air balloon? No, wait, you have a bubble. Sorry. I was confused. And anyway, I think this plot line blows out anything in *The Wizard of Oz*."

Kate and Michael laughed, pulling Claire along with them. Together, they walked through the trees in silence until they stopped in front of a large cropping of rocks, its heavy granite face hanging in front of them.

"I think it was here," Kate said. "Everything was a rush when we left. But it's somewhere right here."

"You're right, my love," Michael said. "I remember it fondly. Just as we were attacked—"

"How do we get in?" Claire asked. "Do giant doors just somehow open like in *Star Wars*?"

And as she said that, something started to rumble, gears and mechanisms in the stone moving so that indeed, a slab of stone began to pull open, revealing a long cavernous hall.

"The Upsilians love surprises," Kate said. "Or they like to appear mysteriously, sending their droids as the welcome wagon."

"Great," Claire said. "But I guess that we're lucky the Neballats aren't the ones driving the welcome wagon."

"Don't be too sure," Michael said. Claire looked at him, and he smiled. "Don't worry. I think we'll be okay."

Claire sighed, hoping that Michael was right. The stone door stopped moving, hanging like a broken tooth against the darkness.

"Here we go," said Kate, and they walked in. Claire tried not to jump when the granite etched its way closed, as the light faded, as the air turned cold. As they walked, their footsteps began to clack, to echo, to sing sharply into the darkness, indicating that they'd left the soft forest floor far behind and were now on solid rock.

So are the pods in here? Claire thought.

They were, Michael thought. *Rooms full of them.*

Do you think that they've got anyone in them now?

Kate shrugged. *Maybe they've turned them over to criminals or basically anyone else they don't want in their society. Maybe there were more of us we didn't know about. I haven't been to one of their cities, and I don't want to ever go to one. I don't even know if this world has different cultures, races. Like ours. But if there is anything other than this—anything better—I'm not even sure I'd want to know about it. I just want to see if our people are here and get the hell out.*

Claire kept walking. Maybe there were other countries here, like there were on Earth. The United States and China and the Philippines and just about every country had fundamentally different views on things, so why would all the Upsilians be like this group in this one small cave on this one small mountain? Upsilia couldn't be like *Star Trek* planets, where the crew would land to find one homogeneous group taking up the whole of a planet. She almost laughed. What did she know? Why would the Earth be the model for everything? Maybe *Star Trek* was ahead of its time.

Claire was about to ask more about the Upsilians when another door about two hundred feet ahead of them began its inexorable climb upward.

"Here we go again," Kate whispered. "Last time, the doors kept opening up to reveal yet another mystery or problem. So much fun."

"Shh," Michael said.

They continued toward the opening door, stopping as light fell onto them, a yellow, diffuse, artificial light that seemed to Claire both like the sun and like an interrogation light from a bad Hollywood police drama.

But then something made her gasp, step back, her thoughts and blood seeming to still. Someone was walking toward them, nothing but the darkened figure against the light, no features visible yet.

It could be a Neballat, Claire imagined, afraid that when her eyes adjusted, she might see the figure's horrible innards, its delicate malignant movements. But there was nothing creepy, slinky, malevolent about the figure's gait. No, there was something self-assured, cocky, steady, firm—Claire gasped. Was it Darl? Was Darl actually heading to her right now? Was it going to be as easy as this? Was she going to be able to grab him and pull him into her arms and then maybe just totally away?

No, came the thought, and the figure slowly morphed from an indistinguishable shadow to a man. A tall, blond, good-looking man, a man who seemed to be unable to take his eyes off Claire, so much so that she stepped back.

But before she could step back or say something or ask

Kate or Michael who he was, Kate was throwing herself around his neck, her cry still loud in the hall.

"Garrick!" Kate said. "My God. You are okay? You're okay. And Mila? Stephanie and Porter? Who else?"

The man—Garrick—hugged her back, his eyes still on Claire. But then at Mila's name, he closed his eyes, and Claire finally understood who he was. Mila's twin. Her sister's twin.

"I don't know about Porter and Stephanie. Kenneth and Whitney are here. Only about forty of us made it here. But not Edan. Not Mila," Garrick said, letting go of Kate and standing straight, his eyes on Claire again.

"Sophia," he said. "It's you."

Claire nodded. "Yes."

"Darl found you?" Garrick said the words, the last of his question changing sound as he realized that Darl was not standing among them. "Where is he now?"

"I don't know where he is," Claire said. "He disappeared. Right when we got to the safe house."

For a moment, they all were silent, their thoughts a mass of loss.

"And call me Claire." She looked at Garrick. "It's who I am. Sophia was someone else, a little girl, from a long time ago."

He flicked her a quick, sad smile, and Claire wondered about this older sister of hers that she had never seen, this sister who had this man. Or did.

"So," Michael said. "What's going on here? Have they put us all in pods yet?"

Garrick shook his head, breathed in deeply, pushed his blond hair away from his forehead. "The Anthros aren't even here. No one. Nothing. No pods. No droids. No machines to scan us. It looks like the Neballats wiped them out or cleared them out or something."

"Are they in the cities?" Kate asked.

"I don't know. I don't know much of anything." Garrick put his hands on his hips, shook his head. "We haven't been here that long. A day, tops. Everyone is not exactly thinking clearly."

"So what's the plan?" Michael asked. "Where did everyone else end up?"

"Earth, maybe. Other parts of this planet. There isn't a lot of guessing there. No underwater worlds or anything. We do need air, or most of us do at least."

Claire stared at Garrick. *Who doesn't need air?*

He smiled, hearing her thought. "A couple of people here can breathe in, shall we say, alternative methods. I don't ask questions about powers, though, except when they save my life. Like what Kate and Michael can do."

Garrick put his arm on Michael's shoulder. "Come on. Let's talk with the others. We are about as confused as you are. Though we do have a spaceship."

"At least there's that, but this isn't exactly what I imagined we'd hear," Kate said. "What I want is a well-formed plan. Lots of options. Someone in charge of all this."

"That's what we all want," Garrick said, but his voice, the sad lilt of it, showed Claire that was not what he wanted. What he wanted was what she wanted. Their twins. Mila and Darl.

"We need to go into the city," a woman was saying, her feelings so strong that Claire wondered if the woman even needed to speak. "Maybe a group of us came here before and then found what we did. Nothing. So they moved on."

Claire sat between Kate and Michael on a bench, in a group of Cygirians. As she listened to the group vent and demand and explain, she wondered how many Cygirians had been found before the attack. Thousands? Hundreds of thousands? Before this, had all of the lost children been rounded up from both planets? But even so, what was a group of about fifty going to be able to do against an entire world? How could they find the other groups that were potentially on Upsilia? How would any of this talk get her closer to Darl? When was she going to be able to figure out if he was okay? When would she learn where he was?

"We don't even know how many of us survived the attack," a man said, and Claire closed her eyes. "No one has sent a message."

"My point exactly," said the woman. "We need to find all who did. Get back together. Figure out what to do as a community, not just as a splinter group."

"It doesn't make sense to trudge through the mountains like some kind of ridiculous scouting expedition," someone else said. "And it's not like a spaceship is going to go unnoticed."

"We don't need a spaceship," Claire heard herself saying. "I could go to the city center right now."

Kate put a hand on Claire's shoulder, *Shh* a thought Claire could hear. But she didn't want to *Shh*. She wanted to scream. She wanted to move, to get out of this cave, to do something, anything.

"I could go in and give it all a good look. Find out what has been going on there." Claire stood up, looking at the group of people in front of her. "I know I don't want to wait for one more second."

Garrick turned to her, looking at her intently. Then he smiled, and she caught his thought.

You are so much like Mila. She would be saying the same thing.

Claire smiled back for a second until her nerves took over, shaking her smile off her face. She swallowed, looked back at the group in front of her.

"My ability is to go wherever I want to. I can't get home the same way, but I can move around a bit. I just need to know where I am going. Get a look at it through someone's thoughts."

"None of us have been to the city," said Garrick. "This is where the ride stops. This cave."

"I could walk until I could see something. Part of it. I just need some bearings."

Everyone listened to her and then when she stopped talking, there were conversations. Kate pulled her around and held her shoulders in her hands.

"What are you thinking?"

"I can't just sit here," Claire said. "I just can't."

"Don't you think everyone in this place feels the same way? There are so many missing people. But to put yourself in this danger?"

"So what are we going to do?" Claire asked. "Wait for those disgusting Neballats to show up? I can look around. I can at least do something. I can send out a message. Move. I can't just stand here and talk about this when he might be—when he . . ."

She stopped, breathing in deeply. It just wasn't going to happen. She wasn't going to allow this loss to be real. All her life she'd lived with things being taken away, and for once, she was going to grab it back. Grab him back. Grab Darl.

Kate nodded and then let go of Claire's shoulders. "Fine."

"Fine what?" Claire asked.

"We'll take you to where you can see. And then we'll go to another spot in the city." Kate paused, thinking, it appeared, to Michael, then saying, "Okay."

She turned to face the crowd. "Listen. Listen. I think that Claire's got a point. She can go scout out a section of the city. Michael and I will do the same. Anyone else who has the ability to move in some way should try, too. That way, we can gather information. Maybe, if we are lucky, we can find our people."

"We have to be careful about sending out messages, though," someone said. "They could hear us."

Claire looked around, waiting for someone to say who the *they* were, but then she realized that it didn't matter who. Either the Upsilians or the Neballats would be bad. Either could make it impossible for her to find Darl.

"That's right," Garrick said, leaning back in his chair, his long legs in front of him. "I think we should keep our thoughts tamped down. Communicate only through language. But be careful with that, too. It's impossible to say what we are going to find out there."

I know what I want to find out there, Claire thought, trying to pull back her thought before anyone noticed she hadn't kept her thoughts to herself, even if the mission hadn't started yet. But Garrick turned to her.

"I know you know. I'm counting on it. I wish you could take me with you, but I know you can't. So I'm counting on you finding Darl and your desire to find him will bring Mila back to me. I thought—I thought we were done losing each other in this enormous universe. I found her, and I keep losing her. I can't keep her safe."

She reached out and touched his arm. She had no business saying this or anything like it, but she couldn't help herself.

"I'm going to find Darl. And my sister. My brother, too.

To know that they exist—that everything I always dreamed of is there but endangered." Claire paused, breathed in, the image of her sad little apartment back in San Francisco floating through her mind. In the next instant, she thought of Annie and Sam, the tiny people who once thwarted her with paint and tears. In just a couple of days, she was no longer that hapless kindergarten teacher, crying in the corner along with the children.

She stood straighter. "I can't not try. I can't fail. I'm going to find them. No matter what."

Garrick was about to say something else, but then the group began to talk all at once, the formal meeting over, members deciding who with what power should go on this mission. Kate and Michael motioned for Claire to join them and two other Cygirians who had walked over to them, and Claire nodded. But before she left, she looked at Garrick, this man somehow related to her through family and feeling and hope.

"I don't know my sister or my brother except through my dreams. For years, I saw them both every night, Mila always sitting in between us. There she was, this older, smarter beautiful child who would take care of me. She and Edan were both there to take care of me, and then I'd wake up without her, without them, feeling more alone than ever."

Garrick gave her a quick sad smile, his thoughtful, handsome face almost set in grief. "She had that dream of you, too. She's always known about you and Edan, from the beginning."

"That's what's going to bring us together," Claire said, knowing she meant it as the words came out of her mouth. "And it's my turn to take care of her."

Garrick took in a breath, swallowed, bringing up his hand and putting it on Claire's shoulder. "And there's something else."

Claire waved to Kate, letting them know she was coming. "What is it?"

"It's Mila," Garrick said. "She's pregnant. There's no place to be safe now in our world, so I couldn't protect her. Or our baby."

Even though Claire didn't really know her sister or this man in front of her, she knew that this baby, this next generation of Cygiria, was important not only to them, to her, but to all of them. This baby was their future.

"I promise I'll find her. There's no choice. We have to find each other," Claire said.

Thank you. I know you can do it. Just close your eyes, Garrick thought. *And you'll be able to find her again. Go back to the dream and feel her as you felt her then.*

Claire nodded once again, and with a last touch to Garrick's arm, she walked toward Kate and Michael, knowing she had to be ready to go. Willing to go and willing to go now.

With Kate and Michael standing next to her at the edge of the city and with the most accurate picture of the city of Dhareilly in her mind—given to her by many members of the group—Claire closed her eyes and imagined, and within less than a second, she could feel the change of place, in the air around her, the noises of city life, the smell of the streets. Food, crowds, some kind of exhaust from some kinds of engines. Voices in another language—soft, low, lyrical— that in some strange way slowly began to make sense to her, flowing into her ear as if the words were English.

Tiny movement by tiny movement, she opened her eyes, hoping not to get hit by a vehicle or a pedestrian. Hoping she hadn't appeared in the middle of a street performance or a farmers' market or a group of preschoolers walking hand in hand down toward some exciting field trip. But no. She was safe on a smooth sidewalk in the midst of a city day.

"No thanks," someone close to her said. Claire whirled and a man moved past her, as did his companion. The man looked at her, his eyes trying to say something to her, urging her—urging her to do what? But then he and the woman were gone, and another voice was in Claire's ear.

"Stop it. We're almost there," a woman said, and Claire whirled back, pushed against a wall immediately by the woman, who was holding the hand of a crying child. "You have to go to group. It's what all the children do. I don't know why you are crying. Just keep walking. Why do I have to tell you this every morning?"

As she passed by, the girl looked up at Claire mournfully, and Claire couldn't help but think of Annie and her tears.

I go a million miles only to be right back where I started, Claire thought to herself, knowing that her thoughts were hers and hers alone, everything wrapped tight to her mind.

Breathing in deeply, Claire began to walk, keeping her gaze on the sidewalk except for furtive looks up, looks she had to force into brevity because she wanted to stop and stare and take everything in. All of this seemed impossible. How were these people just like people on Earth? Yes, things were different in this city, different from San Francisco or Manhattan or Chicago or Paris or London in that the architecture reflected tastes from a different culture, more advanced technology, greater intelligence, or something. Things Claire wasn't even sure of, things like energy systems and wires and building components and advanced knowledge of quantum mechanics or string theory or dark matter or ideas no one on Earth had ever heard about before.

But even with that, these people were people. With lives and worries and children. Invading aliens, too, but Earth had those and didn't even know it. But here on Upsilia, they had the Source. Except that they sent her brother into it. And now they might be planning to do the same or worse to the Cygirians who might have fled here, desperate to escape the Neballats.

She hoped that the other four groups of searchers—Kate and Michael one of them—were having better luck than she, quickly finding out something. This large silver, white, and gray city seemed almost like a painting, something vivid and right in front of her, but something she could not touch.

Claire stopped at a corner, waiting for a flurry of large, white carlike vehicles to rush by, their motor sounds a whirring roar. She blinked into the brisk air, wondering where to go. Where would she hide if she arrived here? Which people looked as if they would help her? Who to turn to? Who would not report her to the pod police who would dump her in some pod somewhere?

The cars went by, a bright white light flickering off and on, indicating it was safe for her to cross the intersection. Or at least that's what it appeared to tell her, as others around her stepped into the intersection. She moved with them across the street, and thought about Earth. Where would she go there? The police would want to involve immigration services—the major immigration chiefs of staff—because she would maintain she was from another planet, the biggest immigration situation to ever befall them. No, not Homeland Security—the police would call mental health professionals, major heavy-hitting doctors who would drug her senseless as she struggled in her straitjacket. So no police. Who, then?

With a loud squirting sound, a truck pulsed by, its whirling brushes cleaning the already clean street. Next, a huge silver vehicle roared by, emitting a smell like laundry soap bubbles. An air-freshening service? She noticed that, in fact, everything was sparkling and shiny, white and chrome and glinting steel. No soda bottles nestled into storm grates, no newspapers clinging for dear life to fences. In fact, there were no fences, no construction sites, nothing that wasn't done already, perfectly placed, perfectly clean. Not a cigarette butt to be had.

Claire looked down again, continued to walk, thinking as she did. Where to go? Where to go? What about the Salvation Army? The Red Cross? The YMCA? The free clinic? And where were those places on this planet? What would they be called? In the city, there had to be those who were down and out, homeless, hungry. Those who needed the services that only the kind and generous could provide.

As she thought, she heard a voice, and she looked up, seeing a man standing still on the sidewalk. He looked like everyone here did—dressed in the clothes that seemed to be in fashion, pants and a long blue top, neat and pressed and tidy.

"Continue to move," the voice said, and Claire realized it was coming from some PA system somewhere. "Do not stop on the sidewalk."

The man stood there, his hands out by his sides, his face turned upward.

"Continue to move," the voice said.

The man didn't move, and the people at either end of the sidewalk started to flume away from him, leaving him alone on the sidewalk.

"This is your last warning," the voice said, and Claire was startled back against the wall as everyone on the street—even the cars—stopped, turned, moved quickly away from the man and the voice.

But the man didn't move. He didn't flinch or change position. And then, in a whisk of energy that Claire could barely see, he was struck down, flat on the sidewalk.

And then, in something like a sizzle, he was gone.

"Oh," she said, sound escaping her. "Oh my God."

"Keep walking," a woman said. "Don't look at me. Keep going."

Claire tried to find her legs, everything inside her wobbling. He sizzled. He disappeared.

"Come, on," the woman said, and Claire began to walk slowly, taking strength from the woman's strong hold on her elbow.

And then she stopped, looked at the woman, wondering if she could even trust her. Or was she one of the people who would sizzle someone like bacon on a sidewalk?

"Who?" Claire began. "What?"

"I'm Lura. Just keep going."

"Are you an Anthro?"

Lura shook her head. "No. Keep moving. You've already stopped enough. If they notice us . . ."

Claire nodded and put one foot in front of the other, barely feeling the pavement under her feet. What kind of world was this? There was no hope here of finding her people. If the Upsilians put them in the Source the first time, now they would just line them up on the sidewalk like sardines and blast away.

For the first time since she lost Darl and heard about putting Cygirians in the Source, anger blasted through Claire, a horrible feeling in the shape of razors.

"Lura, how did that happen? Why?"

They turned a corner down a quieter street, but, as Claire realized, they were all quiet. No people in groups, no people talking on stoops, no businesspeople on cell phones leaning against brick walls. No children staring at dried worms. No one walking a dog. Just people walking past, quickly, fast, going exactly and only to where they were supposed to go.

"It's the law," Lura said. "No stopping on the sidewalks. If you stop, you are asked to leave. If you don't leave, you are killed."

"And that's all right? That's okay?"

"It was decreed," Lura said. "This isn't your world, remember."

Claire swallowed, knowing she'd blown her cover just by walking. Or not walking.

"How did you know?"

"You from Cygiria have been coming back the past two days. I was put here to look for you. To keep you from becoming, well, toast."

"So you know where there are more of us? You've seen us? Can you take me there? Now?" Where Claire wanted to stop before, now she wanted to run. She wanted to go. She wanted to find Darl and fling herself at him. She wanted to hold him tight, put her hands on the sides of his face and kiss him. She needed to see his smile, touch his long, dark hair and love him. Let all of him sink into her, her eyes, her fingers, her body.

More than anything else, she wanted to save him from this horrible place.

"I have contacts who have some of your people in shelter. I'm going to take you there." Lura kept moving, her hand tight on Claire's elbow. "But we have to keep going. We can't stop again."

Claire tried to focus, turning to look at Lura. The woman seemed intent on her task, but not upset by what had happened to the man. Was this because she was used to it? Had Lura become inured to sizzling people? Or was it because she was—what was it? A droid? One of those electronic zombie people that Kate and Michael talked about?

And now as Claire walked down the street, she saw that no one was stalled, still, or even slow. Just like the people who had whizzed by her when she first appeared on the street, everyone was in a rush. There were no happy tourists pointing fingers at architectural wonders; no homeless men or women with signs in hands, asking for spare change; no teenagers sitting on bus benches, singing songs to overloud boom box music or laughing. No, everyone was in motion, scared by the prospect of sizzling. Of dying simply because they were standing. Breathing. Looking up into the sky in wonder.

"Here," Lura said, pulling Claire down an even smaller street. They walked a few steps and then Lura turned into an alley, stopping by a door and knocking once, twice, once.

Claire looked up, afraid that the voice would come, the one telling her to keep moving. But there was nothing but a small slit of sky above her, buildings overcrowding the rest.

Lura noticed her movements, shrugging. "There are dead spots that the net can't get to. That's why we're here. That's why they're here."

"Who are they?" Claire asked. She couldn't help but turn to look behind her periodically, sure that someone would be counting the moments since she last took a stride. One thousand one, one thousand two.

"You'll see."

Lura turned back to the door, about to knock again, when the door opened, light fanning into what appeared to be a small entryway. Claire could see someone behind the door, two eyes wet and blinking.

"It's another one," Lura said.

"A scourge," a man said, but then he laughed, opening the door wide enough for both of them to pass through. "A plague."

While Claire wasn't thrilled to be in this small, dark hallway, she realized that once the door was closed behind her, she was relieved to be away from the voice outside, from the image of the man burning on the sidewalk.

"Follow me," the man said. Claire looked quickly at him, guessing that he was about thirty, thirty-five, his face friendly, happy, his dark hair short, curly, threaded with gray. He seemed animated, energetic, not a droid. Not an Anthro. And now, Lura seemed more real, too. The impassiveness out on the street, Claire realized, had been fear or smarts.

"Don't play the know-it-all role," Lura said, laughing a little, pushing the man lightly on his back. "I have been here before."

"And if I have anything to do about it, you'll stay awhile this time," he said. "Stop bringing in your strays."

"Excuse me?" Claire asked as they walked, the man leading them down the hallway and then a flight of stairs. "I'm not a stray. I actually came here on purpose. I'm here to find my people. I'm here to find my twin."

"Oh, don't listen to Jurgen," Lura said. "He actually very happy to do this work. He cares, but he thinks he's a hardass."

"You've never asked to touch my hard ass," Jurgen said, pushing open a large door down a second hallway. "I think you are finally realizing my hidden ass-ets."

"They are hidden, thank God. And I never will touch a thing on you," Lura said, passing by Jurgen as she entered the room, which was filled with light. Claire gave Jurgen a half-smile and followed Lura into the room, ready to find out who was safe. Who had made it. Darl or Edan or Mila. She didn't really care about this Jurgen jerk. He took her in, got her away from the potential for sidewalk death, and right now—right now!—she might find her love, her family.

She almost pushed herself up against Lura, wanting to be farther into the room, hearing voices, seeing people. She looked around, trying to scan for Darl, or maybe even Kate and Michael, who might have ended up here as well. She didn't really know exactly what Edan or Mila would look like, but she had the feeling that if she saw either, she would know. After all those years of the dream, their childhood faces were in her mind.

But she didn't see anyone familiar. People were smiling at her, people were walking closer, asking questions.

Darl, she thought. *Darl?*

Claire looked at the crowd, her heart beating hard in her chest, and that was when she saw it. Him. Something. After what Kate and Michael had described, she'd thought she'd understood. But God, it was awful. It was horrid, despite the way it tried to conceal itself, its horrible shimmery leg with visible veins, its horrible decrepit body, the huge red eye that peered out from beneath its cloak. But how could it be? How was it possible here, on Upsilia, with all these Cygirians and Upsilians around it?

But it was a Neballat, here, in the room. Hiding. Spying. Waiting to take them all back to its ship. How could they not know? She had to warn them. Her heart pulsed even faster, the hair behind her neck prickling, her knees barely able to hold her up.

She grabbed onto Lura's shoulder, needing to say something, but then everything began to spin: the room, the people, the horrible, horrible Neballat and its one red eye. Just as she fell into darkness, her body crumpling, her eyes closing, she called out one more time.

Darl! Are you there? We're in danger. Tell them. Help us.

And then she felt nothing but air holding her as she fell back into something like relief.

Chapter Six

"If I wanted to go camping, I would have picked Yosemite," Porter said. "Or Yellowstone. Not this horrifying rock."

Darl turned to look at Porter, who sat next to him on an overcropping that looked out toward the city. Odhran had said the city was called Dhareilly, the capital of this province, the name of which Darl had already forgotten. It was hard enough to remember the name of the planet.

"I don't think the resident Dhareillians would appreciate a blob of energy floating into their town square," Darl said. "And we don't want to be picked up by any sensors."

"Truthfully, I wouldn't mind being picked up by just about anything at this point," Porter said. "Aerobics are highly overrated."

Stephanie came and sat down between them, handing Porter a bottle of water. "Please stop complaining before I go on a long spiel about longevity and cardiovascular health. We may have powers, but I haven't met a Cygirian yet who can install a new heart. Sure, one of us could raise you from the dead, but knowing you, he or she might turn and walk away from you."

Porter took the water, smirking at her as he did, and the

three of them looked out to Dhareilly, the buildings tall and silver in the afternoon sun. Darl was itching to get up and go, but the group was a group and in the four or so miles they'd been hiking up over the hills, they'd had to take several breaks. No one wanted to alert anyone or anything to their existence, so the trip had been slow and steady and completely within normal bounds. No powers. No spectacles. No time, space, or energy travel. Just quads and glutes and lungs.

But out there, Darl knew, somewhere, was Claire. He could almost feel her. Hear her, even though they'd been instructed to keep thoughts and reception tamped down. Odhran had told them that all Upsilians had the same ability as Cygirians, so it was important to keep everyone's thoughts quiet. Darl had never felt like screaming before, but he did now. He wanted to jump up this rock and scream out her name. He knew the feeling was stupid, useless, pointless, but he needed to do something more than sit and listen to Porter complain.

"Look," Stephanie said, putting a hand on Darl's shoulder. "We will find her. You can't be impatient. Think how many years it took before you found her in the first place."

Darl shrugged, nodded, took the water Porter offered him and took a sip. He swallowed and sighed. "Yeah, you're right. But I don't think you two know what it feels like to be separated. From what I know, you've—"

"Been stuck with each other since the beginning," Stephanie said, her laugh small and light. "I don't know how you are feeling. But I've seen so many people going through this. We are in a precarious position. We don't have a world. Not even a safe house any more. Our leaders are who knows where. And then there's always Edan to consider."

"He's quite, as you say, 'freaky,' " Porter said, stretching his legs. "I'm never sure how to take him."

"Is Claire like him at all?" Stephanie asked. "You know, kind of ethereal and all?"

At the question, Darl felt Claire's full force, her eyes, dark and directly on him. Her arms around him. Her laugh. Her breath. Her smell of lavender and purple. The magic that they could do together pushing him through space and time.

He let all of his memory of Claire move through him. Darl closed his eyes, and then he shook his head.

"No. Not a bit ethereal. She's like Mila. Completely there. Right in front of you. No bullshit. No mystery. Nothing spooky. Edan, I don't get. But Claire is one hundred percent true."

"Edan isn't mysterious," Porter said. "He's just still in the Source. If you ask me, maybe he only brought half of himself back."

"Of course, no one did ask you," Stephanie said, but she seemed to agree with what Porter said.

From behind them came the groans of the group standing up, getting ready to move into the city. Stephanie took the bottle from Darl and took a long swallow, wiping her mouth when she was done.

"I know most of the time I want to throttle Porter, but I can't imagine him ever being away from me," she began.

"Now you tell me," Porter said. "After all this time, your true feelings finally come out."

"Please be quiet," Stephanie said. "I'm trying to have a Kodak moment, all right?"

She looked at Darl, her eyes not full of humor but of truth. "I want you to find Claire. I want to help. And I know we won't leave this planet until we find her."

Darl smiled, felt her conviction, wished that he felt anything good right now with as much conviction. All he felt now was loss. But he wasn't willing to stay with that feeling. That's not what he was trained to do. He'd been trained to win, to keep playing, to ignore the potential for loss at all costs. He was trained to see the goal and to get there, no matter the pain, no matter the obstacle.

"All right," he said, standing up. "Let's go."

At first, the city looked like all cities: full of buildings and sounds and people moving from one place to the other. But as he listened closely, he didn't hear what he was used to in New York or Chicago or even downtown LA. The hum of cars and motors and construction didn't hang in the air. There was no conversation of horns, the one, two, sit-on-it-hard-until-the-jerk-moved kind of pattern. No motorcycle gunning through the congestion. No boom, boom of an underground subway. And it was clean. Unlike every American city he had seen while traveling around the country playing football with USC, there was no garbage someone was trying to get to with a tiny broom and bin. In fact, even the air was clean, light and full of a laundry sort of smell.

Odhran had told them about the city, as much as he knew. He'd been brought up in one of the many suburbs surrounding Dhareilly, but he'd found himself there before being put into a pod.

"They have the same language ability as we do, so you can speak in English or Spanish or Tagalog or whatever language you have. There are some who study languages for fun. But you will find yourself able to understand, too."

"I wish I'd known about this in French class," Porter said. "I would have done so much better."

"There are many rules," Odhran had said before they'd

set off on their journey. "You can't stand still on the side-walk."

"I can't stand still?" Stephanie asked. "You mean, not even to tie my shoe?"

"No," Odhran said. "Not really. We have to keep moving at all times."

"Whatever is that for?" Porter asked.

"A way of protecting people against crime. The homeless. Beggars. Grifters. Criminals waiting for the innocent. That kind of thing," Odran said. "And if you don't move, there is a punishment."

"What kind?" Darl asked.

"Death. And I mean instantaneously."

No one said a word, all of them staring at Odhran as if he were finally speaking a language they didn't understand.

"What do you mean?" Darl asked finally. "Instantaneously."

Odhran shook his head, looked down.

"You didn't do it," Stephanie had said. "But you need to tell us."

Odhran sighed. "It's a directed energy weapon."

"Excuse me?" Porter said. "Are you some kind of Wellsian fan?"

Not getting the reference to H. G. Wells, Odhran continued. "It basically fries you on the spot."

"French fries," Porter said. "Toast. Chips. Your basic death ray."

What Porter said was true and it wasn't funny, but no one chided him because they could all hear the apprehension—the fear—in his voice. The same feeling they all had.

So now with Cygirians fanned out and walking toward the city center, Darl kept moving, averting his eyes from the Dhareillians who passed him. He imagined that if he didn't think too much until he had to—until he had to act—he could pretend he was in downtown LA, on Melrose Avenue. That was it. He was home, seeing nothing that would flip him out. Buses, not droids. Cars, not invading Neballats with visible stomachs and hearts. No, all was well, wasn't it? He didn't want to see anything to make him pause in wonder. He didn't want to hear anything that made him even appear to stop short and glance upward, his stride changing, slowing. He wanted to keep moving, knowing that the collective energy of this group would bring them to the other Cygirians on this planet.

"They couldn't have known—" he began, but Stephanie shook her head.

Darl flushed, knowing that he wasn't supposed to speak of anything, leave any clue in the air of who they were.

His mind tamped to silent, he tried to push out of his imagination the thought of this terrible energy weapon and any Cygirian burned by it.

Darl!

The thought was sharp and felt like a wedge pushed through his head.

We're in danger!

Darl felt his first misstep and then his next. He reached out to grab hold of Stephanie or Porter, but they were ahead of him, walking in single file.

Help us!

Darl ran, grabbed Stephanie's hand, ignored her gasp. "I have an idea," he said, his voice slow, his fear soft on his tongue. "And it involves my friend."

"What did you say?" she asked as they both continued to walk. "The friend I haven't met yet?"

"Yes, it was something she just said." Darl swallowed,

holding Stephanie's arm. "About something bothering her and her friends."

Stephanie nodded, her face pale. "But you can't really find her at this moment. She is hard to contact, right?"

Darl nodded, his heart seeming to beat unevenly, his feet continuing to move him down the sidewalk. "But I think that there must be a place where I can contact her."

"I'm not sure," Stephanie said. "Let's get to your place to do it."

"Sounds good," Darl said, and Stephanie ran forward quickly to touch Porter's arm.

"We need to go to Darl's place," Stephanie said, and Darl wanted to scream at what he imagined Porter would do or say at this seeming nonsense.

"All righty then," Porter said, turning quickly and walking with them toward a side street, the three of them breaking off from the group.

"Let's keep walking," Stephanie said, her voice soft and full of unconcern she couldn't possibly feel. Not now that she understood what Darl meant.

They walked on, turned down a smaller street, and then another, finally stopping and resting against a hard stone wall.

"What now?" Porter asked, and then from somewhere behind them, there was a sound of concrete being scraped on even rawer, dryer concrete—a squeal of rock and mortar. They all turned, grabbing each other's shoulders and arms, knowing that they could, together, move, but it seemed to be too late to push into energy.

Darl felt himself yanked apart from Porter and Stephanie and was pulled into a dark room. He heard his friends yell, and then the heavy door closed and they were in darkness.

He wanted to think a thought or take in a thought from either Stephanie or Porter, but before he could do either, someone was talking to them all.

"Follow me. We have other Cygirians, and we have a plan."

In silence, Darl heard the slow turning and scraping of feet on the floor, and he moved with the bodies around him. He didn't know who he was with—droids or real live Upsilians. He didn't know where Porter or Stephanie were, and he was hoping this group surrounding him was not a pack of Neballats, taking them somewhere horrible.

For one slow second, Darl thought of home. Not enough to fling himself back there. But there it was. Encino. His house. His couch. His television on to a sporting event. Outside, the lawn sprinklers were chirping their nightly wet song. The streetlights flickered on, the evening creeping into night as it always did. He was sitting there alone, alone. There he was, no one knowing who he really was. Everyone seeing what was on the outside. No one was thinking about him except maybe his mother and his students. He'd never been able to let anyone else in. And most importantly in this home vision, there was no Claire. Not even the thought of Claire.

He couldn't leave now, not with her so very close.

"What is this plan?" Porter asked, the fear barely masked by contempt.

"Just keep walking. You put everything at great risk by coming here. We were about to take control of the situation."

"Yeah, I bet," Stephanie said, and Darl didn't need to read her thoughts to know she was thinking about the Source, the way these Upsilians threw Cygirians in there in the past.

In the darkness, Darl let himself be led, and the only way

he was able to do that—the only way he kept himself from pushing through the pack and toward some kind of safety—was to think of Claire.

I'm coming, he thought, his ideas set to the rhythm of his steps. *I'm not far away now.*

"We are just about there."

"Where would that 'there' be?" Porter asked, but before the answer could come, there was a bang, a flinging open of a door, and light streamed into the hall they'd been walking up.

"Finally," Stephanie said.

And Darl was about to nod, blinking into the light, but something was wrong. Something wasn't making sense. The people who had flung open the door were running at them; the five people whom Darl could now see had been leading them were rushing forward.

"There's no choice right now," someone said, the voice almost in a pant. "We have to. They are here. They infiltrated."

"Okay," a man said, and Darl and Porter and Stephanie were pushed down another hall, the big door slamming again.

"What in the hell is going on?" Darl asked, home and comfort and safety screaming in his ear. But he couldn't leave now. Not now. "Where are you taking us? Who infiltrated?"

"Just be silent," a woman said. "It's too dangerous right now. We've got to get you to a safe place for now. Until things calm down."

Porter spoke, his voice losing all sarcasm. "You aren't putting us there."

And before Darl could think to fight back, everything faded to white, to gray, to pixilated black and then nothingness.

Once in a great while, and especially years back when he was playing football and was often physically exhausted,

Darl would wake from a sleep that had been truly restful. His body and his mind felt rejuvenated, his thoughts a flat, even stream of peace. He would stretch, slowly move out of bed, and float around the house in an alert meditation. The air around him felt calm, warm, even. His movements languid and direct. Not until he had to go out into the world, moving through crowds or in traffic, would it wear off. Suddenly, his sore muscles would ache, noise would jar him into headache, his blood pressure rising with the day, the lovely sleep all gone.

But that moment after waking was like none other, and now, Darl felt that same way, except he wasn't in his house or in any house or any place that he recognized. In fact, it was impossible to tell where he was. Blinking or seeming to blink, he tried to focus on what was in front of him. He moved his arm in front of him, but he didn't see an arm, though he could feel the movement. His phantom limb moved through air that was light and soft and warm. He tried moving his other limbs, and while it felt as though he was moving them, he looked around and saw nothing but gently pulsing light.

For an instant, he thought to be wary. Something had just happened that made him feel that way. Shards of adrenaline crackled out of his body and then dissipated. What was it? He was supposed to fight, but against whom? He should be running, but where?

Darl tried to find a way to grab on to those thoughts, but they slipped away into the light, nothing but calm inside him. No running. No fighting. Nothing but this being.

So he floated forward, letting his idea pull him into the place where the light seemed, well, lighter, opaque and glimmering in the distance.

And as he moved, he felt buoyed by something. Maybe it

was energy or the air simply thickening around him. He wasn't sure, but he knew he'd never felt as safe in his whole life.

Where am I? he thought, not really needing an answer as soon as the thought passed through him. He had the answer. He was here. Here, the place he'd always thought about. The place he remembered without even remembering.

That's right, a voice whispered into his mind. *You're back.*

Darl turned to the voice, and thought he saw a person for a brief flicker. But it was only energy, a pulsing shape of being. His mother.

Mom? he thought, knowing the answer just as he asked the question. He knew it was his mother Joanne.

Or at least part of me is here, she thought.

Where is here? Darl thought.

You know, she thought back, and he felt her as her thought moved through what he imagined was his mind. *The place. The one you've heard called the Source.*

And you're here, too?

What? Humans aren't good enough to come here? Everything is here.

You are still alive, aren't you? Darl thought, his heart pounding at the thought of the house in Olympia without his mother. How many times had he flashed home to find her there, working in the kitchen, the garden? Why hadn't he called her more after he moved to Los Angeles? He sent her cards and presents on Mother's Day and her birthday, but in the last couple of years, he'd felt weary. Growing older had made the gulf between his mother and him grow as well. Joanne wasn't his "real" mother. She was just the kind, warm-hearted woman who'd taken him in, who'd been tricked into raising him as her own. He was the egg planted in her nest that she sat on until she had some of her own. And she didn't know who he was or what he could do.

Of course I do, she thought. *How could I not?*

Huh?

All that popping in and out from nowhere. I'm surprised I haven't had some kind of coronary incident.

Darl felt more than saw his mother's laughter. Really, there wasn't anything to see here but energy, the swarming warmth of heat and movement. And the space was growing lighter as they spoke, flecks of yellow and light pink pulsing with their words.

But you can't know about me in our real life. I can't just talk to you about all of this stuff. About my traveling home.

What is our real life, Darl? This is all our real life. You've always been able to have this part, too, you just didn't know it. And you don't have to be put in a pod to get here. It is here, all around us. All the time.

Darl shook his head, wishing he had arms to cross and eyes to roll. How could this mass of energy be all around him in his real life? He wanted to argue with his mother, but he knew that out there, back where his body was, he had something very important to do. Something . . . someone.

You can find the answers here, she thought. *All the answers that you need.*

Where?

Feel your way to them, Darling. That's always the answer. Close your eyes, turn off your mind, and just feel. That's the way to do everything, not just here. I know you can do it. All you have to do is set your mind to it.

Darl moved toward the energy that was his mother, pressing into warmth he could only describe as orange and soft and warm. He wanted to fold into her, feeling this old, known love. This was such an old feeling, something before even his life, something he had always known. For a moment, they held each other, as energy can push against another force, but then he felt her waft away, leaving nothing but space.

Feel, he thought. *Feel. But what? Feel whom? Feel how?* He looked where his body used to be, realizing that he'd almost forgotten what his body felt like. Where was all his flesh, his bones, his blood? Where was the feel of his feet on the ground, his arms swinging, his spine forced to hold him erect? What weight it all was. How heavy gravity's pull. What a drag, literally, on him all these years. This new nonbody was like floating, his being expansive, full of air and light. How could he feel anything like this?

Again, his question seemed answered as he opened himself up, moving again, floating through the current of lightly buzzing energy, the air alive. He could feel more this way than when he was trapped in his body, his nonbody reaching everywhere, feeling everything, as if he had tentacles that could hold the universe. And the universe seemed to feel him back. There it all was: love, fear, joy, hatred, anger, sadness, hope, compassion. All these feelings coursing into him, through him, around him, all the things that made living real. Everything made sense. Everything was available. Everything . . .

Claire. Oh, sweet Claire.

He thought her name and let himself feel what it had been like to see her for the first time. No, maybe not the first time, but the first time they looked at each other, in her car. Her dark eyes on him, his on hers. The connection between them then was like the connection to everything he felt now. In a short time—no, it was a lifetime of almost memory— she'd shown him who he was. With her, he was himself. Truly Darl. Truly the man his mother always told him he was. He didn't seem as though he were confined to being Darl James. He was part of all of the universe, the people, the things, the plants, the animals, the energy of life itself. And if he was part of that, Claire was, too. And Claire, like his mother, had to be here, too.

Claire! he thought. *Are you here?*

Darl hung in the buoyant energy of the Source, waiting for her, his twin, his partner, his opposite, his equal.

Claire!

If he had lungs to breathe into he would have taken in a huge breath, waiting for her reply. If he had legs, he would have run to the four corners of this immensity to find her. But what he had was the ability to stretch out, to feel the space around him. He moved into the energy, waiting, feeling, hoping, and then he felt just the beginning of heat, a peach-colored flare of warmth, the sound of a word not yet uttered. And then, and then, *Darl!*

Where are you? he thought, pushing himself out even farther in order to find her. The air around him went from peach to melon to orange.

I'm here, she thought, her voice getting stronger.

And then with the eyes he didn't have, he saw her, his Claire. He pushed closer to her, and in his memory and imagination he conjured her face, the lovely line of her neck, the sweet heart shape of her face, her eyes full of his reflection.

As they bent toward each other, energies moving, he felt his atoms merge into hers, every part of his essence tingling as she flowed into him, her heat so warm and delicious and lovely. This time away from her had been more agony than he'd realized. And now it was over.

Yes, she thought, and they twirled into a mix of reds and oranges, merging their energies together. He felt his energy smooth over hers, feeling the heat and light and pulse of what made her Claire. She was soft and full and hot and needful. It was not like skin touching, but it was deeper, different, and Darl moaned into their togetherness.

In this form, their union was not like on the beach in Tahiti, but something different and more profound, a sliding together of their very essence, a mixing of who they were in a way that flesh cannot provide. When they were in the flesh, so much of her was available to him, but here everything was open, arrayed before him, not only their thoughts, but the very beating of what made them alive, this ineffable energy that connected them together, connected them to everything.

In this, rocking, Darl knew the *beat beat* of flickering heat that was this woman he loved. After this, no separation would ever be possible.

He didn't know how long they embraced, time not being a part of this place, this Source, this melding. They could have been together for a minute or a month, but all Darl knew was that this was the sensation he always craved. This closeness. This peace. This happiness.

I'm not leaving you, he thought finally. *I can never leave you again. I will never leave you again.*

With the tiniest of shifts, he felt her pull ever so slightly away from him. His cells, his atoms, ached in the space she was not. All color seemed to fade from the space between them.

Darl, she thought. *My lovely Darl. You have to go back. You can't stay here. At least, not all of you.*

Why not? he thought, trying to move back to the warm place, the totally joined place. But she held herself back.

Because we are people in the world, the tangible world. And you have to go back and find me there.

But how? he thought. *Someone has you. Something bad had happened. I've been captured. I remember it all now. And here, we can go on without all that. This is where we are truly real. This is where nothing matters but this. We won't have to search and fight and—*

Live.

He swirled around her, trying to hold her with his energy, but she pulled back again. If he could see her face now, he knew he wouldn't want to. He didn't know her well enough yet to be able to read the emotions solely on facial expressions, but he could imagine her feelings now. Thinking about how she reacted to him in San Francisco and Tahiti, he could almost imagine the set of her jaw, her mouth pressed tight, her gaze steady.

I didn't know you were so afraid.

If Darl had eyes, he would have blinked. But he felt himself react, hum at a different vibration, something like indignation flaring in him.

I'm not afraid. I just don't see a way out. A way to make this work. The Nebs are destroying everything.

There is a way, Claire thought. *There is a way to pull them to us on that plane. Not just in here. They are here with us. Everything is here with us.*

Yes, they are here, too, Darl thought, remembering what he had been told about the Source. He scanned the immensity for Neballats, half expecting to see their transparent selves, expecting to recoil from their hatred. But all he saw was energy, some parts flickering more darkly, more lightly, more steadily, but nothing that made him afraid. In fact, right now, everything seemed so obvious and easy. The world wasn't supposed to be about fighting and hatred and conquest. It was about this one universal connection, this energy that was all of everything. What he felt right now with Claire was what everyone should feel with every person, every landscape, every creature. Connection. Respect. Love.

But how can we do that out there? he thought. *We can't change the way things are if no one wants to believe in this.*

He waved his imaginary arm. He shook his nonhead. He leaned into the beating energy that was Claire.

No one would believe this was true. No one would understand how wonderful this could be.

It's only wonderful if we can remember it when we are in our bodies. It's the goal. Taking it back. Bringing it to our lives now.

Claire, I don't have a choice. I guess they put me in a pod. I'm stuck in here until they let me out. I've heard of people being in here for years, and they don't seem too upset about it. In fact, it's harder for them when they come out.

Swirls of energy spun past them. Darl was sure he heard laughter. He saw forms pulsing in shades of red and yellow, a wave of sunset colors. He wanted to sigh, to breathe out into the energy before him. He wanted to sleep in here, pull what was Claire and find a way to sleep for a thousand years.

Of course it's harder in life. All that resistance to our flesh. Gravity pulling us down. All the things that aren't clear. But nothing will change if you stay here. We will never have the life we want if you stay. Force yourself awake, Darl. Force yourself to wake up. Wake up, Darl. Just wake up.

But how? he thought, and then he realized that Claire was leaving him.

Tell me how, he thought at her, trying to find her strands of energy with his own. He lunged forward, grasping, but in a flash, she was gone and he was alone.

There was so much that he wanted to do here. He

wanted to find Edan and ask him the secrets that the man seemed to carry into the real world. What had he discovered in here that made him so calm, so accepting, so ready for all the struggle before them? Darl also wanted to find his Cygirian parents, the ones who gave their lives for his. He wanted to find a Neballat and ask why they wanted what the Cygirians had, enough to destroy worlds. He wanted to find his father on Earth, the one who left his wife and family, and kick his ass all the way home. No, that wasn't true. Here, Darl wasn't angry. But he wanted answers. He wanted to find the truth to everything.

The energy spun into the spot where Claire once was. Now there was nothing to see but a whirl of gray and white emptiness. She had told him to wake up. To just wake up.

Wake up, she thought. *Wake up.*

Darl closed his noneyes and talked to himself, thought to himself. *Wake up. Wake up, Darl. Just wake yourself up. Go back and be in the real world.*

Wake up!

Chapter Seven

In the midst of the screams and yells, Claire felt herself shaken into consciousness, as if someone had told her to wake up. Unclear of where she was or what was going on, she stilled herself, listening to the chaos, and then she remembered. The alien.

Without looking for Lura or Jurgen, she pushed herself up on all fours and then into a crouch, moving through the crowd and toward the door.

Claire had never run so fast in her life, bolting out of the room, down the hall that Lura and Jurgen had walked her through just moments before. Instinct took over, and she could barely find her breath; the only thing flowing through her lungs was fear. She had seen it or him or her: a Neballat. She had watched its creepy movements, saw it sliding toward her, just like in a collective Cygirian nightmare.

Here it comes. Here it comes. Here it comes again.

From the meeting room behind her, she heard noises, something like explosions or electricity or wind.

Claire couldn't think, but she ran, finally finding the door and pushing out into the light of the horrible street, this terrible place. But it was better to be outside in unknown territory than to be in that building. Frying or dying. Those were her choices. At least she could keep frying at bay if she just kept moving.

She ran to the end of the street, slowed to a jog, and then when she reached the main street, she slowed to a brisk walk. She was breathing hard, her muscles working, and for a second she was grateful for all her Pilates classes. She was strong enough to keep going for a long while, but as she wiped a thin line of sweat from her forehead, she realized that if stopping was illegal, maybe going too fast was as well. So she switched to a slower gait, kept her thoughts tamped, her head down, and moved.

As she walked, her heart pounding, her body tingling, breath slowly coming into her lungs, she almost started to laugh. Darl would probably call her a "little dense one" again. What had she been thinking? Why hadn't she gone somewhere with her power? Instead of running like an idiot out of the building, why hadn't she flung herself back to Earth? Maybe she couldn't have gotten herself home, but somewhere close. She might not be able to get back to the cave where Garrick and the other Cygirians waited, but she could have found herself some place safer than, well, anywhere than here.

She could go right now. This instant. No more worrying about frying or dying.

A man passed her, and Claire averted her eyes, walking down the almost shiny street, not a piece of paper floating in the light breeze. Where could she go? She didn't want to leave Upsilia because she knew Darl would be here soon if he wasn't here already. In fact, when she'd called out to him just before she passed out, she thought she'd heard him answer her call. Probably she'd been dreaming, but before hitting the floor, she'd imagined him moving into action to find her. For a tiny slice of time, she'd almost seen him, his eyes full of reassurance.

Darl? she thought, pushing her question out as far as she could, knowing she should be keeping her thoughts to herself. *Do you hear me? Are you here?*

She walked and waited, listening for a reply. But there wasn't one. No visions of his face. No reassuring smile. Nothing but silence.

She wouldn't leave this planet, she knew that. Crossing a street and then turning down another, Claire conjured up a place to go. It would be on this planet, and it would be safe. Safe and dark and warm and still. Nothing dangerous for miles around. No Neballats close by, no Upsilians.

As she had prepared for travel to the safe house and later to Dhareilly, she needed to imagine the place so she could get there somehow. Claire looked around, staring at the faces in a bus driving by, knowing she had to think and walk and conjure up this contained, warm, dark place.

But what was this place like? What were its specifications? The floor was hard, the walls something to lean on. The air was warm and soft. She was safe in this place, and without knowing she was doing it, Claire drifted into her way of moving and in the tiniest amount of time, she was there, exactly the place she'd imagined.

"Oh," she said, putting her hand on the wall that was warm and dry and smooth. "My."

There was a sound like a gasp, and then other sounds—clothing brushing against the floor, paper pushed to the side. Claire stared into the darkness, her eyes wide. This time, she was ready to go somewhere fast, ready to conjure any city on the West Coast of California. At this point, she didn't want to put herself into any more danger.

"Who's there?" she asked quietly.

"Who are you, yourself?" a woman's voice asked. "I was here first."

"True," Claire said. "I just want to know—well, are you going to do anything to me? If so, I'd just as soon leave. We can pretend that I was never even here."

The woman laughed. "I'm right there with you. The doing anything part. But your answer is no. I'm not going to do anything to you unless you try something to me. I'm taking a little breather here."

"Breather from what?" Claire asked, the woman's shape forming as Claire's eyes adjusted to the darkness. She was sitting not too far from Claire, leaning against the wall.

"Oh, escaping from people trying to either enslave or kill me. It's hard to tell. Or then there are the ones—" The woman stopped speaking for a second. "Where are you from?"

Claire didn't know what to do. Should she admit right away where she was from? The woman seemed to be from Earth, but at this point, Claire was unsure of everything and everyone. After all, she'd been at a meeting with Upsilians and Cygirians, and a Neballat had slunk into view.

"I just came from the city. Dhareilly. But I'm not from there."

"I'm not from there either," the woman said. "Actually, I never made it to the city. I've been too—I just couldn't leave."

Are you from Earth? Claire thought, opening up her mind.

"Oh, yes," the woman said. "Thank God. Cygirian?"

"Yes," Claire said. "And on the lam from Neballats and pod people."

The woman laughed soft and low, the sound almost seeming to turn into tears.

"You're okay? You aren't hurt or anything?"

"No," the woman said. "I'm just exhausted. I ended up here after the safe house was destroyed. The spaceship wasn't quite right when we took off and it crashed. And . . ."

She stopped talking, and all Claire could hear was the woman's slightly ragged breathing, the sound echoing in the enclosed space. The darkness seemed to lift a little, the air growing warmer.

"Someone—someone didn't make it?" Claire asked.

"Yes," the woman said quietly. "I had to take Alfonso outside. I didn't have the strength to do more than cover him with branches. I wanted to help him. I was desperate to, but my powers aren't good enough to fix that. I don't have that power. God, I wish I did."

Claire was silent for a moment, thinking about loss, her own and everyone's. Losing her mother had been terrible, but it was explained, understandable, clear and orderly parameters surrounding her illness. What was going on now, here, what happened to all of Cygiria, was harder to accept because Claire had no idea how any of it happened, how any of it could be explained.

"My power has been pretty damn useless, too. But I ended up getting myself here, though I really don't know where here is."

"The spaceship," the woman said. "We crashed into this forest."

"What have you been doing?" Claire began. "What do you want to do?"

"I don't know what else to do. So I'm sitting here, keeping my mind turned off, waiting for . . . I don't know what I'm waiting for. I should be moving. I was thinking just now that it was time to get up. It was time to figure something out, and then you were here like that."

Claire didn't have her mind open now, but nevertheless, she could feel the woman's sadness all around them both, the air heavy with sorrow.

"I'm so sorry," Claire said. "I can't help you with the man outside, but I know where the rest of the Cygirians are, and we could walk there. I suppose. We need to get our bearings and see where we should go."

The woman sighed into the darkness. "I should have left hours ago. I couldn't move in this horrible time, and I didn't want to push forward to the future. I mean, what is going to happen next? It can't be good. I feel like there's no hope. I mean, ever since I found out who I was, what I was, there's only been one constant in my life, and now he's gone. I don't know where my twin . . ." Her voice hitched, lurched into a short sob. She breathed in deeply and went on. "I don't know where my twin is. And this sounds stupid—this sounds like something I never thought I'd have the ability to say, but I can't face the world without him. I can't face going on into this war being half. I'm tired of all the Neballats' anger and violence. I thought sitting here and thinking or not thinking was what I should do."

Claire nodded, understanding. In a way, that was how she'd felt at home in San Francisco. She'd been hiding out there, trying to escape real living. It was easier, but oh how those few hours with Darl had changed everything. She needed to get this woman out of the wreck and get moving. She had to find him. She had to warn the others about the Neballats in Dhareilly.

"Listen," she said after a moment. "I know how you feel. I lived my life exactly like that until I met my twin. But now he's not with me, and I need to find him. I'm not ready to give up. I know I haven't faced what you have, but I'm going to keep looking. And I'm going to take you with me, okay?"

The woman seemed to think, moving slightly in the darkness. "How did you end up here, though? Why did you come here?"

Claire shook her head. "What I can do is go somewhere. I can't get home, but I can go. Anywhere I want. It was really hard to deal with when I was a child, but today as I was running from Neballats, all I had to do was think of an image. Something safe and warm. Something, I think, from a dream I've had all my life. And here I was."

"We all have the dream," the woman said.

"But it felt like mine," Claire said. "And there were people—children—in it who were mine."

"What was your dream about? Who was in it?" the woman asked, and Claire tried to press down her irritation. There was no time for this. They needed to leave. The woman was injured, and Darl was in danger.

But the woman had been through something unimaginable, and Claire sighed lightly, looking around. Her eyes had adjusted enough for her to see that she indeed was in a spaceship, with its metal walls, flat surfaces, knobs and buttons and doors. All the accoutrements from a schlocky sci fi movie. The woman was more clear now, too, and from what Claire could tell, she wasn't that much older than she. She was slim, with long, light hair that hung down to her waist, and though Claire couldn't see her expression, she could see the woman's exhaustion in her slumped position.

"My dream starts in a spaceship," Claire began, turning her inner eye toward the story that had come to her night after night for more years than she could remember. "And I'm in it, traveling away from something dangerous. But I'm happy. That's the weird thing. I'm happy because I'm with these two other children who are mine. Family. I think they are my brother and sister, and we are in it together, the three of us, the things that we say to each other. The stories we tell. The feeling in me as I sit next to the girl, my sister. I know there is all sort of stuff going on out in the world, but there is nothing more important than the children and the warm dark space. Just like this."

Claire put her hand on the metal wall, closing her eyes. And for one second, she is in the dream, feeling the lull of the engine under her, hearing the soft conversation of the children around her.

"And that's basically all there is. The spaceship, the children, the warmth."

After Claire told the story, the woman was silent. There was no sound but some faint echoes of machinery going silent after its long flight from the space house, slight and tiny pings and tangs within the walls.

"I think you can go home," the woman said. "With your ability, I mean, not some literary allusion."

"What do you mean?" Claire asked, not understanding the fact or allusion the woman was referring to.

"In a way, I think this was your home. A spaceship."

"No," Claire said, again feeling impatient. "No. The dream might be a fact, but it wasn't my home. And I never can go home with my ability. I don't think you understand."

"Yes," the woman said. "I do."

"How can you know what I mean about my dream?" Claire said, looking at the wall for something to grab to help her up: a handle, a knob, a belt of some kind. This was too much. Now she wanted to get out of here. Maybe she would leave the woman sitting here in the spaceship and find a path back to Garrick and the rest of the Cygirians.

She could fling herself somewhere close and walk the rest. She needed to move, now. Who knew what was happening back in Dhareilly. She hoped that Kate and Michael had not been taken captive, too.

"It was me," the woman said.

"*What* was you?" Claire said. She pulled herself to standing, the light in the spaceship sufficient enough to see the way out. Then it was only a matter of finding her bearings.

"It was me in the spaceship with you."

"Apparently a lot of us were in the spaceship," Claire said, the childhood inclination to say "duh" right on the tip of her tongue. Sad or not, injured or not, the woman was going with her. Or not. But Claire was getting out of here. Now.

"No, Sophia," the woman said. "I was with you. Next to you. I'm Mila."

For a second, Claire didn't even hear the name, her hands on the wall, her feet moving slowly down toward the front of the spaceship. But then the name registered. Sophia. The name Darl had called her when he first popped into her car. And then she stopped moving, hearing in her mind the second name. Mila. Mila her sister. Garrick's Mila. Her Mila.

Claire turned, looking down at the woman and then sinking back down to the floor.

"My sister? Mila?"

There was another pause, one that Claire felt in the air. What should she do? How should she react to this news? Slowly, she slid down along the wall. As Claire sat and settled, Mila put her hand on Claire's arm, and she opened her mind, and there they were together in the ship. Claire looked down and saw their little girl legs next to each other. She turned to see little girl Mila smiling at her, talking to her. The spaceship encircled them in metal arms, kept them safe, moved them toward their new lives. Next to Mila was the boy. The boy named Edan, who was now the man every-one talked about.

"You're my sister," Claire said, and she leaned over and hugged Mila. Her sister, a constant in her imagination, an always in her unconscious. If she hadn't believed Mila's words before, she did then, remembering even in her older body this hug, the feeling of her sister against her body. It didn't matter that that Mila was years older than she had been the last time they were together. This was a real mem-ory from her earlier life. Her real life.

"Yes," Mila said, pulling back, stroking Claire's hair. As Mila did so, Claire watched her as well as she could in the half light. "I have wanted to see you forever. I had the dream, too. I saw every night. I'm an artist, and I painted the space-ship in more paintings than I wanted to, needing to know what my story was. And until I found Edan, I thought I never would know who either of you were."

Claire nodded. "The dream woke me up almost every night. I didn't know what it meant until Darl showed up."

"It was there to remind you. It was there telling you who you were."

Claire sighed, ran her hand on Mila's forearm. "Are you real?"

"As far as I know. Sometimes my life doesn't feel real, I'll tell you that. I didn't know what to do after the crash. It made me feel like everything was over. I could have moved time forward, but to what? To what other bad time? To what other bad place?"

Claire nodded. "I could go somewhere else, but I need to find Darl. And now I've found you. We have to go. We have to get back—" Claire stopped, her words in her throat. She almost coughed, gripping Mila's arm. "I forgot. He's there."

"Who's there?"

"Garrick. Garrick."

Mila blinked into the darkness. "Garrick?"

"Yes, Garrick. At the place where the Upsilians put people in the pods."

Mila pulled away, began to stand up. "Oh, my God. Okay. Okay. Oh." She began to cry, putting her hands in front of her face. "He's all right."

"Yes, he's all right. He's fine. He is worried about you, and we can go there. Not with any powers, but with our feet. Let's go, Mila. Let's go find Garrick."

"I knew he was all right," Mila said, her voice full of air and sadness. "I was just scared to look. To listen. I couldn't take any more loss."

It was then that Claire remembered what Garrick had told her.

"How are you feeling?" Claire asked. "I mean—you are . . . how?"

"I'm fine," Mila said, her voice changing a little, stronger now. "The baby is fine."

Claire put her hand on Mila, wondering if she could actually communicate with the tiny being inside her sister. She wanted to tell the baby that everything would be okay. That she would get Mila out of here to safety, but Mila seemed to hear and began to move.

So together, the two sisters stood in the light gloom of the spaceship, standing together in a way that reminded Claire of always. Here was her dream in her life.

"Let's go," Mila said.

Claire took her sister's hand, and together they walked through the darkness into the light of the Upsilian day.

* * *

"I have no idea where we are," Claire said. She sighed, looking around her at the spindly, dry shrubs of the desert. Everything looked dusty, gunmetal green, lifeless. The wind was warm, wrapping her with hot hands. "I—"

"This might seem impossible now, but there is a range of mountains somewhere," Mila said. She held one hand above her head like a visor against the sharp angle of sun slowly setting in the eastern sky. They had been walking for at least two hours, sweat running in a slim river down Claire's spine. "I saw the spaceship pass over the range on our way down. Not that I was paying that much attention to the terrain."

"Mountains tend to not just disappear," Claire said. "Or I could be wrong. Damnit, I don't know what anything can do anymore. Maybe someone hid them for fun."

Mila shook her head. "I know. After learning about what Cygirians did as a culture, I realized that anything was possible. And for most of my life, the biggest miracle I could conjure was keeping my mother from talking about my love life and fixing me up on blind dates."

"Did any of the blind dates work?"

Mila looked at Claire, almost laughing. "Yeah. I never really thought about it, but yeah. That's how I met Garrick. She'd fixed me up with everyone on the social ladder in San Francisco—"

"San Francisco?"

"That's where I grew up. Lived my whole life," Mila said. "Did the whole social scene there. Private schools, debutante, you name it, my mom had me signed up for it."

Claire wanted to weep or laugh, she wasn't sure. How could she and Mila have been in the same city, county, state, in the same time, for more than twenty years without having ever met or felt or seen each other? All those years of feeling alone could have been erased. To have someone close who was truly related? Who understood all the weirdness she'd lived through? To have someone she could have called and complained that she'd thrown herself down to Disneyland by mistake? To have someone wire her bus money to get home? What would that have been like?

"You'll never believe it," Claire said. "But that's where I grew up, too."

Mila stopped walking, turned to Claire, her face opened up into surprise. "You did? In San Francisco?"

Claire nodded, trying to lighten the mood. "Yes, but it was more like public school, YWCA summer camp, Stonestown Mall shopping for me. You know, I hung out with the Hot Dog on a Stick crowd at the food court. If I was lucky enough to hang out with anyone at all."

Mila smiled briefly and put her hand on Claire's arm. The loneliness they shared in their separate childhoods connected them. Mila tried to say something and then shook her head, unable it seemed to find the words she needed.

"I know," Claire said. "I would have loved a sister. I would have loved anyone who understood."

Nodding, Mila wiped her eyes. "It wasn't until Garrick that I felt halfway normal. I bet that's how you felt when you met Darl."

The sisters looked at each other and kept walking east, toward the sun that hovered low in the sky, orange and heavy.

"You know Darl," Claire said, remembering what Darl had said about her family. How he'd not given her a glimpse of them so that she would have what she had just now: the lovely discovery of her siblings. "You've met him."

"Yes, I have," Mila said, her full smile coming back. "What a character. And what a hottie."

In that instant, Darl's face flickered in Claire's memory. She wanted to reach out and touch him, breathe in his smells. Some deep part of her felt for a second that he was actually in front of her at this moment, talking with her, his eyes dark and serious and full of concern. She could almost hear his voice, sense his questions, his need, his desire.

Darl, she thought, calling out to him. *Where are you?*

For a second, Claire imagined she felt a soft swoosh of his touch, the sound of his round, smooth laugh just at her ear. But then there was nothing but silence. He wasn't close by, not reachable by thought.

Claire rubbed her forehead, focused on her feet moving forward. "Darl saw me in a way that no one ever could. Or has. Or will, I think. And I don't know what I'm going to do if I can't find him."

"I know this sounds ludicrous," Mila said. "But I think you'd know if he were, well, gone. With the way we are connected with our twins, I think that absence would be like the absence we felt before we met them. Do you feel like that?"

And at that instant, she felt Darl again, somehow swirling around her, talking to her. She shook her head, breathing in sharply, tasting sand and dust on her tongue as she did. "No, I don't feel that. I feel like he's with me. Like he's there, here, with me."

Mila nodded. "That's the feeling I was ignoring when I was in the spaceship. I guess I had given up hope. All this struggle, and for what? Well, the very basic answer to that is, for Garrick. For our connection. For us. For our baby."

A bird flew by, something gray, swift, and fleeting. As it disappeared over the slight roll of terrain, Claire heard its call, low and mournful and yearning. Mila was right. Connection to each other was all the Cygirians had. All anyone anywhere had. All this dirt and space and time were nothing without it. And now Claire had not only her connection to Darl but to Mila and to her brother, this man everyone talked about with a sense of awe.

"There." Mila had stopped walking and was pointing to a slight outline of mountains obscured by haze. "That has to be it. I know the spaceship didn't go too much farther before it crashed."

"I'm glad I'm in good shape," Claire said. "I didn't know being an alien would mean so much exercise."

Mila laughed. "Maybe we've been lazy. You would have flung yourself there and I would have pushed through to a later time."

"But then we wouldn't be able to be together," Claire said. "Or I just wouldn't remember anything about it."

"Exactly," Mila said. She took a sip of water from the bottle Claire had found in the ship and handed it to Claire when she was done. The water was warm, but tasted sweet, washing away the grit of their journey. "And I don't think this would work without us both going through it the same way."

She handed the bottle back to Mila, and they started walking toward the range, the haze clearing and lifting, the sun's slanting rays highlighting the mountains.

"Tell me about Edan," Claire asked. "What it is about him that makes people totally unable to describe him. Or if they try, they say words like 'amazing' or 'ethereal.' Makes him sound like an angel or a ghost."

Mila looked at Claire, bit her lip." That's pretty true, I guess. Both words apply to Edan."

"What happened to him to make him that way?" Claire asked.

"You know about the Source, right?"

Claire nodded and then shrugged. "I don't know too much, really."

"I've never been in it, and I am pretty sure I don't want to go. But Edan spent a lot of time there. More than most of the other Upsilians. And either being there made him the way he is, or he was that way and the Source only intensified it."

"What do you mean?" Claire asked. "What is it?"

"It's like he knows something. He seems to see the reason for everything, even things that seems ridiculous or horrifying or scary. I know I can't see things that way. I don't know why I had to go on so many blind dates or why I fought with my mother. I don't know why it took Garrick and I so long to meet. I don't know why Alfonso had to die in the spaceship. I don't know why the Nebs had to destroy the safe house. I don't know why they had to kill off almost all of our race. I mean, I know what they wanted but not why it all had to fall out this way. Edan sees the patterns, the reasons for things. He sees the bigger picture and can actually look at it without going completely insane."

"He's special," Claire said. "I guess that's all people can say. There's no other way to describe it."

The sun was very low in the sky, the shadows long and dark. For a long time, they walked in silence, Claire focusing on her steps, the path in front of her, her feet moving one, two, one, two. Her thoughts were the same, plodding but steady: *Darl, home, Darl, home.* After about a half hour, she looked up, almost gasping. They had made it to the foothills, the earth turning a soft, lovely red, the plants thicker and greener, the air cooler, filled with water.

We aren't too far from the place the Upsilians created for the pods, Claire thought.

Thank God, Mila thought. *My feet are going to fall off.*

Claire smiled. Her legs hurt, her feet hurt, too. She was tired and hungry, her heart carved out by Darl's absence. But they were almost there. Mila would run into Garrick's arms, and she? She would try to find Darl.

We will find him, Mila thought, reaching for Claire's hand.

And in that instant, Claire was back in her dream, back in the spaceship so many years ago. She brought forth the image, the plot so familiar and known. There she is, so little, holding her sister's hand, looking at her brother, all of them going into the rest of their lives. But for that moment they were safe, happy, together.

It will be like that again, Mila thought.

Promise? Claire thought before she could stop the immature plea.

"I promise," Mila said. "If it's the last thing I ever promise, I promise that we will find Darl. And Edan."

Claire wiped her eyes with her free hand, and holding her sister's hand, walked up the mountain, walked on.

Chapter Eight

Darl felt as though he were swimming up from the bottom of a well, the top and safety so far away, the water heavy upon him, the small circle of light above him a pinprick of hope.

Wake up!

That's where he needed to be, that's where he needed to go. He wasn't sure why, but he knew that going up was his only choice. Darl moved toward the light, pulling and kicking and struggling, the water a thick blanket he wanted to shrug off. But he had to make it up, up, up to the light.

Wake up!

Darl urged himself upward, finally feeling his fingertips pull free of the weight of the water, then his wrist, then his arm. He kicked harder, and then his head was just at the surface, just about there, there, there, and he broke free, pushed up, breathed in a huge lungful of air, the water falling off him in a splash.

He breathed in once, twice, hard, and then he hit his head. Darl opened his eyes, blinked into the gloom surrounding him, expecting to see the wet walls of the well, the wavery darkness of the water. But he wasn't in a well, and the water had disappeared. Where was he? When was he?

Darl didn't know what day or time it was, the gloom constant. He had no idea what he was lying on. He was in what? He looked down at his feet, moving his head as much as he could to get a good angle. He was enclosed in a tube, smooth and slim. What was it? A coffin? He shuddered, letting his hands feel the smooth walls that contained him. What had those people done with him?

Moving his hands along the walls, he prayed for a button and switch, something to open this horrible can he was in. If these people were so evolved, he thought, the least they would have was a release button, the way the car companies now put handles in trunks to open them from the inside in case someone was trapped. And Darl was.

He smoothed his palms along the walls, feeling, feeling, and as if Ford had designed the tube, he found a button and pushed it, the cover of the tube sucking open, the sound a release. Darl stopped breathing, listening as the door opened, sure that his captors would have heard the sound, too. But when he slowly looked up and out of the tube, he saw nothing more than many more tubes in orderly rows in the large, dark room.

He shook his head, the memories of the Source coming back to him, the knowledge of what Upsilians did to Cygirians clear. He was a pod person now. He'd been put in the pod and had gone—he had gone to the Source. He'd been where Edan had been.

Pulling himself quietly out of the tube, he remembered the swirling energy of the Source, the images floating back to him. His mother. Claire. Claire and her love and concern and heat. What had she told him to do?

Wake up!

His feet on the cold floor, Darl looked around at the pods next to him. Everyone needed to wake up, get moving.

That's why they had all come to Upsilia in the first place. It was time to stop being victimized. Too many people had done too many things to Cygirians all these years. He knew what Cygirians could do if they put their collective mind to it. He'd traveled from Earth to Upsilia on nothing more than combined energy. That's what they needed to do now.

Walking from pod to pod, Darl pushed the buttons on the sides. As he did, he thought, *Wake up! Wake up now. Don't let anyone control your mind. Join your thoughts with me right now. We are going to Converge. Join me now before anyone sees we're awake. And we are awake! Finally.*

One by one, the pods opened, the sound a fluming pop each time. And as the pod doors opened, Darl felt the minds of the Cygirians join his and then he felt them join him physically as he walked down the rows. There were more people here than in the group Darl had traveled with, and the strength they brought was pulsing, huge, enough to do anything.

Wake up! Darl thought, hearing Claire's voice in his mind as he thought out to all the sleeping Cygirians before him. *We can't wait any longer. We have to change things now. Wake up!*

Toward the end of the rows, Porter and Stephanie emerged from their pods. Porter had no quips, no sallies, no sarcasm. All Darl felt was the crackle of his strong energy joining the group's. Odhran was there, too, and his knowledge of Convergence spun around the group until everyone was ready. They all stood connected, touching, holding hands, their energy almost visible, orange, indigo, violet, yellow, red, blue, green swirls around them.

Where are we going to go? someone thought.

To the people on this planet who can change the way we

are treated. To the people on this planet who can fight against the Neballats, Darl thought, not knowing how he knew what to do. But it made sense. It was time to stop the Upsilians caging and stifling Cygirians. It was time for the universe to fight back against the Neballats, who would eventually destroy everything that kept them from Cygirian skills.

Where is that? someone thought.

Odhran flashed an image, a building in Dhareilly. *The Government of Three. Representatives from all three continents on this planet are there. It's where all the planetary decisions are made. It's where we can tell them what we want. If we can get there, if we can show them what we want and what we can do, then they will pay attention.*

There was a wave of understanding and acknowledgment through the group, the tightening of their desire to be finished with all the running and hiding and fear. For a quick moment, Darl felt for dissent within the group, for refusal, and while there were a few slender threads of fear and regret and maybe anger, there was nothing stronger than that. And in moments, the flush of total agreement was all he could feel anywhere.

We need every single person here, Darl thought, knowing that if his twin and everyone's were in the group, the Convergence would be stronger, more powerful. *We need to call all Cygirians together, anyone who is on the planet right now. Any that didn't go to the Source in the first place. Any who came here after the safe house was destroyed. We need to send a message and have them come to us there, come to us through Convergence, join our energy.*

Yes, the group thought. *Yes.*

And they sent out a message, sent it out with their collected minds and hearts and thoughts. They pushed forward the image of the building, of their plan, of themselves, sending it like a giant billboard out into the universe, asking for people to join them, calling forth all Cygirians to come together in this one place, at this one time. Now.

But that message was dangerous because it would alert any Upsilian who was paying attention. It might alert Neballats, too. So they needed to go and go fast.

Darl cut into the message, urged Odhran to focus them, push them into the full extent of connection so they could go.

And then like the time before as he and the other group left Encino and merged into the great open energy field that was the universe, Darl saw the flickering particles of energy spinning around them. The particles seemed to melt into them or he and his fellow travelers melted into particles. They were becoming the energy they were composed of, just as he had been in the Source. Everything was one mass of energy, and they moved, pulled themselves into the one-ness and moved toward Dhareilly, the place where they would finally change everything.

Then they were there, on the smooth marble floor, stand-ing in front of a podium or large desk, a statue of a flying creature almost seeming to bear down on them, watching them with empty stone eyes. Darl blinked, felt his body so-lidify and become heavy with mass, and then there was the call to push up, push energy back, and he did without knowing why.

And then when he looked around past the statue and saw the energy field that the Cygirians were holding over them-selves, he realized they were under attack. The white-blue light of some kind of ray was bouncing on top of the shield they had quickly created, trying to cut its way in. Darl thought of what Odhran had told them before they'd left for Dhareilly about the people being killed on the streets for standing still. Was this the directed energy weapon, a death ray?

Hold it firm, Odhran thought. *Hold it tight.*

Darl let everything flow through him, let the energy sail up and out of his body where it joined with the others' energy, saving them from being fried like fish, guppies in a glass globe. But the ray didn't seem to abate, its force constant and hard.

We need to push back, Darl thought. *Push it into nothing.*

The group agreed, and Darl could feel their extra push as they tried to force the energy higher, larger, push the ray past its range. But nothing happened. Neither their energy nor the ray budged.

Darl felt that he could push out this energy for a long time but not forever. He looked around the group and realized that while they were able to do this together, eventually, they would all collapse from fatigue. They were biological in this form, needing food and water and sleep.

But in their energy form, they couldn't change this external world, this world of objects not recognized or felt as the energy they were.

We need to call out, Darl thought. *We need to bring them all to us. From everywhere. They need to join with us and fight back.*

The group agreed again, and together, they thought. They conjured forth all the Cygirians, those trapped or hiding or lost. There had to be more than just they on Upsilia, and Darl thought about Kate and Michael, Kenneth and Whitney. He thought about Edan and Jai and Risa. He thought about all the people he met at the safe house, those he'd talked to and laughed with, those he hoped were still alive after the attack.

And then because he couldn't help it, he thought of Claire. Oh, he didn't want her here. In fact, he wanted her safe at home in her tiny Cole Street apartment, watching television and eating leftovers with a glass of wine. He wanted her back in the classroom, where the biggest threat was a spoiled five-year-old with a bladder problem.

But he needed her here, too. He needed her strength, her energy, her powers that made his powers complete. Claire, who made him whole. He closed his eyes and thought about her body, her soft skin, her lovely back, the freckles on her shoulders.

Claire, Darl thought. *Come to me. Come to us. We need you. I need you.*

And as he called out to Claire, he felt the collective call of all in the group, the names sent into the air, the wind, the collective mind of all Cygirians.

Come to us!

For a time, nothing happened. No one appeared right away, the added bit of energy that would save the day. No, they all stood together, pushing against the ray that the Upsilians thought best to use against them. They pushed and waited, and then, finally, Darl saw it. As he stood his ground, he saw four Cygirians appear right in the middle of the group, their swirling, combined energies forming into individuals, individuals who pushed up and back and against the ray.

Darl sighed, feeling the relief even as he realized Claire was not among the group. But then more appeared, using Convergence to bring them where they were needed most. And then again and again, so many appearing that Darl couldn't even see who was arriving. And at that point, he couldn't pay attention because their power was growing, strengthening, becoming more forceful. He could see it pushing up, squeezing away the ray, rendering it thin and weak and useless.

More, more, he thought, as did so many in the group. *Push it away.*

And the more Cygirians appeared, the stronger their energy became. Darl could feel the Upsilians' fear. Just what they had always dreaded was happening. Here the Cygirians were, finally fighting back, pushing into their carefully ordered world, changing everything.

The energy crackled within the group, all this united power working, working, working until they pushed free of the ray, pushed it into nothingness, and then it was gone with a crack, a snap, a whip of white. And then all in the large room was silence, nothing but the sound of his breath and heart in his ears.

"What do you want?" the voice said, the sound large and hard, echoing against the smooth, empty stone. Darl shivered, remembering the way Garrick had described the Nebs and their interrogation methods, telling him how the voice boomed and surrounded and hovered. But that wasn't what was happening now. At this moment, Darl and hundreds and hundreds of other Cygirians were safe inside their energy field, having destroyed the ray the Upsilians tried to destroy them with. They weren't harmed or even at the mercy of the Upsilians. For a change, they were in control.

The Upsilians had hidden somewhere, but the voice remained.

Darl felt the words on his tongue, the need in his throat.

"We want you to join with us. We want you to help us fight the Neballats."

"They wouldn't be here if you weren't," the voice said. "We have no trouble with them if you leave."

"If we were gone, how do you know the Nebs wouldn't come looking for what you have to offer?" Darl said, feeling his conviction sink into his skin and bones and blood. "How do you know you'd be safe for one second? Your world is just as fine as Earth. It has the atmosphere they need. And you have powers Earth does not. What is left but you?"

The rest of the group pulled around him, their thoughts mirroring his. He didn't wait for the voice to answer, pushing his words into the room.

"We want you to release us. To let us be. To join with us in order to get rid of those assholes," Darl said, stopping, realizing that they were likely not understanding the idiom. From somewhere in the group, he heard Porter's snicker.

"We want you to help destroy them," he finished. "Enough of fearing us. Fear what is real. Fear what wants to hurt you."

Darl stopped talking, he and the group waiting for the voice's reply. As they waited, he could hear thoughts and worries and fears.

They don't trust us.

They will kill us.

They will betray us.

They kill people on the street, for God's sake!

Darl agreed with what everyone was thinking, but he knew that the Upsilians offered the only salvation possible. Earth was defenseless, backward, behind. There were no spaceships, no weapons, no one who even believed that other worlds existed, except, of course, for nutbars who liked sci fi. Nutbars, Darl now realized, who were right.

But in any case, Earth would be captured, along with the Cygirians who had tried to mobilize forces there. Upsilia had defenses, people with powers, and knowledge of both the Neballats and Cygiria. It had to work. There really was no other option.

Darl scanned the room, waiting for something. Maybe an attack, a group of armed soldiers coming at them with portable rays, streams of heat everywhere. But instead, the voice spoke again, and as it did, a group of people walked out of a door in the far corner, coming toward them very slowly.

"We will agree to talk," the voice said. "But you must remove your energy shield. You must agree to negotiation terms."

"Such as?" Darl asked, and as he said it, he had a brief thought of how his football team would stare at him right now in complete disbelief. Darl wasn't telling anyone how to run the ball but informing an alien world how negotiation talks would commence.

"None of you will use this power," the voice said.

"And you won't use your fabulous death ray," Darl said.

"Agreed."

Darl felt for the group's feelings, and felt the "Yes" on his tongue. "Agreed."

The voice continued. "And none of you will partner with your double to create any kind of power during the talks."

"Agreed," Darl said. "And you will release any Cygirians still locked up or in the Source or hidden somewhere for these talks."

The people standing before them seemed to be thinking. Darl leaned into the energy of his group, hearing the affirmations of his fellow Cygirians. He didn't know how he'd managed to speak for them all, but he was, and they appreciated it.

"The other lost ones will be brought to Dhareilly," the voice said. "You will wait here until that time."

"Agreed," Darl said. He spun his thoughts around the group, hearing no other request come forth. It would be okay. They wouldn't end up as toast, and all of them would be together for the talks. All of them would be together if there were trouble, too, but if Claire were on this planet, he would see her soon. Maybe she was among those who had arrived while they were here. He wanted to rush through the crowd to look. He wanted to see her, pull her to him, kiss her sweet mouth.

He felt his heart beat faster, pounding a quick rhythm in his chest.

"Wait," Darl said, as the people moved back toward the door they had entered from.

"Yes?" the voice asked, an edge of anxiety running through the question.

"I think," Darl said, feeling the necessity and ridiculousness of his request, "that we could all use something to eat."

The people turned around, and one woman could barely contain a smile.

"Food will be brought to you," the voice said, and then the people were gone, the door closing behind them.

The Cygirians sighed, literally and in their thoughts, and then without saying a word or thinking a single thought, they let go. The energy shield they had created together flickered and then slowly evaporated into nothing but air.

"Great work," a man said to Darl, and as he walked through the crowd, he felt pats on his back and heard murmurs of thanks.

"Thanks," he said, once, twice, more times than he could count, but all the while he was looking for Claire.

Claire, he thought. *Where are you? Are you here?*

In the midst of the noise, he stopped, listened, waited for a response. Darl could almost feel her, could hear her laugh against his ear, her lips just at his neck.

"I can't believe it," she had whispered to him on the Tahiti sand. "I can't believe I found you."

"Believe it," he'd whispered back, pushing her down against the soft white beach, his lips on hers.

He swallowed, looked around, kept his mind open for any word, any thought, any flicker or trace of Claire.

But there was only the din of the room, the Cygirians planning for the talks.

"She'll be here," Porter said. "Unless she's on Earth."

Darl turned to Porter, who stood with his arms crossed, shaking his head. Porter continued on. "What would be more trenchant to discern is what the Upsilians are really going to do to us."

"They're going to get us food," Stephanie said.

"Right," Porter said, but Darl could tell that Porter wished Stephanie were right. And there was the collective understanding that if something weird should happen, if something looked off in any small way, they would hook themselves together in energy and fling up and out of the building. They would have to find another way. But with or without the Upsilians, they were going to fight back against the Neballats.

There was a sound of motors and grinding, and Darl clenched his stomach, reached out for Porter and Stephanie, who did likewise, but he found himself smiling. No death ray smashed through walls or no other kind of weapon he had no name for. It wasn't a legion of troops in space-age amor riding in on horrendous beasts with snarling teeth.

No, it was a retinue of servers bearing trays of what already smelled like food. Darl almost laughed, wondering how the options of death or dinner could be similarly obtained.

Just ask, Stephanie thought. *They'll either kill you or make you a brisket.*

Why can't they just bring me Claire instead, he thought back. *Who needs the food?*

"Poisoned, no doubt," Porter said. "Sleeping potions so they can throw us back in the Source. Or something painful like cyanide or botulism or rabies."

"You're sick," Stephanie said, but Darl could see that she didn't quite trust the food that was being laid out carefully on tables.

"Clearly, they had a caterer on call," Porter said. "How convenient."

Darl looked around, realizing that many of the Cygirians were grouped around a person, all seeming to listen intently.

"Probably Jai or Risa," Porter said, trying to feign boredom. "Just arrived. Undoubtedly filling us in on a mighty plan."

"Do you think they have one?" Darl asked. "I was just hoping to make it through the meal."

Porter's face changed, became serious, focused, his eyes intent. "I do. I think they will be able to help us with these negotiations, provided that the salad doesn't do us in."

As Porter spoke, Darl noticed that Cygirians were arriving through conventional portals such as the doors in the room or just appearing, as they often did. As he often did. As Claire often did.

"Do you see her?" Darl started to walk, moving away from his friends, feeling something pulling at him. "Is she here?"

He moved through the growing crowd, the noise level rising. He looked around, hoping that even though everyone was distracted by finding friends and twins and loved ones, they were still focused on the Upsilians and their potential to kill them at any moment.

Hello! Remember the death ray, he thought. *Remember that before the lovely food service was imminent death.*

But so much now was taken over by reunion. Reunion. Claire. God, he wanted her, to reunite with her, and a death ray couldn't slake his need to see her.

Are you here? he thought, gently pushing past groups talking and hugging and exclaiming. *Do you hear me? Did you come back to me?*

At first, he thought the sound was a whisper next to him, a small murmur from someone he passed by. He turned, looked around, seeing nothing but the noisy crowd, noting that more and more people were arriving.

Claire, he thought, gently pushing through the crowd. *Are you here yet?*

And then he didn't hear anything as much as see Tahiti, feel the sand under his back. He could taste salt in the air and on Claire's shoulder. He could hear the waves lapping at the shore and the small, tiny cries Claire made as he entered her for the first time.

Water, he thought. *Movement. You.*

You, she thought back, the sound of her so far away.

You, he thought back. *Where are you?*

Here, she thought, and then Darl turned. He wondered even as it happened if he would remember this moment forever. Of course, he would never forget his first glimpses of her when he was invisible and deciding when to approach her. He would never be able to forget her face when he appeared to her in the car. The way she watched him, her eyes dark, accepting, and lovely.

But this? This meeting was more like the first time he saw her than the first time had been. This was the moment where he got her back. When he didn't know if he'd find her again and then did.

"Darl," she said, reaching out and touching his arm. His skin jumped, electric. Was this real? Had he finally found her?

"I'm here," she said. "But I'm not sure you are."

"Trust me, I'm here."

"Will you promise to stay for a while?" she asked.

"I'm not going anywhere but closer to you," he said.

Darl took her arm and pulled her close to him, holding her as tight as he thought he could. He wanted her next to him. He wanted to feel her body against his, her breasts against his chest, her tight stomach against his, her ass in his hands, pushing her toward him.

And he wanted more than that. He wanted to be connected to her through their bodies for sure, but his longing was deeper than that. He wanted the connection of the true understanding they had of each other. He wanted that force of feeling that came when he realized that when Claire looked at him, she saw everything. Completely.

But his body seemed to be the messenger of his feelings, and he felt himself harden, push against her, want her right now, even if that would be just a huge embarrassment and absolutely ridiculous.

Get a room! Porter thought from somewhere. *Good Lord.*

But Darl ignored Porter's thought, and the world tunneled into nothing but Claire, knowing that she felt him, his need. He couldn't get enough of her. Her hair in his hands, her mouth on his, her arms wrapped around his waist. He kissed her as if he had never kissed before; he kissed her as if he never would again. She tasted like she smelled, sweet and light and almost too good to be true.

"Where did you go?" she whispered, kissing him in between words.

"Nowhere useful. Home to Encino. It's all I could think to do after you disappeared, and you know how I manage to only get myself home," he said, breathing in a large breath of her smells, salt and lavender and sugar. "Then I had to find my way back to you."

She kissed him on the cheeks, the nose, the lips. "Don't go home again without me."

"Wherever you are, is my home," he said.

She held him tight, and he could feel her tears come, her body lightly shaking. He looked around to see if anyone was paying attention to them, watching them reunite, watch Claire cry against his shoulder. But it was as if they were in a bubble, a snow globe, the snow falling around only them, the world reduced to this hug, this feeling.

"Don't cry, sweetheart," he said. "Don't be upset. You know, we have to pay attention. Any minute we could be toast. Fried by the death ray. We have to be ready."

She laughed lightly, pulled back, and smiled nonthreateningly. Then she breathed in. "You aren't kidding. I saw what they can do. And it's not a joke."

"So what do you think they're doing with us now? Do you really think they will negotiate with us?"

Claire wiped her eyes with one hand, the other holding onto his. "Why would they? What would they have to gain?"

Darl shrugged, but then he looked around. More and more Cygirians appeared, the room swelling with his people. Many were eating and drinking, clearly appreciating what the Upsilians gave them. But the room was full of his people. Their people. Aside from his football teams, Darl had never felt so proud of being part of a group. They had struggled, survived. They had been left alone to fend for themselves. And yet, here they were, more and more appearing as he watched the room. More and more sets of twins coming together. More and more power each second.

"Either they have a way to obliterate our converged power," he said, "or they realize they can't send all of us to the Source. Maybe finally, Upsilia is ready to deal with us."

"Pod people," Claire whispered. "I don't want that."

"I was there," Darl said.

"What?" Claire stared at him, her lovely face still with surprise.

"I went to the Source," he repeated. "And while I don't think I want to vacation there regularly, it was, well, pretty damn amazing."

"How can you say that? It's just their way of confining us. Of punishing us. It's like a prison."

Darl touched her cheek with the back of his hand, wishing that—as Porter suggested—they did have a room.

"I saw you there," he said. "And you were like you are in real life. So smart. So strong. So right."

She opened her mouth about to say something, and then she seemed to understand. "I think I know when you were there. When I was walking toward the mountains with Mila, I felt you. For a second, it was as if you and I were having a conversation. I could feel your body next to mine. Around mine."

She blushed, and Darl took in a quick, sharp breath, re-membering what it felt like to swirl into Claire's energy, her heat.

"I guess there's a way to bring the two places together," Darl said softly. "But I think I could feel you no matter what universe I was in."

Claire kissed his cheek, next to his ear, his neck, and he closed his eyes, wanting her more than he ever had before. But clearly, this was not the place. He struggled up from de-sire and looked around the room quickly. "You've met Mila? What about Garrick? Did they find each other?"

"They are back together," Claire said. "But it didn't seem like it would happen. I had to convince her to get out of the wrecked spaceship—"

"What? I'm pretty confused now about everything. But maybe we should start with how you got away from the safe house and end with Mila."

Claire smiled. "Not now. It's a long story. But yes, I've met my sister."

Darl leaned forward and kissed her. "One day we will have a lot of stories to tell our grandchildren."

Assuming we survive the death ray, Porter thought. *Pay attention, people. Our Upsilian contingent is coming through the door.*

Darl turned to the front of the room and, grabbing Claire's hand, maneuvered so that he could see the Upsilians walk-ing toward them.

Here we go, he thought, looking at Claire, his heart bump-ing around in his chest as he did. *Whatever you do, don't let go of my hand. We are not going to be separated ever again. Not for a second. Stay with me. And if anything happens— if the group powers fail, if we can't Converge—take us out of here, to anywhere.*

Claire looked at him, nodded. *I don't want to be without you again. I can't.*

Darl gripped her hand tight, and the Cygirians quieted. From the midst of the group, Darl watched as Odhran pushed his way to the front, followed by Jai and Risa, Kate and Michael, Mila and Garrick.

Get up there, Porter thought in a hiss Darl could hear. *You started this negotiation.*

Hearing this thought, too, Claire smiled. "He's right. I don't know who those other people are, but you did get us into this little chat."

So together, Darl and Claire moved to the front of the group, standing next to Odhran. The seven Upsilians in front of them were dressed in gray outfits, no difference between the men and the women, their grim faces mirroring the starkness of their clothing. They appeared to be unarmed, but as Darl considered them, he wondered if they were, in fact, Anthros, androids sent forth to do the work the Upsilians should do themselves. Androids were expendable. Androids could easily be destroyed.

But as Darl stood with his love, his twin, his double, and with these brave Cygirians, he felt their strength spill over and fill him. Somehow, he knew that the Convergence energy was still a flickering flame amongst the group. If the Upsilians tried to do anything to them, Cygiria would rise again and fight back.

"Why have you come to us like this?" an Upsilian asked.

With his thoughts, Odhran asked for permission to speak, not wanting to usurp anyone's position. Darl felt that as a Cygirian raised on Upsilia, he would be the perfect one to speak for them, and the group agreed, pushing forth waves of support.

Odhran took a step forward. "My name is Odhran Amalie.

I was raised on Upsilia by Rangor and Melma Amalie in Dharstad. I was put in the Source and then recovered by my fellow Cygirians."

He turned, looking back at the group. Darl could feel his pride, his happiness, his relief at finding his people. And as Darl held Claire's hand tight in his own, he recognized that he had the same feelings.

"Since you have been 'recovered,' why did you choose to come back here?" a man asked.

"Our safe house was destroyed by the Neballats."

"So you bring your war to us? For so many years, that's what we have been dreading."

You've been dreading us, Darl thought. *You've been dreading us more than the Neballats. You are worried about what we will take from you.*

One of the Upsilians looked at him, her eyes squinting as she seemed to take in his thought.

"Together," Odhran said, "we can defeat the Neballats. We have learned from the mistakes of the generations of Cygirians before us. They did not strike back at the Neballats. They allowed discussion. But there is no discussing with them. They attack and hope to find what they want amongst the ashes."

The Cygirians pulsed together with heat and in agreement to all that Odhran said. Darl wanted to rush forward and shake all the Upsilians, forcing them to say yes, to work with them. He wanted that eighty-yard punt return touchdown. He wanted that perfectly caught Hail Mary.

"What would you have us do that would not endanger our people? Our world? Why should we take you in any further than we already have?"

A whoosh of disapproval floated through the group.

Right. That's what you did. Took us all in, Claire thought. *Turned us into pod people.*

Something pulled Darl forward, away from the front line. He let go of Claire's hand as he moved, the absence of her heat and touch a pain throughout his body. Reaching back, he grabbed her hand as he spoke.

"You took us in before we knew how to mobilize. How to work together. You were afraid to give us the chance, so you put us in a place where we wouldn't bother you. But the truth is, you can't contain us. Your weapons are useless. You may be technologically advanced, but your greatest fear is realized. No matter what you say here, now we can take what we want."

For the first time, the Upsilians showed some emotion, turning to each other, communicating among each other through thoughts. The room, for all the people in it, was silent.

Odhran stepped toward Darl as well, Claire moving to his other side, the three of them facing the Upsilians.

"We don't want what you have," Odhran said. "We want a place from which to fight this battle. We want to be given the right to be here on this planet while we determine the best way to fight back. But we will do no harm. We are not like those we fight. We are not going to take anything away from you."

"We want to fight together," Darl said, a pulse of emotion running through him. And in a small bright glimmer, he saw it: he saw the battle they would engage in. He saw them here, on Upsilia, battling the Neballats, the sky purple and red with heat and explosions. In the sky, the enormous Neballat ships hung like ominous metal clouds. Darl found himself standing on an open plain, a machine of some kind in his hands. He looked around, wondering if this was, in fact, his—his memory, his vision, his idea. Where was it coming from?

As Claire squeezed his hand, the vision cracked open and disappeared. Darl took in a sharp breath.

"Together, we could stop them."

The Upsilians listened, talking again through thoughts. Finally, one of them spoke.

"This is not something we can decide upon alone. We need to contact other officials from other provinces. There are also more Cygirians on their way to you. Probably from Earth as well. So we all need time to contemplate this situation."

Odhran stepped forward. As he did, the Upsilians almost seem to start. "And we will not be harmed. You will not try to destroy us as you did earlier," he said, a statement not a question.

"We will not harm you," one of the women said. "You will be given shelter and food until we come to a decision. But we say the same to you. You will not try to destroy us."

Odhran nodded, and the Upsilians turned and walked out of the room, a strange single-file line.

Anthros, Porter thought. *Those weren't Upsilians. They would have been too afraid to send in real representatives. Or they would have brought in portable death rays as a fashion statement.*

Darl realized that Porter was likely right. *But at least we have the answer we want.*

For now, Porter thought. And then Porter's thoughts were drowned out by the wave of sound of all the Cygirians talking at once.

Darl looked around the room briefly, still amazed by all his people. They might be in a hostile place, surrounded by others who would rather see them shut down or possibly dead, but here they all were. The air was alive, crackling, electric with power, with energy, with sound, and Darl felt it everywhere. He turned to Claire, taking in her lovely face, her soft skin, her wide-open trusting eyes. He put his hands on the side of her face, kissed her gently.

We need to take his advice, he thought.

Whose advice?

Porter's.

And what fine words might those be, she thought, her lips turning up, parting, exposing her white teeth. And then just the thought of her teeth made Darl think of her tongue and he knew he couldn't go on much longer being vertical and dressed.

I've heard a lot about Porter from Kate and Michael, Claire thought. *What could he have possibly advised at this point?*

He told me that we needed to get a room.

Well, Claire thought, *they did promise us shelter. He might be more reasonable than I've heard. Maybe we could request a king-sized bed? And a view. Maybe room service, too.*

Darl kissed her lips, wanting that tongue, wanting her breath. Wanting her.

It doesn't hurt to ask, he thought. *But it won't matter in a few minutes where we are or what death threat we are under. I need you. I need you now.*

Darl could feel her under her hands, almost as if she weren't wearing clothes. She was shimmering with heat and feeling, and he pressed himself against her, pulling her tight. He kissed her harder, more, longer, pushing away all of their thoughts of anything other than this kiss, this moment, now.

* * *

They stood together in a very small room, looking around at the cold, windowless space, empty save for a bed.

"It's like a dormitory room. Or a jail cell."

"But smaller," Claire whispered against his ear. "If that's possible."

Outside in the hall, Darl heard the sounds of movement as other Cygirians were led to their rooms by what were clearly Anthros. After the flush of arriving in Dhareilly via Convergence and the relief at being allowed sanctuary, everyone was pretty much exhausted, though Odhran, Jai, and Risa and a small group had gone off with what appeared to be "real" Upsilians for further discussion.

But so far, no one had been harmed, even as more and more Cygirians arrived. Darl wasn't sure how many were now in Dhareilly, but it had to be in the thousands.

"Don't get me started thinking about what they could do to us," Claire said, holding on to his arm. "We're like sitting ducks here, all in our neat dormitory rows. They could be in league with the Neballats. They'll get a finder's fee or something like that."

Darl ran his hand up her arm, feeling her shiver under his touch.

If we are sitting ducks, we may as well enjoy it, he thought, bringing his hands up to her blouse buttons and slowly undoing the first, the second, the third. He saw her take in a sharp breath and close her eyes.

"But what if it is just a trap?" she whispered, her voice sticking a bit in her throat as Darl finished unbuttoning her blouse and pushed it off her gently. "What if there's no warning and we can't Converge? What if it ends, just like that?"

"Shh," he said, letting his fingers trace her body, feeling her collarbone under his fingertips. He leaned forward, letting his lips play on her skin.

No more talking, he thought.

But, she began.

No more thinking. Just feel.

Darl moved his lips up her collarbone to the dip of flesh at the base of her throat. He heard her hum, purr, open her mouth to a slight *Ahh*.

He slowly slid his hands from around her rib cage to the small of her back, feeling her smooth flesh, the softness of her skin, and pulled her close. He knew she had to feel how much he wanted her, and she pressed back, holding him tight.

Too many clothes, he thought, and together, they took off what they wore in the slight gloom of the room. But Darl didn't need light. He could find her heat just by being in the same room. She smelled like lavender, sweet and light and delicious.

He looked up to see that she was just about to take off her panties.

Wait, he thought. *Let me.*

And he knelt down, facing her, seeing her stomach quiver as he lightly placed his hands on her hips. With just the slightest movements, he pushed down, allowing himself this wonderful vision. This beautiful view of her as the cotton slid down her thighs.

He had to stop, close his eyes, breathe, hope that he could make it past this moment so there could be others. He was so hard, wanted her so much, being this close to her was ecstasy.

Taking in a deep breath, Darl slid her panties all the way

down her legs and helped her as she stepped out of them. He tossed them to the side and then brought his mouth to her, his lips on her, taking her in.

God, she was wet, ready for him. Claire put her hands on his head, her breath quick. Darl felt her desire, felt her grow under his tongue. He held her beautiful ass in his hands as he sucked and licked her, feeling as he did how she was having trouble standing. She was having trouble staying quiet, moaning between his strokes, pulling his hair slightly.

And then she pushed against him, her body contracting, holding on to his head so that she wouldn't fall back. She moaned loudly, and then Darl felt her pulse with heat and energy, and then relax, slowly, her body jolting slightly.

"Oh," she whispered. "Oh, my."

Darl stood up, grabbed her around the waist, and carried her to the small bed, putting her down softly, but he didn't stop. He needed her, and it wasn't going to last long. He spread her legs and slipped right into her. She was so wet, so ready for him. And he kissed her, letting her taste herself, moving against her body, feeling how she matched his movements. Together they moved until the world folded into nothing more than Claire's body, his body, and the heat between them. The heat and movement, and then the joy. Oh, the feel of it.

Claire, he thought, letting himself think her name loudly as he came into her. *Oh, my lovely Claire.*

Chapter Nine

The sun had moved over Dhareilly, setting in the east, and the room was now completely dark. Still, Cygirians were arriving, and Claire and Darl lay in bed together, pressed close, not only by their desire to feel each other completely, but because of the size of the bed.

"I know this is a camp dormitory for kids. The four-year-olds sleep here," she said, rubbing her hand over Darl's chest.

"We can only hope that they behaved better than we did," he said, stretching next to her and throwing a leg over her thighs. "And if they didn't, I don't want to know about it!"

She smiled, unable to really believe that after being separated, they were actually together again. One touch, one taste of Darl had been enough to make her want him forever. This closeness, this skin, this contact was what Claire knew she could no longer live without.

"I hope there's more you can't live without," Darl said, his fingers lightly tracing lines under her breast and down her stomach. "Your skin is amazing, but there are some other, deeper, inner parts I am keenly interested in."

He brought his lips to her shoulder, moving down her arm. Claire closed her eyes, knowing that she couldn't send herself anyplace better. Nowhere in the universe was as absolutely perfect as here, right now, this.

Darl laughed. "You like the digs here?"

"The Upsilians didn't outdo themselves, that's for sure," she said, turning a little on her side so she could see him better. "I don't want to even see the bathroom."

"I think it suited our purposes just fine," Darl said, his hand skimming her hip. "It's all I ever want in a room."

Claire smiled, felt herself blush in the darkness. "Yes," she said. "I think you are right. And after all we went through, to actually find each other. God, this place is horrible. I saw a man fry to death on the sidewalk. If it weren't for that woman Lura saving me, I would have been toast. I mean literally. And then after I saw that Neballat—"

Darl sat up, a dark shadow above her. "What?"

Claire swallowed, feeling the fear that she had before passing out. There it was again, its slithery, see-through limbs. "Lura took me off the street and brought me to where—to where I guess you'd call the resistance is. Sort of a band of Upsilians protecting us. And fighting against this government and all its rules. Anyway, there was a meeting going on, and as I was listening, I saw it."

"A Neb. You saw a Neb. Here."

"Yes," Claire said.

"So what happened?" Darl was sitting up now, his voice low and intense.

Claire closed her eyes, wishing she could have done more than pass out. "I fainted. But I came to while everyone was freaking out. And I ran."

At that, Darl chuckled. "You of all people ran?"

Again, she blushed, but this time out of shame.

"Oh, no," he said, leaning down and pulling her to him.

"No. I just meant in a second, you could have been any-where."

"Don't you think I know that?" she said. "It was ridicu-lous. But I was scared. I've never seen something so horri-ble."

He kissed her neck, smoothed her hair back and then kissed her forehead. "You know me. I would have flung myself back home. Neballats could be invading the world, and I'd be home on the couch drinking a beer."

She smiled, leaned against his chest. "And then I thought of someplace safe. Someplace warm. And there I was, inside a spaceship with a strange woman."

"Mila," Darl said.

"Right. And after I finally managed to get her out of the ship, we hiked to the mountains. After we found Garrick and the rest, we were called to the city. And the rest," she said. "It's all here. It's all you."

"But what about this Neballat? You know what they say about vermin. If you see one, there are a thousand some-where close by. In the walls. Crawling on the ceiling. We should tell the others. I think that's a bit of information they need to have."

Claire lay back on the bed. Of course this lovely interlude had to end. They were, after all, in the middle of a war. But after so many years of feeling alone and weird, Darl was like—well, he was like heaven. And she just wanted heaven to last a little longer.

"It will," he said. "I promise. But now, we've got to go tell Risa and Jai and Odhran about the Neballats. The Up-silians need to work with their resistance to find out where they are hiding. Where they've infil—"

Darl paused. "My God, that's what they said to me before putting me in the pod. Infiltrated. The resistance knows. They have the Neb or know where to find it. Him. Whatever."

Claire really didn't understand what the Neballats wanted. Of course, she'd heard from Kate and Michael and even Darl that they wanted the Cygirians' powers to fix their world, their lives. Their bodies, even. That they'd gone through the universe destroying what they could not have. Why hadn't Cygiria helped them in the first place? Why couldn't the generations before her have said yes?

If they had, none of this would be happening now.

"You don't know that, Claire. They might have taken what they wanted and then destroyed Cygiria anyway. They don't seem like the most rational people."

"You call them 'its,'" she said. "You make them not people by using that pronoun. You make them not people by calling them Nebs."

Darl was silent, and she felt him pull away from her slightly, feeling his confusion at her words. Her words confused him. Except for floating in space as the safe house exploded, seeing the Neballat was the most frightening thing that had happened to her. It wasn't just his creepy body but the fact of what his presence meant. All Cygirians were in danger. From all sides. Any moment they could all be killed. Poof! And then nothing.

"How does anyone stand living with all of this?" Claire asked, thinking about the first twins, Jai and Risa. "It's like being a rat on a wheel but the wheel is going to fly off into the air."

Darl didn't have to speak. He simply pressed himself against her, letting her feel his body, his breath. She breathed in his smell, felt the current of their power between them. She heard his laugh in her ears, touched the smoothness of his skin, the hardness of his muscles and bones underneath. She wondered if she listened hard enough if she would hear his blood in his veins.

Claire could still feel the rub and pulse from their sex, the wetness of him slicking her thighs. Her nipples pricked, tingled at the memory of him over her, in her. Knowing her. Seeing her.

This—this knowingness, this bond, this feeling—was what made it possible. This was what made going on a possibility.

He bent down to kiss her on the mouth, holding her face as he did. "You are my beauty. You are the one I love. And that is what makes things worth anything. Anything. Everything."

Darl kissed her again and then he stood up, rustling around for his clothing. "We have to go. We have to tell the others what you saw. This is important, Claire."

For a moment, Claire felt that if she left the bed, she would never have this warm, safe feeling again. She would never have Darl again. She wished she had Garrick's power, the ability to move time backward over and over again. If she did, she would replay these past couple of hours like a favorite movie, lingering over specific scenes.

But she knew she didn't have that power, and even if she did, Darl was right. They needed to tell the others about the Neballat.

And then Claire laughed.

"What?" Darl said, looking over at her, smiling as he buttoned his shirt.

"I keep thinking about something a colleague used to say to me," Claire said as she stood up in the darkness. "When I would complain about my class, Yvonne would say, 'Now,

Claire, it's not all about you. It's about these poor, neglected children.' But then we'd laugh. But it's true now. It's not all about me."

She bent down to pick up her clothing, but Darl grabbed her, brought her to him. "No, it's not all about you. It's about us. And it always will be. No matter what happens. Us."

"So in the midst of this group meeting, there was a Neballat?" Jai asked.

Claire nodded, looking around at the hastily assembled group, everyone weary, red-eyed, exhausted by the events of the past few days. Mila stood at the side of the room with Garrick, and Claire could feel Mila's presence, hear her thoughts.

It will be all right, Mila thought, and Claire nodded, the sound of her sister's voice in her head so known, so familiar. Instantly, Claire pushed back in time, back in the spaceship, sitting next to Mila, both of them listening to Edan. The memory made her want to cry, to lean over and mourn every single dream she had of the dark place, celebrate the reunion she'd just had with her sister. She wished she could meet Edan, finally see this boy who'd somehow been able to be strong and sane at four.

But Claire couldn't cry. Not now.

"They brought me in off the street," she said. "The resistance or whatever they call themselves. The group that is fighting the government. The establishment. I had just seen a man killed by that ray, and a woman urged me to keep walking and then led me to a building and then inside. They were having a meeting, and during it, I saw the Neballat."

"And then you fainted," Kate said. "Couldn't you have

stayed awake for another minute or two and got a really good look at the Neballat's disgusting self?"

Kate smiled at Claire, who actually didn't feel like being teased. She felt irritable at having to be parted from Darl's skin, tired from the running and hiking and searching. Tired of being scared for her life, scared in a way she never had been before. When would she have had to? When the crayons broke? When the paint ran out? When the children cried and screamed and wet their pants? Maybe she'd been afraid when her mother was sick, but nothing like the terror she'd felt when floating above a destroyed asteroid, the safe house blown to bits.

Claire wanted to talk more with Mila. She wanted to find Edan, and together, try to conjure their family life back home on Cygiria. She wanted to know about her parents, her mother and father and grandparents on both sides.

But again, she realized she had to focus. What she would tell the group was the information that was going to change things. Change the negotiations. Change the course of Cygirian action.

Sorry, Kate thought. *I'm not trying to be stupid. It just comes naturally.*

It's okay, Claire thought back. *I'm tired.*

I am sure I would be too if I'd been doing what—

"How can we find this Neballat? How can we find out what he's doing here?" Risa asked.

"I think we need to find the group of people who were helping me," Claire said. "I don't know if they are willing to work with us now that we're with their government. But they must know something."

Darl reached over and took Claire's hand, squeezed it, and then spoke. "When I was brought to the same group, I heard them say they'd been infiltrated. I think they were talking about the Neballat. Or Neballats. I'm not sure. I was put into the Source right after that."

"We go to the Source," Odhran said quietly. "Everything, everyone is in the Source."

"Why hasn't everyone figured everything out already, then?" Kate said. "Enough people have been in there long enough to stop a hundred world wars. So why haven't they?"

"I know that the concept of the Source sounds ridiculous to those of you who have not been there," Odhran said. "But let me say if we knew there was information we had to get from the Source, we would find it. When we were put in, it was to make us disappear from this society."

Claire held on to Darl's hand, remembering what he'd said about the Source, remembering how she'd felt when he was in there. She'd felt his body, his heat, his mind, even as she and Mila hiked toward the mountains. There was a connection between the two places, the two worlds. There was an interface.

"And these are the people we are going to trust right now?" Kate asked. "We want to join forces with people who want us to disappear from this society? They use this thing—this probably holy thing—as a punishment. As a way of getting rid of those who don't fit in."

"It doesn't seem like a punishment when you are in there," Darl said, his voice crisp and urgent.

"But did you want to go into the Source just then?" Kate asked. "Didn't you have other things on your mind?"

Darl let go of Claire's hand and moved into the middle of the group. "I didn't ask for it. I wouldn't have gone into the Source. But once I was there, I learned things."

Claire saw Darl look toward Odhran, who nodded at him, encouraging Darl to continue.

"When I was in the Source, I received information that helped me out here in the conscious world. Helped me," he said, turning to Claire, "find Claire."

"What does this have to do with now?" Michael asked. "Aren't we supposed to be thinking about the negotiations? About the Neballat in our midst? About our battle plans?"

As she listened to the group, Claire knew what she had to do. She was the one who had seen the Neballat. She understood what Darl was saying to the group.

"It has to do with information," she said, walking to Darl and taking his hand again. "And I can get it for us. I will get it for us. All I need is to go into the Source to do it."

The group went silent, and she felt Darl's hand clench hers.

"You want to go to the Source?" Kate said. "On purpose. Of your own volition?"

"Claire," Mila said. "Don't go."

Turning to her sister, Claire saw what Mila was really saying—after all this time separated, how could Claire choose to go somewhere else, somewhere that Mila wasn't?

It will be all right, Claire thought. *Just like you told me.*

"It's not dangerous," Odhran said.

Porter laughed. "As if all the ramifications of danger in the Source have been documented. No one has put out a Foder's guide for the Source yet."

"But will it get us what we need?" Jai asked, ignoring Porter's comment.

"Who cares about that?" Darl said, interrupting. He turned to Claire, his eyes opened wide, his mouth a slim, grim line. "What about Claire all alone in there?"

"Go with her," Odhran said. "You know what it's like. And she knows the energy of the Neballat. Together, you can find the answers. Bring them back to us."

Claire pulled on Darl's hand, and he moved closer to her, wrapping his free arm around her.

You don't need to go with me, she thought.

Wherever you go, I need to be. Wherever you go, there I am.

Together, they stood in the middle of the group, Claire feeling all of Darl's love, his concern—and then, all of the group's. In a small blip of time, she'd found so many people to love. Darl, Mila, Garrick, Kate, Michael. In such a short time, she'd found a whole group of people to call her own. Claire knew what it was like to go through life without all this love, and she didn't want to lose it now. She would do anything to keep this connection alive.

So she and Darl would go into the Source, into the primal energy bin they all came from, and find the answer that would save them all.

"Do we know what we are doing?" Darl asked as they followed the two Upsilians down a long corridor. They had been led from the dormitory building, through an underground tunnel, and then up into another building. Accompanying them were Odhran, Mila, and Kate, sort of the oversight team.

"The protect-your-ass team," Kate said earlier. "The watch-those-insane-loonies team."

Mila had just held Claire's hand, and Claire was happy that her sister would be there for this journey, too.

"You are doing a great thing," Mila said now as they walked. "This is our way into the Neballats' plan."

Darl turned to look at Claire, smiling, his thoughts warm visuals right now, like soft thought kisses.

Claire's and Darl's thoughts were not open to the other Cygirians. Somehow they managed to learn to transmit their thoughts to each other without others hearing them, imagining they'd pulled off some amazing feat. But when Darl mentioned the trick to Porter, Porter snuffled with glee, and started to tease Darl, calling him "the magician."

But the good news was that as they walked, she and Darl could communicate without bringing in the minds of the Upsilians in front of them. And they were walking a long way. To Claire, it seemed as though they'd walked more than three city blocks down this corridor alone.

"I thought I'd already hiked enough for a lifetime," Mila said, smiling at Claire. "You basically had to pull me up the mountain. Kept me from terrible morning sickness by giving me water every half hour."

They should have let you get us here, Claire, Darl thought. *We'd be there by now. All this walking is so overrated.*

But then we'd just have to wait. And I'm already nervous, she thought.

Don't be nervous. I showed you what it was like. I showed you how it felt to be in the Source. It's like water. It's like a wave.

Claire nodded, remembering Darl's thoughts. To her, the Source felt like floating. Moving through Darl's memory into the image of the Source, Claire felt the boundaries of her body blur, disappear, float into the molecules and atoms of the swirling energy. Darl was right. It wasn't scary, it was just that she not only had to dissolve into energy, she had to find a strange Neballat at the same time. And she had to find that Neballat in order to save her people.

One problem at a time! he thought.

I'm trying to plan for the future, she joked.

Darl took her hand as they walked. *We both are. That's what we're doing here.*

As if able to hear her worry, Odhran looked at her.

"Going into the Source is easy. When you arrive there, you will feel as though it were something you've done your entire life."

Claire closed her eyes for a moment as they walked, letting Darl guide her. She knew that she could go with him anywhere and feel safe. After all, she'd taken him to Tahiti and back. She'd transported them to a destroyed safe house. She was with him on an alien planet. So going to the Source was really nothing out of the ordinary at all.

Claire opened her eyes and then the Upsilians stopped in front of a door. They all stopped behind them, Kate giving Claire a look that seemed to say, *Give me the signal, and I'll get us out of here.*

Smiling, Claire shook her head. She was going to do this, though right now, even Kate's and Michael's crazy bubble travel seemed preferable to the unknown that lay before her.

With a quick scan of one of the men's eyes, the large door pulled up, light pouring into the dark hall.

The man turned to the Cygirians, and Claire felt certain this was really a man, not an Anthro, a droid, a robot of some kind.

"We have the transporter cells in here. We don't use them often. Our main facility—"

"Is in the mountains, far far away," Darl said. "I've heard. But you've managed to keep some around town for special purposes, I know."

"Good for keeping people quiet," Kate said. "The big deep freeze."

The Upsilian stared at Darl and Kate and then sighed. "I know our ways are confusing to you, but you aren't from here. It's not a good practice to judge what you don't understand." The man looked at Odhran. "You should be able to explain this to them."

"There are things I will never understand about Upsilia," Odhran said.

Claire almost laughed. "I can pretty much say that frying someone for standing still is hard to understand."

All three of the Upsilians were now looking at her. Claire felt her mouth keep moving, words forming on her tongue and pushing out into the air. "Frying people for exercising their own free will is wrong. And putting people anywhere they didn't ask to go is wrong."

"You aren't qualified to judge our world," a woman said. "You don't know our rules."

She's got to be real, thought Darl. *Kinda bitchy!*

"You both are going to the Source on your own volition," the man said. "We didn't come up with this plan."

"This time I am going on purpose," Darl said. "But you are the only people I've ever heard about who use heaven as a punishment."

"Heaven, as you call it, is a relative term," the man said. "As is punishment. Now, if you will follow me to the transporter cells."

I don't trust them, Claire thought. *There is something completely off with them. How are we supposed to stay here on this planet? How are we supposed to believe that they won't put us in the "cell" and leave us there? And the word cell. I keep thinking about San Quentin.*

We don't have much choice. It's either them, the Neballats, or the unconscious people on Earth. At this point, I think they are the better choice.

The lights in the room brightened even further, and as they all moved into the room, Claire saw a row of about eight pods, gleaming and white, cylindrical.

"This gives me bad flashbacks," Kate said. "And I hate the pods. They look so weird."

Giant Tylenol, Darl thought.

Claire smiled, the feeling strange on her nervous face.

The man walked over to two of the pods, pressing buttons. Machines began to whir, and then the doors on each pod opened up with a whoosh. Claire heard noises she imagined should reassure her—the smooth metal purr of well-working mechanisms; regular, steady beeps—but she felt uneasy, shifting back and forth on her feet, as if part of her body wanted to run away.

One of the women brought in two robes, handing one to Darl and one to Claire.

"You can put these on. You will be more comfortable in the transporter cell," she said.

I want to be able to run out of here when we get out, Darl thought to Claire. *Let's keep our clothes on.*

"Thank you, but we're fine in our street clothes," Claire said.

The Upsilians motioned for Claire and Darl to walk over to the pods, and as Claire began to walk, Mila reached out and took her hand.

"This is an adventure I am going to want to hear about," she said. "I wish I could go with you."

Claire wanted to say, "You are with me. You always have been," but the words were caught in her throat. So instead, she nodded, smiled, squeezed her sister's hand, and walked with Darl toward the pods.

They stopped in front of the first pod, and Claire reached out to touch it, the surface smooth and cool under her fingertips.

What happens to us in there? Why do we need these pods? Why can't we just close our eyes and go into the Source? Claire thought, her brain whirring as fast as the machines in front of them. She looked up, realizing the Upsilians were giving them stern, focused looks, the kind Claire hadn't received since grammar school.

Claire, Claire, Darl thought. *I've told you what I know. Odhran went through it with us as well. There's something about lowering our blood pressure, calming our brain waves. The only thing I can point to is look how many of us have been in there and look how many of us have gotten out.*

Claire turned to glance at Odhran, who nodded at her. He'd survived. Darl had, too. Edan apparently had lived years in the Source and come out in better shape, safer than he'd been in the world of war between the Neballats. There were hundreds of Cygirians who had emerged from the pods, from the Source, and all seemed to be all right.

So why was she so afraid of the Source?

She remembered the time her mother had given her a sleeping pill on a red-eye flight to visit relatives in Boston. Claire had looked at the little blue pill in her hand for a good half hour, absolutely certain that when she swallowed it, her life would change. Her brain would never be the same, twisted by pharmaceuticals. She'd be like Alice in Wonderland, growing too tall or too small, depending on what she ingested. Images of the long-necked, giraffe-sized and itsy-bitsy, teeny-weeny Alice floated through her mind.

Claire had spent all of her life trying to hold herself together, trying to be what she was not: normal. And to have her own mother hand her something that might release her weirdness was too frightening to think about. What if she talked in her sleep? What if she didn't sleep at all but acted drunk, loopy, spilled every strange story she had? She could walk through the plane, telling the other passengers what they were thinking. She might completely lose control of everything.

But finally, Claire had taken the pill with a sip of Diet Coke and awakened at O'Hare fresh as could be and clearly still herself. Not too tall or too short. Just exactly the same.

"Okay," she said to Darl and to the Upsilians. "I'm ready."

Darl bent down, kissed her gently on the lips. "I'll see you in a few seconds."

"You'd better," she said, trying out a smile and finding that finally, it fit. She wasn't nervous anymore.

One of the Upsilian women held out her hand and Claire took the assistance into the pod. As she lay down, making herself comfortable, she had an image of the luge, the winter Olympic sport. They looked more like space travelers than she did, dressed aerodynamically in neoprene suits, stiff straight in their sleds.

Claire looked down at her feet, feeling like she was sort of in a sled, a time sled, going on a ride that the lugers could hardly imagine.

It is quite a ride, Darl thought, and Claire looked up as the Upsilian woman leaned over to check on her one last time.

"Just breathe naturally," she said, and then the door on the pod closed, the vacuum sealed, and Claire blinked once, blinked twice.

How do I get there? she thought, and before an answer could come, she was there.

Or she thought she was there. Where else could she be this light? This translucent? She lifted her hand, seeing it stream through the energy, her movement a wave she could follow. She wasn't a body any longer but bits, parts, molecules, atoms. She tried to run, but her movement was more like floating. But it felt so good, so buoyant, so free. Her body was completely without weight, without pain, without strain. Exertion didn't bring heart rate increase or heavier breathing. Everything seemed effortless, so Claire moved farther, faster, feeling the streams of energy pouring around her.

Hey! Hold on there! Where are you going?

Claire slowed, turned, and behind her saw a pulsing form, the energy full of reds and oranges and yellows.

Darl?

Who were you expecting? he thought.

Claire sailed toward him. *I don't know. Mother Teresa. Jesus. Muhammad. God, even. Goddess, for that matter. Everyone. Everyone I've ever known. Oh! Oh!*

Claire paused, realizing that if this Source was what everyone could promise, she could find her mother. She could tell her mother about her life finally. After all these years of hiding, she could explain all the weird behavior, the calls from bus stops and BART trains as Claire fought her way back home after flinging herself all over the Bay Area and sometimes more distant parts of California. She could explain the times she hid herself in her room, not wanting to leave the confines of that small place because she was afraid of where she might push herself. She would tell her mother how sometimes she avoided her because of all her mother's pain during her illness, her mother's thoughts too sad and desperate to not read.

Claire, Darl thought.

I have to find her. I need to talk with her. It's finally time. I have so much to say.

Claire.

If Claire had been in her body, she would have been panting, anxious, needing to get going, her whole body leaping with need. How could she waste this opportunity? There were so many things to talk about, so many things to remember, apologize for, forgive.

We have work to do, my love.

And that's when Claire remembered. That's when she realized that she might not have much more to tell her mother if the Neballats found all the Cygirians and destroyed them. She wanted to tell her mother the whole story—the story about Darl and Mila and about a race of people brought back together.

If the Source was truly available to them, she could come back. Assuming that Upsilia still existed, that the Neballats didn't destroy everything here, she could come back and say what she needed to. She could find her mother and tell her everything.

So Claire turned and followed Darl's flickering red form, feeling his energy fan out behind him, enveloping her.

How do we find one Neballat in all this matter? Claire thought. *How do we find anything in here?*

I think we ask for it, he thought. *I think we simply think of what we want and it comes to us.*

That's convenient, she thought. *I wish there was a way to do that in the real world.*

There is, Darl thought.

What do you mean?

Well, he thought, turning to her, his energy swirling around him like a cape, *I wished for you and I finally found you. It might take longer in the "real" world, but it can happen if you are patient. I only had to wait twenty-six years.*

Darl moved close, and Claire felt something she had never really felt before, not even when they made love. In the Source, they were connected in a way that was impossible in the flesh. As he moved closer, closer, next to her, he seemed to move into her, their very atoms merging, his consciousness merged with hers, their thoughts truly *their* thoughts. If she had breath, she'd sigh with pleasure. She did anyway.

For a few moments, Claire and Darl flowed together in one steady, rich, colorful stream. Claire knew that this connected energy was what everyone, everything was. Only in the flesh was everything separate, isolated, cold, removed. Not here, though, in this warm, lovely place where everything made sense.

I don't want to leave, she thought. *I want this forever.*

Now you can see why Odhran and the others weren't that upset about it, Darl thought.

Yes. Yes. Claire let herself be buoyed in the stream. *Yes.*

We can do this together, he thought. *Think of the Neballat. Bring him to us.*

With some effort, Claire pulled herself out of the pure joy of being in the Source and remembered. She thought of the meeting, the people crowded in the small room. She saw the slight movement that caught her eye, the movement of his see-through, slithery body.

I need to talk with you, she thought, her call light and untrue. She didn't want to talk to him at all; she had to.

We need what you know, Darl thought. *Come talk with us.*

His thought was strong and real, and Claire joined him in his strength of conviction.

Come talk with us, she thought. *Everything depends on it.*

Together, swirling in the energy, Claire and Darl called out again, asking the universe to provide. Where was this one soul that could help them save their people? Where was this one Neballat who could change everything?

Come, they cried out together. *Come.*

Time spun and flumed, the colors bright and changing and alive. Then Claire felt something prick what would have been her neck if she had one, the atoms of her being flicking with fear and dread.

The air around them seemed to change, fill with a darker, heavier color.

I know what you want, the voice thought.

Chapter Ten

Darl reached out his hand, trying to grab for Claire's, but he didn't feel her wrist or fingers or palm. He felt her heat, her energy, but when he went to squeeze her, he felt only the melding of their two bodies. He loved that melding, that complete joining, but now, with a Neballat in front of, behind them, around them—somewhere, somewhere close.

Stay with me, Darl thought, pushing his energy close to Claire's. *Don't move.*

Where is it? Claire thought. *I heard it, but I can't see it.*

Why is it that you Cygirians never look at what is right in front of you? came the answer.

Darl spun, fluming particles as he did. *Where are you? Come out so I can see you?*

Even as he thought the words, something darker began to pulse in front of him. Slowly, the shape began to take a slight body shape: a head, arms, legs. But this must have been a trick the Neballat learned to do because there were no shapes in the Source. Maybe it was the only way people just entering the Source could understand things.

Ah, so you are figuring things out.

I was hoping irony and tone weren't a part of the Source, Claire thought. *This is heaven, after all.*

The shape laughed, the thought a deep, booming pulse.

Heaven, as you call it, is made up of everything. Not just joy and mirth and forgiveness. Everything that is on the reality plane is here, too. War and greed and need and desire. We just understand them here a bit better. We see why we use them on our worlds. All those things have a purpose.

And as the Neballat thought, Darl looked around, seeing things that he hadn't before, certainly not the first time he'd been here. As if he had just learned to see, his eyes—or the part of him that could see in the Source—picked up more shapes, light and dark and some even moving along the edges of his vision. What were they? More souls? People assuming a form? Animals? Or just wafts of unattached energy? Maybe trees and plants and water and clouds assumed a shape here. Maybe here was all there really was? Maybe life elsewhere was simply a game they all played at.

Something in Darl made him want to slide away, follow the lights, merge back into this matter undifferentiated, unshaped, unformed, uncaring of anything that was going on on any planet. But he could feel Claire pulling him back, forcing him to remember their mission.

You are the Neballat who was at the meeting? she thought.

Yes, I was. Am, really. I am still there in my other form.

What are you doing? Why did you show me who you were? she thought. And though she was being forceful, brave, clear, Darl could feel her fear, her anxiety a ripple he could almost see as color.

It's really ridiculous, the Neballat thought. *We are trying to find the power base on Upsilia. We are tired of searching for the lost Cygirians slapdash. It's time for a home base, a home planet, so why not the only place that makes sense?*

And we can use the Cygirian power to give us back what we lost.

Lost? Don't you mean destroyed?

Semantics are often a matter of perspective as well, the Neballat thought.

Darl stared at the pulsing purple shape. *So you are going to fight them for their world? You are just going to take it all?*

After what we've done to your people, I'm not sure why you are surprised.

So much fighting, Claire thought.

Well, it won't be much of a battle. Yes, they are more evolved than the creatures on what you call Earth. But they don't have our technology.

Darl felt a deep hurt, something so old and heavy he wanted to sink to his knees. All this fighting. All this constant war. And it wasn't just on Earth where things were bad enough, people killing each other over land and oil and religion for the entire history of people. But it existed away from Earth, too. It was in the sky, in space, with different people, all of whom wanted something from the other. Even the Cygirians, who wanted a base to fight back from, were taking space and time and resources from a planet and group of people who simply wanted to be left alone.

How long do we have? Claire thought. *What should we prepare for?*

Space, the Neballat thought.

Space? Darl thought.

We need room to do what we want to. It's important to have structures still standing. So we need space. Openness. Expanse.

As the Neballat thought, Darl could feel Claire's anger grow, her pulse deepen.

What are you talking about? Why can't you just tell me right here what is going to happen?

Just think, the Neballat thought. *Where could we find the space to land undetected? Where could we go without being detected for a little while?*

Darl wanted to run over and shake the Neballat free of his knowledge. How could he play so coy with them in the Source? And just as he felt he might do something stupid with a nonbody he didn't really know how to move here, he felt a memory pull over him. What was it? He was standing on an open plain, a machine in his hands. Above him, the sky burst with color—red and purple—enormous ships marking the terrain with bulbous black shadows.

Darl pushed himself into the memory. Where was he? Who was he fighting? What was he holding? He knew that he had only seconds, instants to see this, so he looked up and saw the dry, flat land in front of him, remembered that this was a memory of a vision. Not of something real. Or at least, not something that had actually happened.

But he knew where he was. He knew where the battle would begin. He hoped he knew where the battle would end.

Turning to Claire, he pushed into her heat.

I know what to do, he thought. *Let's go.*

He couldn't really see her, but he felt her surprise by the jumps in her energy.

I haven't figured anything out yet. He won't show me.

The Neballat laughed again, loud, the sound pulsing through the Source.

You know everything you need to know already, he thought. *Why are you still here?*

And then, slowly, his form backed away, shimmered into an increasingly lighter color until he was nothing but the background from which he initially came.

He's a total ass, but he's right, Darl thought. *Let's go back. I know where we should go.*

But something was wrong with Claire. She was moving slowly away from him, her form slowly seeming to leak into the fabric of energy all around them.

Where are you going? Darl lurched out, trying to grab hold of her, press her to him, keep her from leaving. But it was too late, even as he grabbed for her. In less than a second, she was gone.

Claire! he cried out into the full vast nothingness in front of him. *Claire! Come back.*

But there was nothing in front of him anymore but particles and waves, energy like a river that Claire, his love, his true love, had sailed away on.

Darl was unsure about time. Maybe a minute had gone by since Claire slipped away, maybe an hour, maybe a week. Maybe an entire lifetime. Maybe he'd died and come back to the Source for good. He'd almost forgotten what he was doing here or where he was, really, because nothing seemed to matter much anymore. He floated, floated, turning in the warm hold of the energy all around him. At first, he'd been nervous, worried, desperate to find Claire and bring her back. They had something to do, something very important.

But why? She had to be feeling as wonderful as he was. And he thought he could probably just call out to her and she would come to him. The edges of his need to move, to go, to fix something blurred, wore down. So he waited, knowing that when it felt right, he would call to her. That's what he would do. Sometime soon.

And in a strange way, he was able to be with Claire, even though she was gone. He could feel her, almost touch her smooth skin, breathe in her lavender, citrus smell, hold her warmth in his palms. She was not by him but in him, memory as alive as time.

He thought her name, *Claire, Claire, Claire,* loving the sound, the feel of her in his thoughts.

The world around him was orange and yellow and red. Now and then, darker shapes would flicker by, and Darl thought that maybe he heard voices, words, sentences. He didn't care if he understood, not feeling afraid, forgetting that he might be afraid of something or someone. He knew there was something he was supposed to do, but he knew it could wait.

Why would anyone want to be anything but this? he thought. *Why would anyone want to have a body? It hurts too much. It's such a burden. There is too much to lose.* Everything about living was about loss.

A thought nagged at his mind, reminded him that he'd lost Claire in here, in this place that wasn't really life. Or maybe it was total life, or the real life, and everywhere else was fake, a tiny piece, a mirage. So there was loss here, after all. But as soon as the thought began to develop steam, it died, flattened, blew away.

Darl stretched, he sighed, he spun into a flow that was made of him and made of so much else. All the energy of everything seemed to be flowing through him. Or he was flowing through it. He turned and felt a smile somewhere inside him, but then he felt something behind him. A shape, an energy, a voice, and it wasn't a Neballat's.

I guess you've been wanting to talk with me for a while, the voice thought.

Darl felt a pull, a tug, a wrench into denseness, solidity, hardness. He knew that voice, though he hadn't heard it for years, even though—for a while—he had wanted to.

I really haven't, Darl thought back. *I've wanted to beat the shit out of you, but other than that, I don't think we have too much to talk about. You aren't worth the effort.*

So you don't walk around holding anger toward me? You don't think about me? You just said you wanted to beat the shit out of me. I think that qualifies.

No longer feeling loose and stretched out and flowing, Darl turned to face his father, or his father's energy. The man he'd known—tall, blond, sturdy body, blue, cold eyes—wasn't there at all but Darl felt the same feeling he had when he was a little boy, wanting to run into another room, cower under a blanket, and wait until he left. Not because his father Pete would do anything violent or mean or hurtful. Just because there was a space of discomfort between them, a silence of no words or feeling.

Yeah, I guess you're right. But there's nothing you can say that I really want to hear. You left Mom and your children. You went ahead and made yourself a whole new family and forgot about us. It's by Mom's sheer will that we all got through school. That we are self-sufficient. That we aren't criminals or derelicts or homeless. You don't really deserve my attention at all, good or bad.

His father's energy bobbed and flowed. Pete's form and feel weren't as dark as the Neballat's had been, but Darl could see his distinct outline against the streaming yellows and oranges of the Source.

You aren't interested in why I left? This hasn't been one of the driving forces in your life? This isn't your unanswered question?

Your story is just the story of another loser, Darl thought. *What's interesting about that?*

Oh, his father thought. *So very much. You know, it was I who found you.*

Darl felt everything that was him go silent. *What?*

I was the one who was asked to take care of you. I was the one who put you in your mother's arms for the first time.

When Kate and Michael first found Darl, one of the things he had never understood was how the Cygirian babies were placed with families on Earth.

"What happened?" he had asked. "Babies on doorsteps? With a long, weird note?"

But Kate had explained how there was power at work with each placement, Earthling parents suddenly convinced of their own parentage of the children now in their arms. They'd brought the babies and toddlers into their homes, convinced mostly of their own parenthood. Sometimes the story didn't stick, but by then, the parents were in love with the children, keeping them in the home and safe. Safe and hidden from Neballats. Darl's mother had never kept up a façade, pretended. All she'd ever said was, "I am lucky to have you. One day you will know who your parents are. They will somehow find you."

And in a way, they had. Through Kate and Michael. Through the safe house. Through Claire. He'd found them by finding what they had left behind. Culture, life, love.

But now, staring at the energy of the man who had taken him from Cygirian hands, Darl wanted to know the story. Needed to.

My Earth-bound self doesn't remember this except with a slight feeling of headache, Pete thought. *The memory is still bound in a magic that is too confusing.*

So what happened? Darl moved closer, wanting the words to pass through him, fill him with a clear understanding of this moment.

I was standing out on the cul-de-sac in front of the Acton house, watching the weather. You know, the way the clouds would roll by there, over the trees. And then it seemed to me that the clouds were moving a bit faster than usual. Crazy like. Tornado like. But there was no wind, just movement. And then out of absolutely nowhere, a door opened out of nothing, and a woman rushed down a plank and handed you to me. Just like that.

Darl knew that if he were breathing, he would stop right now. This man, his father, had watched a spaceship land, a door open, and took the toddler an alien handed to him.

So that didn't seem a little bit strange?

Pete's energy seemed to shrug, to laugh, everything about this moment clearly still right in front of him.

Naw, it was the nicest thing. Sure, I wasn't expecting to see a spaceship or an alien, but there you were. A cute little kid. My own kid that I could take home to my wife who seemed to think she couldn't have any. And that's what I did.

So what did she say about your happy package?

Pete seemed to float a little. *Aside from your crying at night for a while, those were the best months of our marriage. She never asked any questions about where I found you, and I didn't offer up any story because I forgot. And it must have seemed normal to all our friends and family because no one ever asked. It was that alien magic.*

Darl needed tears and voice and his body. He wanted to scream or bend over and weep. Where did this life go? The one that Pete described, this happy little threesome of people? This wasn't the family that Darl remembered: the anger, the fights, and then the silence.

Why did you leave? he thought, his feelings ragged and hard.

I didn't want to. But things just got out of control. It was three more kids, boom, boom, boom. Three more kids in just as many years.

You seem to like kids, Darl thought, *having a few more after us.*

Yeah, Pete thought, *but it was your mom I lost. To all of you. I could never get her back. Not since I gave her you. She was made for being a mom, not really a wife.*

Darl spun back, pushing away from his father. *Did you ever ask her? Did you ever tell her that?*

Pete seemed to float away a little more, his form fading into the yellows and oranges as if he were slowly being erased.

Some things you don't need to ask. I know here I should have done things differently, but my being on Earth? Doesn't have a clue yet. We know what we are supposed to do when we leave the Source, but applying it on Earth, trying to re- member through all that atmosphere, all that gravity, all that flesh is a little more difficult. So I'm kind of the idiot, bumbling along.

Darl wanted to bark out a laugh, but then something stopped him. Pete wasn't any different than anyone else on the planet. Everything was so clear in retrospect. And this Pete had the added advantage of being here in this place, in this Source of all things.

So Darl didn't say anything, instead staring at the fading form of his father.

Go to me on Earth when you have the chance.

If I have the chance, Darl thought. *Things aren't looking so good for us Cygirians.*

Pete didn't acknowledge this, simply repeating himself. *Go to me. Talk to me. You were the best thing I ever had. A gift from heaven, I thought then. A prize I could never get again.*

Darl felt the heaviness of tears form, but there were no tears here, just the feeling of them.

Anything else? he thought as his father began to float away.

Yeah, Pete thought. *Go get that girl of yours and get the hell out of here. She's something else, and you have things to do. You need to survive if you are going to help me out on Earth!*

With that, Darl felt his father's laughter in his cells, and then Pete melted back into the energy that was all around them. He heard his father's words, trying to think of the last time he heard his father speak to him on Earth. Nothing sounded as clear as this. Nothing as true.

Darl opened his feelings, his thoughts, and called out to Claire, knowing that his father—at least here in the Source—was right.

Where are you? he thought.

Hmmm, he heard Claire mumble, somewhere close to him, just by his ear.

Claire? Claire? he thought. *Is that you?*

Yes, she thought back.

We need to go, he thought. *We need to get out of here and tell everyone about the Neballats.*

I've just been waiting for you, she thought.

Darl spun and turned and moved right into the warm splash of Claire.

Where have you been? he thought.

Everywhere. Right here. Are you all right?

Darl wanted his body back so he could hold her. He barely knew her but he knew her completely. She was there with him, supporting him, but letting him do what he needed to do.

I'm okay. That was pretty damn strange. You know, father/son reunion in the middle of the Source. Talking through particles and waves. Talk show hosts would have a field day with this, he thought, pressing into her warmth, feeling her press back, allow him in, accept his energy as her own.

How do you feel about it? she thought, her words soft and lulling against his thoughts, comforting him.

He paused. He didn't really know how he felt. There was too much information here in the Source, answers to things that took lifetimes of Earth years to be revealed. He probably could have died a very old man without having ever heard his father's side of the story. Maybe it would have plagued him forever, though, and now Darl knew the story, knew what he never would have had he waited for Pete James to show up and confess his parenting sins.

Maybe someday, he thought, *after the big war and our amazing, come-from-behind victory, I'll go back to Earth and look up my father.*

You'd be lucky to be able to do so, Claire thought. *See him in the flesh.*

They were silent for a moment, and Darl knew she was thinking about her mother.

Did you find your mother? he thought.

No, she thought, her idea slow and tiny.

What have you been doing? he thought.

Oh, this and that, she thought back. *Let's go, okay? Let's get this all started. Let's go back to our people.*

Our people. Darl savored the thought, and then as he had done before, he let go of the Source, the energy that connected them all together, and opened his very self so that he could go back to his body, go back to the Cygirians who were waiting for him, go back to Claire and her lavender scent, her wide, welcoming smile, her eyes taking in all of him. He opened and drifted and waited for the darkness to carry him back home.

*   *   *

The second the pod doors opened, Darl looked up into the faces of Kate, Michael, and Porter, all of them staring down at him through the evaporating whoosh of white misty oxygen.

"Welcome back, Traveler," Porter said. "We bid you a kind hello."

"Will you shut it?" Stephanie said as she came up to his side. "How are you, Darl?"

"How long have I been out?" he asked.

"Oh, so long," Porter quipped, "that I about pined away."

"God!" Stephanie said, pushing at him and looking at Darl. "About three hours, I guess. I think the time in matches the time out. Unless, of course, you can move time."

"I can only go home. And I thought once I was there, I should stay a while," he said, sitting up and looking over to the other pod. Odhran, Jai, and Risa stood over Claire in the same manner, and behind them stood the Upsilians, who were talking quietly amongst themselves.

"Did you find the Neballat you were looking for?" Odhran asked.

Pushing himself up and then stepping out of the pod, Darl nodded. "Yes, we did. And we need to get together with all the Cygirians and the Upsilians and figure out a plan."

"Is it war?" Porter asked.

"What else could it be?" Stephanie said. "What other alternative do we have?"

"It depends on what the Upsilians are willing to do with and for us," Darl said. "But yes, it is war."

Darl put his hand on Porter's shoulder and then walked over to Claire, helping her out of her pod.

Are you ready for battle? he thought.

I'm ready for anything with you, she thought back, and

together with their group, they followed the Upsilians out of the room, down the hall, and back to their group where they would make the plans that would change everything.

It was late. Darl and Claire lay side by side in their small bed. Outside in the hall, they heard newly arrived Cygirians being led to quarters, a bed to sleep in before the new day brought something most of them had never encountered before. There were some quiet conversations, some laughter, but mostly everyone seemed focused on getting to a room and waiting for what would happen next.

"Who would have ever thought we'd be involved in interplanetary warfare?" Claire asked. "It's certainly not anything I'd ever imagined."

"Nobody ever expects interplanetary warfare," Darl said. "War maybe. Mostly, we expect bad politicians and ill-fated wars against small countries with oil. But this is something new to just about everyone."

"Do you think we can do it?"

"If the Upsilians hold up their end," Darl said. "If they stay on our side. If they don't decide to capitulate and agree to Neballat terms. But these are the people who kill pedestrians on sidewalks."

Darl pulled Claire close, still almost disbelieving that he held her in his arms. She fit so perfectly next to him. Not just her lovely, soft body, but her personality, her character, her very self. As he held her, he felt their connection of flesh, power, and mind, and knew that no matter what happened, he'd had this, this absolute perfection in life, in his body. Not in the Source, but out here where he could really feel it.

"It's not over," Claire said. "You're thinking like it's going to end. We've really just started."

"Are you spying on me?" Darl kissed her hair. "Are you listening to me?"

"It's like you're broadcasting on all frequencies," she said, rolling on top of him, her hair draping them, her eyes obsidian sparkles in the dark room.

"There's really only one channel I want you to hear." Darl pulled her close for a kiss, tasting her mouth, feeling her excitement as she pressed against him, feeling his own desire pulse through him as he let his hands wander the soft planes of her back.

"And what channel might that be?" she whispered against his lips.

"It's WDARL. Or KDARL. But wait, it's not a public access channel, I can tell you that. It's private. All mine. An audience of one."

Claire laughed low and ran her hands down his sides, feeling his lats, his obliques, her fingertips tracing the ribs underneath. Darl felt himself harden and put his hands on her rear and pulled her close, arching up a little against her.

"I think I'm hearing the station now. Hmmm . . . something is coming in loud and clear," she said. "It's quite obvious that I need to listen to this show for a long time."

Straddling him, she lifted herself up over him and found him with her hand, guiding him into her body.

Oh, Oh, Darl thought, losing his ability to speak. *You are so warm, so amazing.*

She slid down him slick and slow and began to move, taking her time at first, letting each of them enjoy the sensations of the friction between them before moving faster and then faster. Darl grabbed her smooth hips, guiding their movements, pushing into her so that she could feel all of him.

Claire moaned lightly, sitting up, moving on top of him.

For a second, Darl wondered if he was in a dream, a vision. This woman was too good to be true. He had so much feeling, so much desire, such a deep connection that he wondered if he'd moved into an alternate world. Anything was possible these days. There could be an entire planet just for this feeling alone.

But no, this was his body and hers, and they were moving together. Her lovely breasts were above him, her body fitting him tight and warm, her moans in the room like song.

"Yes, my love," he whispered. "Yes."

And he felt her contract, pull around him, squeeze with longing and pleasure and excitement, and all of that made him do the same, pulsing into her body.

Yes, Darl thought, pulling her close, holding her against his chest, feeling her chest move up and down as she took in breath.

Yes.

Chapter Eleven

Claire held Darl's arm as they stood in what she could only call a hangar. But instead of looking at giant 767s or Airbus A300s, they stood in front of a ship that was meant only for space. Together with Porter, Stephanie, Mila, and Garrick, they all stood almost under what might be called a wing, gaping upward. The ship was sleek steel and massive, full of tubes, pipes, wires, engines, portholes, the external texture, smooth but busy, like its own cityscape.

Behind them were seven more of the same ships, the farthest away seeming to be located in another county. There were five other such hangars in Dhareilly, countless more in cities all over Upsilia.

"They've been holding out on us," Garrick said. "they could have taken care of the Neballats long ago."

"Oh my God," Claire said. "It's like something from a movie."

"Three football fields," Darl said. "Easy."

Though Claire had traveled to places simply by thinking herself there, the idea that this gigantic machine could break through any atmosphere seemed to be a true miracle. How did it even get out of the hangar, she wondered.

"More importantly," Darl said. "How do we get into it?

The old-fashioned way, I mean. There doesn't seem to be a boarding ramp. Or an elevator."

"Wouldn't it be great if they flew this between JFK and Heathrow? SFO to De Gaulle?" Porter asked. "I don't think there is an issue with legroom in this contraption. And I bet they can actually make real food in it. No little packaged junk food. There's a whole galley in here. Maybe five."

Stephanie rolled her eyes and shook her head. Claire smiled and walked forward, farther under the wing, looking up. Again she was struck with the notion that while this looked like steel, it might be some other metal altogether. She was on another planet that had undergone different geological experiences, and nothing was the same as it was on earth.

Yeah, Darl thought. *No spaceships on Earth.*

Claire leaned into him, feeling his strong shoulder muscles under his clothes. She took in a breath of his wonderful scent of soap and skin, his long dark hair still slightly damp.

"Seems sort of strange to have gotten up this morning, taken a shower, and prepared to get in a spaceship for a fight with the aliens who destroyed our parents," Claire said. "I wonder when I'll wake up."

"You are awake, my love," Darl said. "And this might be the most important day of your life. Except, of course, the day you met me!"

Claire laughed, but she knew he was right about both days.

She kissed him on the chin, the cheek, feeling her connection to him overwhelming her. Where had this deep feeling of love been hiding all her life?

You were waiting for us, me. And here it is, Darl thought.

Do I have to say it again, Porter thought. *Get a room!*

Claire was about to tell him to shut up, when they were

suddenly approached by a group of Upsilians and an even larger group of Cygirians.

"Here we go," Garrick said. "It's time."

Claire looked over at Mila and reached out her hand. Mila took it, and Claire realized that for the second time in their lives, they were going to fly together in a ship. For an instant, Claire was back in her dream, heading somewhere with her siblings. They were afraid but together, heading toward something they wouldn't have been able to comprehend. All they had was that short time and a memory, a memory that would last them until just about now.

Should you be going? Claire thought. *Are you sure it's safe?*

No, I'm not sure, Mila thought back. *But nowhere is safe, really. And if my baby is to have the life I want him or her to have, I have to help. I have to help make all our lives better.*

Claire shook her head, worried, imagining what the battle might be like.

We can do this, Mila thought, her dark eyes on Claire. *It's like the promise we had to fulfill to our parents.*

I know, Claire said. *All I want is for this to be over. To be finished with fighting. To be with Darl. And you. To meet Edan.*

He's coming, Mila thought. *I can feel it.*

Where is he? Claire thought.

Close. Almost here. Almost ready to be with us, Mila thought. She seemed to want to give Claire more, but Garrick and he were urged forward by the Upsilians.

"Time to board," Darl said. "Do you have your boarding pass out? You don't need your photo ID."

"I have a feeling that they'll let me on," Claire said. "After all, I am with you."

"Yes, you are," Darl said, running a thumb across her cheek, kissing her nose, her forehead. "Yes, you are."

The plan was simple, but Claire wondered if she was missing something. She could certainly create a lesson plan, make papier-mâché pigs out of balloons and paper cups, and think about a child's developmental stages, but waging war on a genocidal troop of raging aliens was something she never learned in college. But even to her, finding the enemy on a desert plain and engaging in battle seemed, well, a bit simplistic.

"Find the enemy and kill them," Porter had said earlier. "Cops and robbers. Cowboys and Indians."

Stephanie had rolled her eyes. "It's not a game, Porter. Think of it. Jews and gentiles. Christians and pagans. Muslims and non-Muslims. Natives and non-natives. It's an us versus them thing."

"I'd prefer to kill them before they kill me," Porter said.

"You've never killed a thing in your life," Stephanie said. "Don't get all warrior on me."

The Upsilians seemed to be ready for the Neballats, as if war was commonplace. And now, Claire and Darl sat next to each other, strapped down in chairs clearly devised for take-off and landing, the belts around them sturdy and thick. Porter and Stephanie were close by, as were Garrick and Mila and hundreds of other Cygirians and Upsilians.

Claire almost felt safe, and as she looked around the room at the hundreds of people in the ship, she wondered how they would go about killing Neballats.

"What else can we do with them?" Darl asked. "What other language do they speak? Violence is their first language. Unfortunately, we're learning how to speak that as well."

She shook her head. "I don't know what else we can do. It just seems that with all this power we should be able to do something else. I mean, with the Convergence, we don't need to be in the spaceship at all. In fact, with the number of Cygirians here, we would be amazing."

Shrugging, Darl sat back. "Maybe the Upsilians don't want to see that. You know, there are three groups of people here, all with separate agendas."

Underneath them, the huge engines of the spaceship rumbled and groaned, and a hum went through the ship, through Claire's very bones. She glanced at Mila, who nodded, remembering that other spaceship one more time.

"So we surprise them and attack," Claire whispered, not wanting to feel so inept. "And we can win that way?"

Leaning over, Darl took her hand. "I hope so. We have the Upsilian strength and ours. If the conventional weapons don't work, we have time and weather and electricity and place and life and death and everything at our call. We can finally use the powers that the Neballats have always wanted. The powers we just didn't know how to use."

She wanted to say so many things to Darl. She wanted to tell him that she didn't want to fight, even the very culture who wanted to kill off her own. What she wanted was the peace and love she'd found with Darl in this short time. What she wanted was the life she knew they would have together.

We can't have that until we fix the outer world, Darl thought. *Otherwise, there might be no us to enjoy it.*

The ship began to rumble harder, faster, and then it seemed to almost begin to glow, the inside of the craft alight, gold, orange, slightly hot.

An Upsilian voice came over the intercom, announcing takeoff, and Claire grabbed on to Darl's arm.

No matter what happens, she thought. *I am so glad I found you.*

You can't lose me, he thought back. *No matter what. I know that now. Even in the Source.*

If she wasn't on a spaceship about to launch into the air, hover over Upsilia before attacking evil aliens, Claire would want to cry. But to cry for joy. Even with all this impending fighting and struggle and potential harm, she had so much.

Claire smiled, sat back, and moved her hand down to Darl's, holding tight. The ship rumbled and seemed to move slowly and then pulsed in a flare, up and out into what Claire could only imagine as space.

She was about to turn to Darl to say something about the ease of the liftoff when the ship began to shudder, shake, move at sharp angles that she never imagined possible from a machine this big.

"What is it?" she cried out, grabbing Darl's arm again. But her voice was lost in the noise of engines and screams.

What is it? she thought.

I don't know, Darl thought. *Let me try to find someone's thoughts, someone who might know.*

Claire hung on, her organs feeling shaken from the inside, her legs almost dancing on the ship's floor. Her whole body hurt with the thrusts and swerves and bounces, and it seemed as if the ship were being batted back and forth between two giants.

They laid a trap in space, Darl thought. *We're going down. We're crashing?*

No, not yet, Darl thought. *We're landing. Maybe not as smoothly as we would like, but we're not crashing. Don't worry. It will be fine, love. Please, don't worry.*

As she took in his thoughts, the ship began to make an even louder, whining noise, the kind of whine only some-

thing heavy and metal and in distress could make. Something heavy, in trouble, and falling.

She let go of Darl because she couldn't hold on to him
any longer. She tried to reach out, but her hands were forced
to her side by something she might have understood had she
ever taken physics. Claire closed her eyes, trying to stay connected to him by her thoughts, but even her brain seemed a
bit scrambled, her head being pushed around despite the seat
and the straps that held her down. Everything inside her hurt,
bones, muscles, tendons. Pushed and pressed, squeezed and
flung, Claire tried to remember the mission, the reason for
all this, thinking over and over, *Protect our people. Make a
place for ourselves. Find our place in the universe. Be with
my love. Live happily ever after.*

She kept repeating the thoughts and using them as a
mantra, hoping she could ignore the pain she was in. All she
felt was the separation from Darl, even though when she
opened her eyes, she could see him. Closing her eyes against
the shaking and torment outside her, she wondered how she
could believe in a happy ending. How was a happy ending
possible with her and Cygiria past? *Darl may be here now,
and he may be in the Source . . .*

The ship seemed to almost flip over on itself, stop, and
thrust out in a different direction. Claire's head banged
against her chair, her body thumping into the sides, and she
tried to find breath. She looked over at Darl, and he was
being flung around just as everyone else was. She wanted to
reach out and calm him, but she couldn't move her arm. She
was shaking so hard she could barely see straight, but she
thought she saw blood on his temple.

Darl? Darl? she thought, but she knew that her thoughts
were as jumbled as everything right now. He couldn't hear
or think of her. Not now.

Above them, chunks of what seemed to be metal paneling were falling down almost on top of the passengers. The air was filling with swirling smoke.

Focus, she thought to herself. *Focus*.

The sudden, hard, jerky movement continued, the cries from the passengers ringing in her ears. She hoped that Mila was all right. Mila's baby—Claire's niece or nephew—meant so much to them all. The first baby, the first of the new generation. Hope. Mila and the baby had to be all right. They had to make it through this.

Claire took in a breath as the ship seemed to pull away, float. But just as it seemed that the jerky movements had smoothed out, the ship seemed to lose its environment, the air suddenly and completely cold, the smoke sucked away. All the instruments around her radiated freeze.

What to do? What to do? she thought, her mind too unclear to think in a straight line. So Claire tried to imagine a calm, soft place. She thought about stillness and warmth and heat and energy. She thought about somewhere where her body wouldn't hurt, where she could relax and forget about all this danger. All she wanted to do was float. All she wanted was to not be afraid.

Claire breathed in a full breath, finding her lungs for a second, and thought of the safest of places, the calmest, the place where she wouldn't ever have to worry about aliens or loss of pain in her body. A place where she and Darl could be together without worry. Where they both would be safe. She wanted peace and hope and freedom and knowledge. She wanted to be completely who she was, entirely.

As the ship screamed down to the planet, blasts from somewhere outside the ship, in a flicker of thought and hope and fear, Claire thought about the Source, opening the image briefly in her mind like a photo and shutting it, quick.

*   *   *

Startled into consciousness, Claire opened her eyes into streaming reds and oranges, the colors alive and warm and rushing past her. Breathing in, she pulled what felt like a true breath, something so full and rich, she imagined she was like a baby being born, taking in that first aching breath.

After a moment of that luscious feeling, Claire slowly made a check of her body to see if she'd been injured in the crash, but as she thought of her head and neck and arms and chest, she realized she didn't have those body parts to really check, just the memory of them. Here she was, back, in the Source, without pain, without strife or stress or fear. But wait. How was she here? Something very bad had happened to get her to this place, she knew that. No Upsilian had thrown her in a pod during the crash landing. So . . . so? What had happened?

She must be dead, she thought. That had to be it. She wasn't visiting the Source with a little bit of her soul. She was here completely, all of her, for however long one stayed here. Claire had never bothered to ask anyone how long a Source visit was, so it might go on and on and on for eternity. And how long was eternity? Was there more than one?

For a second, she was gripped with sadness and fear and loss. She would never know what happened on Upsilia. She would never be able to live to that conclusion, finding out who won the battle. It was clear she would never find out if Cygiria could reclaim itself, its people, its world. Or maybe she would find out while she was here, but it wouldn't matter.

So that's that. She was dead.

Claire teetered on the thought that would bring her from sadness into acceptance. Could she let go? She could. It had been a great ride, but it was over.

Ahh, she thought, letting herself fall backward into the flow, streaming herself into the wave of energy that was holding everything together. It was wonderful, really, this Source, this energy, this floating. She cast everything off and gave up, whirling into the feeling that would be all she had now.

Sweetheart, came the thought. *Sweetheart, time to wake up.*

Mom, I'm tired. I'm too tired. I want to sleep in today, all right? I don't want to go to school. I want to stay home with you.

Claire, you need to get up. You can't miss this.

And now she knew where she was. She was at the house in West Portal, asleep in her bed in her bedroom. Her mother Susan was still alive, downstairs, yelling up at her. Once again, she was missing school, hiding under the covers instead of dealing with the popular girls and the stares from people who thought she was strange. Turning away from her mother's voice, Claire just wanted to sleep.

Tomorrow. Tomorrow, I'll go. But I want to stay here now.

Her mother must have walked away from her place at the foot of the stairs, leaving Claire to sleep through the whole school day. It was too hard out there. There were too many possibilities for embarrassment and feeling awkward. The next thing she knew, she might be in a different town, city, country. All she wanted was this bed . . . bed? Was she in a bed? She didn't live in West Portal any more. Her mother was dead.

She knew she was at home again, safe, finally. But that couldn't be right. Something was off, wrong, but she didn't want to face it.

Claire, her mother thought. *You don't have to go to school.*

Thank you! Claire smiled to herself, spun in the covers more.

It's a little more important than that. You have to go back.

Back? I can't. I can't see those kids . . . I mean, I can't go back anywhere. I'm dead. I died. I didn't make it through the flight.

Claire pulled herself into consciousness, trying to find her mother in the energy.

No, no. You didn't die, her mother said. *In fact, you aren't here at all. You aren't at the house, you aren't even in San Francisco.*

Mom, you aren't making sense . . . Mom? How can you be here?

How can I not?

Claire thought the last word with almost a sob. *Where are you, Mom?*

Here. Here I am, sweetheart.

And then Claire felt her mother swirl around her, moving into her.

Here. I've always been here.

Are you all right?

I've always been all right, Susan thought.

Claire felt a relief she'd never felt before. The last time she saw her mother, Susan was in such pain, such agony, the cancer so far gone she'd refused treatment. But she'd been alive, there, in Claire's life. Her mainstay, her support.

That was the reason she couldn't go back to the house and the reason she couldn't sell it. It contained the last of her mother. It was all that Claire had left.

I didn't want you to suffer so much, Mom.

I know, sweetheart. I know you didn't want that. That's why I left and came here.

Claire paused for a moment, floating in the bobbing waves. *You say I'm not dead? So why am I here?*

You flung yourself here, her mother thought. *You simply wished yourself right here, with me.*

I can do that? Claire thought. *And leave my body behind?*

Apparently, Susan thought, the sound containing appreciation, humor, joy. *You have amazing strength.*

Why did I do it?

Probably because you were afraid. But it's always frightening away from the Source. It's a miracle that any of us are born at all.

Claire was confused by this, but she didn't care. All she wanted to do was stay here with her mother and float. Whatever had happened before wasn't worth losing this feeling, this connection with Susan.

I don't think you mean that, her mother thought.

What?

I think you have a big reason to go back. The best reason you've ever had to be alive.

Claire felt her energy stop, hold still, and she remembered. All at once, the last image before she flung herself into the Source flashed into her mind. Darl in the spaceship, Darl hurt, her people hurtling toward disaster. And there was Mila, and Edan, the brother she hadn't met yet. There was also the hope that the Cygirians could be together again as a group, a people. But would they even survive what was happening?

That's the risk you have to take, Susan thought. *It's the risk we all take when choosing to live. Sometimes, things don't go that well. But you'll end up back here, no matter how it turns out.*

Claire nodded, but she felt the pain of living in the body, the hurt, the confusion.

The happiness, Susan thought. *Like when I was given you.*

You remember that?

Not until I arrived here, her mother thought. *But then I could see the woman handing you to me, the tall beautiful woman with the blond hair. She placed you in my arms and told me you were mine. And you were, are.*

At that moment, Claire wanted her body back so she could hold her mother. All her life, that hug—even when Susan was wasted from illness—was what kept her going.

No, it's always been your strength. I wish I could have helped you more, but I didn't know how to then. But I do now, Claire, and you need to go back. Go back to your life, no matter how scary. Live your life as much as you can until you can't. And then you'll be here again, with me, with everyone, and you can start again.

It was all too much to contemplate, but it didn't matter. Claire felt the rightness in her mother's words, knew that like always, her mother was right.

But I can't get home! That's always been the problem. I can go everywhere but can't get back.

Claire heard Susan's chuckle. *Yes, you can.*

I need Darl.

Knowing that you have Darl is enough. He is your other half, can do what you thought you couldn't. But he's already given you what you need. Opened up your power. You've done the same for him.

Oh, Mom, she thought, swirling around Susan's energy. *I love you.*

I love you, too, Claire. But stay in life while you can. Stay in there as long as you are able.

With that, her mother rushed around her in a twirl of orange and red and was gone.

Claire almost lunged forward to grab at her, but she didn't have the arms to catch what was impossible to catch. So she remained still, tried to calm herself. She got here the way she moved to places, but she'd never been able to go back where she came from. She'd fling herself as close as she could get, but it would never be right. So how? How?

Her mother had told her that Darl made it all possible. That Darl had opened up her power to fullness. She didn't want to think about the crashing spaceship, the explosions all around her, the screams of panic and fear from her fellow Cygirians. No. So Claire slowed herself down, tamped down the energy that made up her form here, and thought of Darl. She conjured forth his lovely, long hair, the curl under his left ear. His eyes, laughing at her, his hands touching her. She heard his voice in her ear, his laughter all around her. And she felt him, his chest, his back, his legs. She remembered what he felt like when he entered her, hard and wonderful and lovely.

Snapshot memories of their short time together flashed in front of her: Geary Street, Tahiti, Upsilia. She focused on what was good and right and wonderful about every bit of being with him, even through dangerous moments, even through times she wasn't with him, even when she was worried. The thought of him was what had kept her going as she ran away from the Upsilians and as she tramped through the desert with Mila. The idea of him was what had kept her going all her life before she'd even met Darl.

Darl, she thought. *Darl. I'm coming back now. I'll be there as soon as I can. Don't give up on me. Don't leave me. Darl? Darl?*

Chapter Twelve

Darl wasn't sure when it happened or why. In a way, he didn't know where he was, only what he was looking at. Nothing else mattered. Not the battle, the emergency crash-landed spaceship, his friends' voices in his ear and mind.

The only thing that mattered was that Claire was in his arms, lifeless. Darl closed his eyes and pulled her to him, letting a low sound out of his mouth. He held her tight, feeling a moan pulse in his throat, chest, entire body. He didn't care what sound he made. All he wanted was for her to wake up, come back.

This can't be real, he thought. *This can't be happening.*

She didn't seem to be breathing, though Darl had a hard time figuring anything out. They'd just skid-landed somewhere, explosions banging all around the outer shell of the craft, people running, screaming, the big ship door opening to smoke and light and more sound. Some Cygirians had used their powers to stave off an attack from outside and run outside to see what they could do.

But as soon as he'd been able to, Darl had wrenched off his landing belt and pulled Claire out of hers. As the ship went down, he was sure that she had fainted, but she wasn't conscious, didn't seem to be breathing. Her arms dangled at her sides, her head turned almost lifelessly to the side.

Claire? Claire? he thought. *Wake up, love. Wake up. Don't go. Don't leave me here without you.*

He laid her down, put his head to her chest, but it was too noisy to hear anything. Heavy metal scraped against metal, engines accelerated, something exploded, the ship reverberating with the hit.

Darl put a finger to her lips and was almost certain that he felt her breath—but then that feeling disappeared.

Find Whitney! Mila thought, running over to them, her hair a flame of blond, her face smudged with something dark, her shirt ripped. Otherwise, she looked fine, and Darl tucked away his worry about her baby.

She kneeled down, put her cheek on Claire's chest.

Oh, find Whitney! She can bring Claire back. That's her power. Oh, my God.

Whitney could bring those injured back to life, but Darl had only met Whitney briefly. He couldn't leave Claire here, like this, on the floor of this cold ship.

"I have to do CPR," Darl shouted. "I can't feel a heartbeat."

"Do it," Mila shouted, just as Garrick came up, his cheek bleeding, his knuckles red, scraped, the skin raw. He kneeled down, too.

"Let me go back in time to see what happened," he said, almost seeming to have to throw his voice out of his chest to be heard.

"What?" Darl shouted back, pulling open Claire's jacket. He'd done CPR only on the dummies he'd taken in the first aid class as part of his teacher training. He'd never had to use it, not with any member of the football team, not anywhere. But he remembered how. Lean or rock forward with elbows locked, and apply vertical pressure to depress the sternum. Mila could do mouth to mouth. He could do it. They could do it together to save Claire. They had to. He put his hands on Claire's chest.

"Let me go back in time to see what happened," Garrick said again.

Darl didn't pay attention, but then he was holding Claire, his face wet, his heart pounding. He put her down on the floor of the spaceship, trying to wake Claire, feeling Mila suddenly at his side.

Oh, find Whitney! She can bring Claire back. That's her power. Oh, my God.

Darl wasn't sure about where Whitney was or if she was even on the ship. Even though she could bring back someone from death, he certainly didn't have time to look for her now. All he could do was CPR, and he was about to start, when Garrick was at his side, putting a hand on his shoulder.

For a second, Darl had the strangest sense of déjà vu.

Don't do CPR, Garrick thought. *She doesn't need it.*

"What?" Darl shouted. He put his hands on Claire's chest. Thirty compressions to two breaths. He looked up at Mila, who was staring at Garrick, obviously listening to her twin's thoughts.

Mila turned back to Darl, putting her hand on his wrist, stopping him.

The Source, Garrick thought directly to Darl. *She's not injured. I think she flung herself into the Source during the attack. I saw her just sort of go away. Nothing hit her. Nothing hurt her. She's too young to have had a heart attack. No one came and did anything to her.*

"How could she have gone to the Source?" Darl asked.

"I didn't know she could do that. She's always had to take her body with her wherever she goes."

That's what it seemed like to me. I could go back again, Garrick thought. *I could take another look.*

Darl looked down at Claire, and then leaned over to put his ear against her mouth. In the din and mess and fighting, he closed his eyes and waited and listened and hoped for a sign.

Let me feel your breath, he thought. *Claire, show me what to do. I don't want to hurt you with CPR. If you are in the Source, come out. Come home. Come back to us. Help us get out of here.*

Darl held her close, and Mila put her hands on her sister's arm. He felt them both calling to Claire, begging her to come back. And they waited, even as the ship rained down parts around them, even as it grew dark outside from the number of ships in the sky, from the smoke from destroyed engines.

Come back, Darl thought. *Come back to me.*

At first, he wasn't sure that he felt it, but then . . . yes. Yes! She moved, her lips twitched, her fingers moving slightly. A pulse in her leg. And then her breath deepened, her exhale clear, full of sound.

"Claire," Darl whispered, knowing that she couldn't possibly hear his words in the midst of all this noise. *Claire. You came back. You came back to me.*

And then she opened her eyes, blinking, staring up at Darl.

"Together," she said, her voice so soft he knew he was reading her lips more than hearing her.

Together? Darl thought.

He looked at Mila and then back at Claire.

"What, love? What?" he asked.

"We can do it together," she said. "Convergence. Will work."

She sat up, her dark eyes full of an idea. "We can create a barrier, just like we did at the Upsilian headquarters."

Darl pushed her hair off her forehead. "But that was against one ray, love. We have a whole Neballatian army out there. Ships everywhere. And we need to get out of this spaceship sooner rather than later. Things aren't holding up very well."

And as if to prove a point, an explosion rocked the ship, fine white dust falling down on them as they huddled around Claire.

"Doesn't matter," Claire said. "Same thing. We need to get everyone together."

"First we need to get out of here," Darl said, pulling her to her feet, Mila helping him. "I don't know how much longer this ship will be a ship. It's turning into flour."

The four of them walked and then ran to the door of the ship, glancing skyward out to see it full of metal, Neballatian and Upsilian ships hanging heavy and huge in the blue. They swerved, maneuvered, shot at each other, and on the ground, the same thing was happening, but there were also waves of what looked like protective shields, sent forth by the Cygirians.

"We have to do that. All together. Push all at once," Claire said, her voice much stronger than just moments before.

"How can we get everyone's attention?" Garrick asked.

"Have you ever played telephone?" Darl asked, thinking back to his days in elementary school. "We tell the next group of Cygirians we see and then have them pass it on."

"You know what always happened with telephone. I'd

say, 'My mother likes silk,' and it would end up being 'My brother wears kilts.' "

"We don't have a lot of time to discuss it," Claire said. "But I know it will work. There is enough space for us to really spread out. That Neballat in the Source was right."

Darl shook his head. "How can you say that? He trapped us. He lied to us. They knew that we were coming."

"I don't think he lied. He knew something that we didn't. I think this is exactly where we are supposed to be," Claire said. "So let's do this."

Darl shrugged and closed his eyes, finding Claire's, Mila's, and Garrick's thoughts. Holding hands, their combined energy whisking through them all, they created the message about the Convergence.

Band together with this thought. Concentrate. Push forward with all your power. Push up. Push forward. Create the safe space. Don't stop until it's over.

And with that thought, with their energy, they threw the thought toward a group of Cygirians huddled under the ship to the side of the door. As he watched, Darl saw them take the message, look around, bring it inside themselves, hear and feel it. They stood up despite the explosions, despite the huge ships overhead, and held hands. And then they must have passed the thought on because each time someone took in the message, the energy inside Darl grew stronger, a strong *beat, beat* in his body.

And as it continued, Darl knew why the Neballats had always been so afraid of Cygiria. Look what they could do. All along, all they'd had to do was connect together and push back. But it wasn't easy to connect a world together. And maybe his parents and their parents hadn't wanted this connection, wanting only to go about their lives with their specific powers, enjoying their separateness, their differences. Maybe some people didn't appreciate others' powers, didn't want to be associated with anyone not the same. Darl didn't really understand that impulse, the same that was on Earth, but had their forebears done so, Darl and Claire and all the rest wouldn't be standing here on this desert pushing back at enemies they'd all had for a lifetime. It would have been so simple to push back for one connected minute and be done with it.

He stopped his thoughts, feeling the message spread. There! There! More and more of them were hooked by thought, their power growing, expanding, strengthening.

He wanted to talk with Claire, share his amazement, but he knew that they should be focusing on the message, pushing their energy upward. So Darl pushed, connected his feelings with everyone else's.

Push, push. The energy radiated out of them and into the energy radiating everywhere. It all began to connect, and overhead, he saw that the sky fighting had slowed, the explosions fewer, the maneuvers slight. And then the traffic stopped altogether, the ships pressed upward into the sky, tossed gently, almost, up and away.

Push, they all thought. *Press them away. Space. Give us a place. Give us a space to live.*

There was a surge, a wild swelling of power, a push that was more than a push. It was a wave, a huge, enormous wave that seemed to pull everything higher. Darl wasn't sure what had happened, but he knew that it was a good thing, a forceful, needed thing that showed their power, their might, their desire to be left alone.

The Upsilian ships pulled away, moved toward the horizon, the Neballatian ships stuck like toy bots in a bathtub, bumping together. They stopped firing their weapons, they stopped offensive maneuvers, hanging like giant bobbing balloons in the sky.

Darl didn't know how much time passed. He'd finally stopped thinking, only feeling Mila's and Claire's hands in his own, hearing the thought in his head, the energy in his body. He focused on this empty space just for Cygiria. He imagined what their lives would be like if they had a space, a world, a place to call their own again. At least for now.

And it could be here, right here, he thought. *We want this desert as ours. This flat plain, this dry earth where we could just be. We would know who we were and we would have a place to learn to be Cygirians again.*

So with all of those thoughts, with Claire's hand in his, Darl James pushed his energy into the mass of energy they all created, and after some time, he forgot to think, forgot the feel, only being the energy that would save them all.

"Darl?"

He heard his name, the question, as if from a great distance, as if he were underwater.

"Darl?" It came again. "Wake up. Please wake up."

And as if he were digging himself out of a hole, as if he were pulling himself up a ladder out of a deep pit, Darl headed for the light, the bright spot at the very end of his vision.

I'm on my way. I'm coming, he tried to think, not sure if anyone could hear him. *I'm trying to find my way.*

I hear you. Keep coming. You're almost there.

And the voice was right. He was, the bright light growing wider in scope, illuminating everything. One more rung, one more pull, and he was there, at the top, the light all around him.

Darl opened his eyes to see Claire staring at him. He

blinked against the overwhelming light, but opened his eyes again so he could see her.

"Is it over?" he asked. "Did we do it?"

Claire held out her hand and he took it, sitting up from where he had been lying on the sand. He looked around the vast stretch of desert and then up to the empty—yes, empty—sky.

"They left." He turned to her. "We did make it happen."

He looked around and then back toward the desert. "Where are Mila and Garrick?"

"I told them that I'd take care of you," Claire said. "They wanted to go join the crowd. I just wasn't ready for it."

"You do take care of me," Darl said.

"No," Claire said. "You take care of me. You called me out of the Source."

"It worked, though. All of it. The Convergence worked."

"Yes," she said, sitting down next to him, leaning against his shoulder. "I guess so."

"Guess?" Darl said, holding her close to him. "You were right. They were literally pushed out of the sky. It was you, Claire. You saved us."

Claire shrugged. "My mom told me how to do it when I was in the Source."

Darl started. "Your Cygirian mother?"

"No. I didn't meet her there. I didn't even think about that. My Earth mother. My mother."

Darl knew what she meant. Even though he knew another woman gave birth to him, his mother Joanne was the woman he'd always recognize as Mom. She took what was given to her and never regretted it. He didn't think that he felt the same way about Pete, but he didn't have to. Someday, maybe, now that he knew about the Source and how to navigate it, he might go back and try to find his Cygirian parents. To learn what had happened to them after he was left on Earth. Maybe he'd find out he had some siblings, but he didn't have the kinds of memories Claire had about Mila and Edan. But who knew?

For now, he wanted to live in this time, this space, this place with Claire.

"So how did your mother know about Convergence?" he asked.

"I'm not sure exactly. Things seem possible in the Source that aren't here, you know. In that place, everything seems to meld together. It's all one thing. Humans, Cygirians, Upsilians. Neballats. Probably people we can't even imagine. It's just one fabric."

"Sort of like Convergence."

Claire sighed. "Yes, it was amazing what happened. What we can do once we put our thoughts to it."

For a moment, both of them looked at the tableaux in front of them, the ships landing in the distance, the Upsilians and Cygirians talking together. Darl was shocked to see so many Cygirians. Hundreds and hundreds and hundreds of his people. Maybe thousands. No wonder they'd been able to push away the Neballats. If only they would stay away until Cygiria found its foothold, because they had power now. True power.

"Did you feel that swell during the Convergence? That kind of wave of energy?" he asked.

Claire nodded. "Yeah, I did. That was pretty wild. I don't know what caused it, but it worked."

Claire nodded. Darl hugged her tight again, and then they both looked out to the desert in front of them, the Convergence shield still hanging above them all in a protective glowing arc. It seemed to Darl that there was some sort of clump of excitement in the middle of the group, a rush toward someone or something. Part of him wanted to get up and search out the mystery, but more than anything, he wanted this amazing sense of peace with Claire.

"What do you think is going to happen now?" she asked.

Watching his people mill about, seeing the Upsilians accept them as a big group, Darl realized that the hope he had during the Convergence just might come true. This might be their place. This might be where Cygiria started over.

"I don't know," he said. "I just know that I'm going to be with you through it all."

And he leaned down and kissed Claire, kissed her in the desert, kissed her as the world around them sorted, changed, turned into something good.

After the battle was over, the ships landed, friends found and greeted and hugged, the Cygirians dropped the Convergence shield, and slowly, they were flown out of the desert and back to the enormous hangar they'd been in before the battle plan had been drawn up. Darl and Claire sat in a ship just after landing. Darl reached over and took her hand, pressing it gently, feeling the smoothness of her fingers. He listened to her talk to Mila and Garrick, smiled when Porter and Stephanie walked over. Kate and Michael were sitting in another row of seats, talking with the famous Whitney and her twin Kenneth. Darl felt relaxed, full of endorphins, as satisfied as he ever felt, as if he'd played the longest football game of his life, made every touchdown, the win huge, beyond belief. But this wasn't football. It was his life, and he was *with* his life, Claire.

"You don't see that every day," Porter was saying. "Actually, you don't see it at all. I felt it. Right through me."

"That's more than the effect I ever have on you," Stephanie said, half smiling.

"My dear, the effect you have on me is immeasurable," Porter said.

"But what was it?" Claire asked. "What made the Convergence so much stronger?"

"I don't know," Mila said. "But whatever it was, it shook me to the core. And seemed to bring out more energy from the group."

"Maybe it was just mass. The weight of all of us. We've never had so many Cygirians together all at once. Critical mass," Garrick said.

The conversation continued as they all discussed what had happened during the Convergence, an eddy of good feeling pooling in Darl's chest. He followed the conversation like a wave, but then he noticed the same stir and swirl of people he'd seen down on the desert. But there were fewer people on the ship, and now he could see that the people were surrounding a man. A very blond man. And then he recognized him, turning to Claire, his heart pounding fast. He wasn't jealous, wasn't nervous, wasn't hesitant about telling Claire what he knew. But he also understood that once Claire saw who had just come in the door, nothing would ever be the same.

"Claire," he said.

She looked up at him, her brown eyes so full of love, he wished he could leave right now and keep things from changing. And he could leave. Finally, his power would help him. Darl could pull his love to her and land them back home. But then, he wasn't sure where home was these days. The safe house was destroyed, Encino seemed like a long-ago dream he once had, and while his mother was in Olympia, the old saying was true—he truly couldn't go home again.

There was always Claire's San Francisco apartment, but

that life seemed as far away and slightly ridiculous as his own. And Darl knew he couldn't take Claire away from what was rightfully hers. Of course, he couldn't do that. It was settled. Darl James knew that her future as well as his own had just walked in the spaceship door.

"What?" she asked. "What is it?"

"It's Edan. Your brother is here."

Chapter Thirteen

Without having to say a word, Claire turned to look at Mila, who was already smiling, standing up, and holding out her hand to Claire, who took hold. But before Claire stood up, she looked at Darl.

"I'm going to—"

Darl took her free hand and kissed it, his lips lingering just long enough that she felt a twinge of pleasure inside her belly.

"Of course. Of course, you are going to meet him."

And then they stood up together, Claire staring into Darl's amazing dark eyes.

"Okay," she said, kissing his cheek. "I'll be back."

"And if you weren't, I'd go find you," he said. "Probably, you'd have no choice. I think I'd have the all-points bulletin out. Or at least Kate and Michael on patrol."

Mila pulled on Claire's hand, and Claire smiled at Darl, feeling her heart skitter around her chest like a small animal. Then they walked toward the group that surrounded Edan. Her brother. Just the little boy in the spaceship, but somehow something more. Someone more. No one Claire had met since she and Darl left Earth had anything normal to say about him. He was otherworldly, spacey, different, powerful, amazing, odd. He was, she acknowledged as they walked closer, damn-good looking. Blonder than both hers and Mila's, his hair seemed to glow in the bright light inside the spaceship. His eyes weren't as dark as theirs, more of a gray, and Claire could see the penetrating, steely quality of his gaze from here. He was tall and muscular and looked strong, though there was a sadness in his face, something heavy and deep that made him look older than twenty-nine or thirty, the age she supposed he was now.

That one slight aspect didn't seem to detract from his looks. On Earth, he could have been an actor or a model or some celebrity type up on that obnoxious billboard next to the Ninth Street exit on Highway 80. The Gap would have loved him in khakis and a too-small T-shirt, an artful, smug smile on his handsome face. So it wasn't surprising to her that over half of the people surrounding him were women, women whose doubles and twins were standing in the group as well, but not as happily as they.

But even with the group surrounding him, as she and Mila approached, Edan looked up over their heads and smiled.

It's you, he thought. *Finally.*

And then he gently pushed his way through the crowd, coming toward them.

"He's really normal," Mila said, squeezing Claire's hand repeatedly. "He completely freaked me out when I first met him, but he's, well, he's our brother."

Then he was right in front of them, and then she was folded into his arms, hugged tight, held by the boy who'd reassured her in that long-ago spaceship, held by the boy who was now a man, a man who seemed to be destined for something bigger, something else.

The images from Claire's dream flooded past. She saw their

legs out in front of them as they sat on the floor, their little stick children's legs, Edan's the longest. From her memory, she heard his childhood voice, explaining to her how things would be all right. In the dream, she is pressed next to Mila, but it's Edan's strength that keeps them all safe.

But they weren't safe, especially Edan, who was raised here, feared by this strict culture, living all those long years in the Source.

I'm fine, he thought. *I'm fine now that I've found you and Mila. I have both of my sisters with me.*

He pulled back and looked down at her. "You were so little when I last saw you. Tiny. I had to think with you more than talk because you didn't have too many words."

Claire nodded, hearing her baby words echoing from her dream.

"And I remember you were called Sophia."

Claire wiped her eyes. "I guess my mother on Earth broke that hold. I ended up being Claire. And I think I'm used to it now."

He rubbed her shoulders, staring at her, and Claire realized how powerful his gaze was. She knew his power was to be able to age himself, but he seemed to have something else, too, something that went beyond mind reading. Maybe it was a power he himself didn't even understand.

"Claire," he said, her name sounding different in his mouth. Not better. Not better than when Darl said it or even when Mila said it, these two people who loved her. But almost magic in Edan's mouth.

Mila moved closer now, touching both their arms. "Where have you been?"

Edan shook his head, his voice deep and serious. "After the safe house was destroyed, I ended up in a place I never thought I'd be. A place no one will imagine."

Claire wanted to laugh, seeing that while her brother was otherworldly and slightly magic and maybe divine, he did like to tell a dramatic story.

"Where did you go?" Mila asked, but as she spoke, Edan seemed to want to interrupt her. But instead, he stared at her.

"You're pregnant!" he said finally.

Mila's mouth opened in surprise, her face turning a slight rose color. "How could you tell?"

Edan laughed. "Oh, I have so many powers. I am amazing—"

"Garrick told you, did he?" Mila asked. "That rat."

Edan nodded, smiling, and then pulled Mila in for a hug.

"This is so wonderful," he said. "I think this is exactly what we need."

"So where *did* you go?" Claire asked after he loosened his embrace, his arm still around Mila.

"I was with the Neballats."

At that statement, both Claire and Mila stopped still.

"You were? You were on the ships that came to attack just now?"

Edan shook his head. "No, not on a ship. I was transported to what had to be something like our space house. A place on an asteroid."

"Did they hurt you?" Mila asked. "What did they do to you?"

At her question, Edan smiled, and in that smile, Claire felt safe. Everything about him radiated safety, comfort, warmth, love. He wasn't terrified, worried, upset after being taken away by his mortal enemies. Unlike Porter, he wasn't using sarcasm to feel the void, cover the unknown. Unlike most everyone else here on Upsilia, he wasn't using force to push back.

"They didn't do anything to me but tell me about themselves. Tell me of their losses. Tell me of their travails."

"Why?" Mila asked. "When they took me, all they wanted to do was make me tell them everything. They wanted all my power, my information. Made me tell them where Garrick was so they could have us both."

"This was a renegade bunch," Edan said. "As it is on all worlds, there are those who don't go along with the main group. These Neballats have come to terms with their lives, their bodies, the situation their forebears created for them. They want to join us peacefully. All they are asking for is help."

Claire thought about the Neballat she saw back in Dhareilly, the one she talked to in the Source. Could he have actually been trying to help? Could he have been a member of this renegade group of Neballats? She'd thought that he had given her bad information, but somehow, everything had turned out okay. Just as the Neballats had been about to attack, they'd found a way to push back. And then there had been the surge of power that had made the Convergence really work.

And why had that happened? What had that been? Claire looked at her brother, wondering when he'd arrived on Upsilia.

"So, was it you who caused that surge?" Claire asked. "Were you responsible for all that power? The reason the Neballats left?"

Edan pulled her close. "There is so much that we have to talk about. So much I want to know about you. So much that you have to teach me."

Claire smiled into his shirt, hugging him. She knew she didn't have anything to teach him, but she was glad to hear the words. She was a teacher. That's what she did, but she'd never been able to teach much to her kindergarteners. They had tolerated her and calmed down for an hour or two a day as if there had been a collective decision to give her a break. But she hadn't managed to impart much wisdom or information to them other than how to hold a pencil and tell time. Claire hadn't been able to share who she really was with them, and that kept her from sharing much of anything.

Somehow, she'd held herself back from just about everything until the day Darl James appeared in her car like magic. It was magic. All of this was. Here she was with her siblings and her true love, everyone in one place. So what if the happy reunion was occurring on a spaceship in the middle of a battlefield? It was true nonetheless.

Slowly, Claire and Edan pulled away, Claire looking over to Mila, who still stood next to them, smiling.

"So," she asked Edan. "Did you find her?"

"Find who?" Claire turned back to Edan, whose face was no longer as beatific and composed.

"My double. My twin," he said, his voice low and sadly still. As he spoke, Claire was filled with a thin sweet sense of loneliness, a loneliness tinged with hope and need.

"No. No, I haven't found her. Or she hasn't found me. I'm not sure which is correct."

"Where can she be?" Mila looked stricken, her face pale, her eyes wide. "Everyone else is finding twins all over the place. Now that we are together here . . ."

Mila stopped speaking and reached out a hand to touch Edan. "You'll find her. Soon."

Edan nodded, turned his head, seemed to scan the crowd in the spaceship. "I don't understand why I don't feel her. Not even in the Source."

From somewhere outside of her or so far inside she'd never been able to sense it before, Claire found a thought, an idea, a truth.

"She's here. You just have to stop looking," she said, surprised by her own words.

Both Edan and Mila stared at her.

"What do you mean?" Edan said.

"Don't look for her," Claire said simply. And she thought of how many hours she'd wasted thinking about the perfect man, the right man. All the nights in her apartment dreaming of a life she'd not managed to live one second of. And then, when she was at the point of not believing what her friend Ruth said about love and what Yvonne said about what Claire deserved out of life, the life and love she deserved just showed up.

Mila laughed. "She's right. We may not be on Earth with its strange dating rules and bizarre social customs. No Date.com here. And nobody fixing us up on blind 'twin' dates, hoping that powers somehow mesh. But I think she's right, Edan. Stop looking."

Edan looked back and forth between them and started laughing with Mila. Claire put her hands on her hips.

"I'm being serious, " she said. "It's no laughing matter!"

Edan pulled both his sisters to him and hugged them tight. "Oh, yes. In this one thing you are incorrect, Claire. Everything is worth laughing about. Everything."

Later, long after the sun had set, Dhareilly gone quiet for the night, Claire and Darl found themselves in the same room they'd set out from earlier. Entwined—and not just because the bed was so small—they lay in each other's arms, one of the two moons shining through the window, the light a calming blue-white against the walls.

"So, you have your whole family with you," Darl said. "You must be happy."

"I never had any siblings, so it feels, well, amazing," she said, realizing that amazing was exactly how it felt. She kept expecting to turn and have someone standing there telling her that, in fact, she'd imagined both of them—Mila and Edan. Mila was simply a hallucination she'd invented to help her get through the journey to the mountains and Edan was some kind of Christ figure she was conjuring to allay her fears about being destroyed.

"Siblings can be overrated," Darl said, a laugh in his voice. "I love mine, but sometimes we all wanted to kill each other. Several times a day, especially when it rained and we were stuck in the house from dawn until dusk. And it always rained in Olympia. So you can just imagine the potential for bloodshed."

In the semidarkness, Claire smiled. It was hard to imagine that so much had happened. She'd found her siblings. The Cygirians had won the battle with the Neballats, at least for now. Not only that, they'd forged an alliance with Upsilia, which was allowing the Cygirians the space in the desert to build a compound, a small city really. Already, Cygirians with certain powers were out in the desert creating water and moving earth and forming materials that would help the Upsilians with the building process. Within weeks, the thousands of Cygirians who had survived the Neballat attacks all these years would be able to live together in a group. They would be able to re-form their society. Together with Upsilia, Cygiria would fight back for hopefully the last time.

"Probably we will need to recreate our society from scratch," Darl said. "I'm not sure we did such a great job of it the last time, considering the outcome."

"There's a lot of that going around," Claire said, snuggling closer to him, loving his warm buttery smell, the feel of his smooth skin against hers. She could just stay right here for the rest of her life and be happy. She ran a hand along his chest, loving the definition of muscles and bone, the slight whisk of hair under her palm.

"What do you mean?" he asked, his hands on her ribs, pulling her closer.

"I've looked at four cultures in just about as many days, and between Earthlings, Upsilians, Cygirians, and Neballats, I can't tell which group is doing worse. I mean, I'm still not sure a death ray is going to fry us into breakfast meats."

Claire shivered, held Darl tighter. That poor man—that poor man on the sidewalk.

"I don't know," he said. "They seem to be putting away all of that. The ray. The pods. The sequestering of Cygirians. But—"

"They think they were right! I don't know how we can ever coexist with people like that."

Claire was ready to stop talking about Upsilia. At least on Earth, she had a clearer notion of the "bad" people. Why it was bad to stop moving on a sidewalk was still completely unclear to her. Why someone deserved to die for it was completely beyond her ability to reason.

"Each culture thinks it is right. Each knows what it wants and the best way to get it, no matter the cost."

"I wish we could change things," she said. "I want to."

She felt Darl's shrug under her cheek. "Seems to be the nature of living to make about a thousand mistakes per lifetime. Probably more. But we can try. That's what we get to do here in the flesh, in life. We have the opportunity to try."

"And then we can figure it all out later in the Source," Claire said. "Then we can come back again and give it another go."

Darl ran a hand up and down her back, his fingertips tracing a lovely pattern on her skin, her body tingling. In fact, he made her tingle everywhere, even her kneecaps.

"I'd love to give it another go," he said, moving over her, cupping her face in his hands. "And then I'd like to try it again and again."

He bent down to kiss her, and Claire was once again amazed by how her body reacted to him, how she felt the need for him *now!* even as he simply touched her face. Her whole body flushed at his touch.

She opened her legs, allowing him to slip inside her, this feeling of him so known but never unsurprising. She breathed in, closed her eyes, let him move slowly in her. Then she met his movements, pushed back, wanting him, all of him. He was so hard, filling her in a way she had never believed she could be. She was full with his body, and full of his love.

"I don't think the Source is heaven," Darl whispered against her ear.

"Why?" Claire asked, her hands pulling him toward her, in her.

"Because we can't do this there. And this, my love, is heaven. Pure heaven."

And Claire moved with her twin, her double, her partner in life, moved to the waves of their skin and flesh and blood and bone, felt the power that each of them had in this very simple, wonderful act. And when she came, she clutched at him, forgetting everything that had happened except him, except Darl, except this, oh yes, this.

After Darl guided them back home from Upsilia and she'd found her apartment key behind the wilted orange geraniums just where she'd left it, Claire opened the door to apartment 5 at 28 Cole Street and breathed in stale air. She'd convinced Darl that she needed to go home for a quick visit, worrying still about loose ends and unpaid bills. He'd agreed, as long as she was okay with taking a side trip to Seattle afterward.

"I think I need to pay a little visit to my father," he'd said. "At least, that's what he told me to do in the Source."

"Sounds good," she'd said.

"I guess," Darl said. "If you're one for interventions or conflict."

But Claire knew that settling things from the past, letting go, was crucial to their new lives. For instance, now she also knew she could find a real estate agent to list her mother's house in West Portal. There was no reason to keep it anymore—her mother wasn't in the house. And while Susan was in the Source, Claire knew she was really carrying her mother in her heart.

Claire and Darl walked inside, and while he made a dash for the kitchen, Claire stood and looked around the place she called home.

"Seems with all that I had to think about," she said, "I forgot to open the windows before we left."

"I think you get a pass on that," Darl said, as he opened cupboards. "I was asking you to change your entire life."

She walked over to the living room window, letting in a cool breeze that seemed almost wet from the fog that rolled in from the ocean. Standing up straight and looking around, Claire wondered who had lived here. Everything was so orderly. Couch, chair, coffee table, the television that had been her weekend friend. A couple of photographs of Susan on the mantel piece. There were her *New Yorker* and *People* magazines and paperback books in neat piles on the table, her newspapers in a pile by the door, her grade book

from school, a couple of droopy plants. Her message machine blinked the number 5, probably all the calls from
Yvonne wanting to know what was truly going on.

"Did you finally find your life? Did you finally meet a man?"
Yvonne would have asked. "What is he like?"

As she thought about Yvonne, she could hear her kindergarteners' questions.

"Where is Miss Edwards? When is she coming back? Where
did she go?"

But then after a day or two of a good substitute teacher, it
was likely Miss Edwards had been forgotten, as if buried
under so many Crayolas.

So this had been the extent of Claire's existence. Was this
all that she had? And now? Everything was different. She
had a clear purpose, something she wanted, something she
had to fight for. She had family. More than anything else,
she had love.

Her reverie was broken by Darl foraging in the kitchen.

"Don't you have something disgusting like Cheetos? I
could really go for something imbued with artificial color
and flavor. Something salty. Something wildly orange or
even purple. Maybe blue. Or maybe something incredibly
sweet. We've practically been on a health food diet. Sticks
and glop and leaves. Alien sticks and glop and leaves. No
beer. No chips. No chocolate. It's more than a man can handle."

Claire laughed, walking over to the kitchen. "I have a secret."

"What? You've been keeping something from me?" Darl
looked at her in mock horror. "Now you decide to drag the
skeletons out of the closet?"

"Yes, it's true. I have a secret. It's my biggest, deepest,
darkest secret. A rather creamy secret, too."

Claire bent over and opened a lower cabinet, pulling a box from the back. "My hidden stash."

He watched as she put the box of Hostess cupcakes on the counter.

"There. Now you know everything. I will completely understand if you never want to see me again."

Darl pulled her in his arms, moved them to the middle of the kitchen, and twirled her around and around. Claire closed her eyes, feeling the velocity of his spin, his arms, his body against hers. She was in her old apartment but with a whole new life, one that was dangerous and strange and entirely new, but one she wouldn't give up. Not for this old life. Not for her friends or students. Not for all the Hostess cupcakes in China.

Laughing, Darl put her down and pressed her close, kissing her temple.

"Now go do what you need to do here. Tie up those loose ends. While you do, I'm going to have myself a little feast. And all I can tell you is that dessert isn't going to be one of these tasty chocolate treats." Darl held up something even better. "And it starts with a C."

Claire smiled, held him tight, knowing that dessert was now, right here, this moment. The tastiest, most delicious dessert she'd ever had.

BEING WITH HIM

They are here among us . . .

Far from home, gifted with special abilities, hunted for their powers. And they are desperate to find their other, the one who completes them . . . before it's too late. . . .

Sometimes, Time Really Does Stand Still

Mila Adams has always known she was different. For as long as she can remember, she has had the ability to shift time, and who would believe that? Certainly not the obnoxious blind dates her mother keeps foisting off on her. But Mila can't help feeling there's someone out there for her, a soul mate who might understand her unique ability. And when she looks into the dark eyes of financial whiz Garrick McClellan, she can't help but feel her time has finally come.

Any man would lust after a beauty like Mila, but the moment Garrick touches her—feels her shifting time just as he can—he recognizes her as his partner in power. Their connection is immediate, passionate, raw, and beyond anything either has ever experienced. But who are they? What is this gift that joins them so intensely? Are there others like them? And why do they feel that time is running out?

If you liked this Jessica Inclán book,
try the series from the beginning!
Turn the page for an excerpt from
BEING WITH HIM . . .

"Your painting," he asked, his words coming from him slow, as if he had to pull each word out of his mouth by a string, "the one with the purple swirl?"

"*The Ride*," she said, changing her gaze, moving it from his hands to his face. She was startled by his pointed expression. "What about it?"

"What does it mean?" he asked. And when Mila looked at him, she could see such an intense curiosity burning from behind his indifference, she wished she could open the car door and fling herself out. No one had ever looked at her like that before, not her parents, not a lover. No one ever paid that much attention to her, all at once. "What is it saying? Where does it come from?"

"It's just something from my imagination. Something I think about. All the time."

"Why? Why do you think about that shape? That color? What do you think?" He was leaning forward now, his face alight, his eyes filled with something like heat. "It's like there's movement there. Like the shape is going some place. Like it's carrying people, important people."

Mila blinked, startled. She'd only ever talked about *The*

Ride with her art instructors, the museum gallery director, her classmates. "I don't know why you care. You certainly didn't show any interest earlier."

"I—I . . ." Garrick stopped talking, shaking his head. He jerked his head up and noticed where the car was. "Never mind. I shouldn't have done this. I never should have come, Linda or not. Driver."

"His name is Mr. Henry."

Garrick leaned forward. "Mr. Henry, you can let me out here."

Mr. Henry didn't turn but said, "It's a mile yet."

"That's fine. Right here. Let me out here." And when Mr. Henry didn't seem to slow down, Garrick almost yelled, "Stop."

Mila sat flat against her seat watching this beautiful angry man do everything in his power to get away from her. If it wasn't so upsetting, she thought, she'd be able to craft some kind of story about it to tell her friends at the beginning of open studio, recounting the evening with verve and style, a jaunty yarn about the blind date from hell. The man who endured asphalt raspberry burns rather than ride a final mile in a one-hundred-thousand-dollar limo with her.

"Here we go, sir," Mr. Henry said, and Garrick opened the door, and he started to push through to the outside. He stopped for a second, and she could see him take in a big breath.

"Look," he said, turning back to her, one foot already out on the pavement. "It's not about . . ."

It's not you, it's me. Yadda, yadda, yadda, Mila thought. *Get out of the car, jerk.*

Garrick stopped talking, and she thought she heard him laugh. But his eyes weren't happy.

"Good luck with your painting," he said, leaving for real this time, the door closing heavy and hard.

As the car pulled away, Mila watched him as long as she could, until Mr. Henry turned left down the hill, heading toward the Mission District.

"Well," Mila said finally as they sailed through traffic. "That was so much fun, I hope I can do it again next Saturday!"

"He seemed a little strained," Mr. Henry said. "A little tense."

"He needed—well, he didn't need me, that's all I know."

Mila sat back, letting the ride home take her over. If she wasn't laughing, she would cry. And vice versa. It was too ironic. Here was a man who if he hadn't acted like such an ass, she actually would have loved to see again. And for no good reason, except for a strange feeling she'd had ever since he walked into her parents' living room. Some kind of zing, a flurry of energy in her body.

But his good looks and some kind of chemistry weren't enough to overcome his clear lack of manners or caring. So now it was over. She'd survived the dinner, her mother would likely not try a setup for months, and Mila could scratch another San Francisco bachelor off the long list her mother seemed to keep on file. Maybe now after this debacle, Mila thought, it was a good time to kiss that list goodbye.

She didn't even have a chance to look at the clock before picking up her cell phone, fumbling in the dark bedroom to find the button to answer it.

"What?" she asked, blinking into the early morning light, her blankets piled around her.

"I have to see you," he said.

Mila forced herself into total consciousness, taking in small breaths, keeping her eyes open. What day was it? Or what night? Was it the weekend? "Who is this?"

"It's Garrick. Garrick McClellan."

Mila rolled onto her back. "You have to see me? Didn't—didn't you just jump out of a car to get away from me?"

There was a pause, and Mila wondered if she'd fallen back to sleep, but then he said, "I'm—I'm sorry. I want to explain. And I want to ask you something about . . ."

"What? About what?" Mila asked.

"Us," Garrick said. "Us."

Sitting up, Mila leaned against her pillow, her mouth open slightly. *Us?* What was he doing calling her like this after a night like that? After he almost made himself roadkill rather than sit next to her? She wanted to laugh at him. To tell him to take a hike. But then, through the phone, she felt so much that she wanted to lie down flat on the bed and weep. Images were coming to her, feelings, thoughts. Garrick's. So much hurt and loss and pain. He had been so alone. So afraid.

"Oh," she said, trying to find words. "Oh."

"Can we meet?" he asked, unaware of what she was pulling in from his mind.

"Yes. Yes," she said. "We can meet."

"When?" he asked.

What time was there? she wondered. What time was there but this moment? She knew from wasting time how valuable it was.

"Now," she said. "Come over now."

And keep an eye out for Jessica's next book,
coming in September 2009. . . .

There was a movement behind him, and Edan turned his head, looking behind him at a group of five people moving along the dried pathways with a cart of food and water that seemed to float with them. As he watched, he breathed in a sweet aroma of fruit and butter, of other things savory and tasty and rich with flavor. The air tasted so good, his mouth began to water.

"Damn, it's about time," Siker said. "I've been dying for some of that chick's food. It's like so good. Awesome. I mean the best stuff you've ever had. Makes working in this heat almost worthwhile."

Turning slightly to follow Siker's gaze, Edan found his eyes holding the figure of a woman. He blinked, wondering why he couldn't get her in focus. For some reason, he couldn't really see "woman" at first, only her blur, only her essence, like the way he could taste the food that was coming without even eating it.

He blinked again, trying to find a focus, feeling as if he were underwater or in a dream he couldn't wake up from. Slowly . . . slowly. There. There! He could bring her into view. But he didn't see her form. What he saw instead was color—white and gold and red. This twirl of color, this amazing vision of her hit his eyes, and he felt the impact of the sight in his head, throat, chest. For a moment, he imagined that he was paralyzed, his feet like lead, his body stiff. He wanted to move forward, but could not, nothing in him seeming to work at all.

"What's up, man?" Siker said. "Are you okay? Is it sun stroke or something? You need some water? Man? Are you going to make it? Should I like call someone?"

Edan took a breath to steady himself and tried to nod, but he was stuck in stillness.

"Dude?"

Again, Edan tried to nod, his chin moving a little.

"Okay, then. But you look like you've seen something totally freaky," Siker said, his voice trailing off as the woman, the cart, and the four other people came toward them. As they did, they handed out food, the smell growing more delicious as they approached.

"Hey," Siker said to the woman. "You have any of that like tart thing?"

Edan couldn't move, couldn't speak, watching as the woman came toward him. He wanted to call out her name, but he didn't know what her name was, though he thought the sound of it would feel good on his tongue. Her name would be as tasty as the food she was handing out, something soft and lovely and delicious. There would be heat and softness to it. And beyond her name, everything else would be wonderful, too. The citrus taste of her, the smell of the delicate skin behind her ear, the warm feel of her skin under his palms. She would whisper to him, her voice a lazy cat in his ear. He wasn't sure how he knew any of this, but he could almost feel the silky smoothness of her upper arm, the shimmering slope of her neck, the dip of her lower back.

How could his hand know that? How could he know anything about her at all? How could he have sense memory of
someone he had never touched?

"Man," Siker was saying from what felt like a million miles
away. "Are you like hungry? You should get some of this."

The woman came closer, her blond hair a wave flowing
behind her, her dark brown eyes taking him in. Edan knew
her eyes, had seen her gaze before, as if she'd looked at him
before, so serious, so calm. Her face was smooth, unlined,
flawless, so clear and clean he wanted to reach out a hand
and touch her. But at the same time, he almost wanted to
hold up his hands to avoid her direct gaze, her eyes seeming
to dig into him and beyond, into the desert behind him. She
was seeing too much, taking him in as he was taking her in,
and he managed to tamp down his thoughts, not wanting
her to hear and know any more than she already must.

"Would you like something to eat?" she asked, her voice
just as he imagined, smooth and low and assured. But there
was something faraway about her, too, as if she'd thrown
on some kind of protective covering, thoughts, feelings, and
even air seeming to push past and around her.

Edan struggled to find his words, wondering if his tongue
would move to form the fricatives, plosives, and bilabials
that would make words that she might understand. If he
didn't focus, he realized he might find himself grunting like
an animal, a primordial, prehistoric beast.

"Please," he said, pushing the word out too fast. "Yes."

Her eyes still on him, she handed him a package, the food
warm in its wrapper.

"I hope you'll like it," she said.

"Do I—do I know you?" Edan asked, gripping the food a
little too hard in his hands, the soft contents underneath his
fingers slightly squishing.

The woman stared at him with her same still look, and then shook her head. "I don't think so."

"Where are you from?" He was almost barking out his words, and she stepped back once, twice, staring at him as she did.

"Here," she said. "Just outside Dhareilly."

"Were you in the Source?"

She shook her head, her eyes narrowing. She put a hand on her hip, shrugged slightly, her mouth in a slim, irritated line. "Why are you asking me this?"

Edan wanted to put his hands on her shoulders and shake her. Where had she been? Why hadn't she shown up before this? Why now in the desert? How could she be here, now, finally? Where had she been all this time? How could their meeting be as silly as this? Now she shows up carting food around, unable to truly see him. Her twin, standing right in front of her.

But maybe he was wrong. Maybe he was just lonely and tired and desperate to discover her. Maybe he was suffering from heatstroke, dizzy from dehydration, needing nothing more than a cool shower to calm his nerves. Despite his limited vocabulary, Siker was right. Edan needed rest, food, and water. That's all.

"I—" Edan began, about to introduce himself, but then a group of workers rounded the corner from the other side of the building and approached the cart, laughing and eager to eat the delicious food, the smells wafting everywhere.

Distracted, she turned toward the approaching people, and Edan stepped back, trying to find his breath.

"Man?" Siker said. "Looks like you've got a major thing going on. Some kind of animal instinct. Some kind of tribal reaction. Like you are about to—"

"Eat," Edan said. He turned away slowly, wondering where

he could go to run away from this feeling, this impulse, this need. He wasn't sure if he could, but he put one foot in front of the other and moved, heading back toward the temporary shelter Jai and Risa had allotted him earlier.

The hot desert air against his face, the sun at his back, Edan found it hard to breathe, hard to concentrate. He needed to go back to the city. Working here in the intense sun had been the wrong idea. He was dreaming up his twin out of the sand and shrub and wavery lines of heat. He was trying to find what he hadn't in all his years in the Source. How could he possibly guide his people to anything if he couldn't even recognize his twin? If he was imagining that a woman handing out pie was the woman he'd been waiting for his entire life, how could he ever be a responsible leader?

"Man?" Siker called out from behind him. "Where are you like going? There's more to lunch than this."

Edan held up a hand, unable to turn around, unable to answer Siker. He didn't know where he was going except away, except out of here.